Sledge vs. The Labyrinth

Sledge vs The Wendigo *(coming soon)*

When Jack Reacher goes to sleep, he checks the closet for Sledge Laukkanen . . .

a novel by

Nick Horvath

Published by SISU Press, New Zealand.

First Edition, October, 2023

ISBN 978-1-7385984-0-3

Cover design by Jemma Cheer Design.

To the grind.

"Theogenes was the greatest of the gladiators . . . . Then, as now, violence, suffering, and the cheapness of life were the rule. The sort of boxing Theogenes practiced was not like the modern-day boxing with those kindergarten Queensbury Rules. The two contestants . . . were strapped to flat stones, facing each other nose-to-nose. When the signal was given, they would begin hammering each other with fists encased in heavy leather thongs. It was a fight to the death. Fourteen hundred and twenty-five times Theogenes was strapped to the stone and fourteen hundred and twenty-five times he emerged the victor."

-Thom Jones, *The Pugilist at Rest*

"The world is run by gangsters. Agent Orange, the guy in Brazil, and Putin. They're gonna do whatever they wanna do. They have no morals, no scruples. That's the world we live in."

-Spike Lee

1

Kiira clambered out of the pines looking like she'd won a fight. And fair enough, she'd just battled through five treacherous miles of hip-deep snow without breaking an ankle or being eaten by a wolf. No mean feat in the middle of January in my neck of the woods.

I stood in the doorway of my cabin and watched her slog toward me. She'd dressed appropriately in multiple layers beneath a gore-tex shell. Hat, gloves, ski goggles, and a pair of carbon-fibre snowshoes that probably cost more than my truck. I knew what was underneath it all, and wouldn't mind seeing it again. She carried no rifle, but I figured that lump on her left hip for the Glock 20 I'd given her a few years back.

"You need quicker access to that thing," I said when she got within ear shot, nodding at the lump.

Kiira trudged another handful of steps and came to a stop, glancing back through the trees.

"Lots of starving white tail wandering around," she said. "The wolves are fat and lazy this time of year."

My mouth curled, ever so slightly. No fooling this one.

"Doesn't mean they'll pass up a free meal," I said. "And who says I was talking about the wolves?"

Kiira looked up at me and smirked.

"Who says I'm a free meal?"

I laughed through my nose. It was good to see her. But something was off. There was a reason she'd hiked through five miles of wolf-infested wilderness to visit a known murderer.

"Aren't you going to invite me in?" she said.

"No."

Her brow furrowed.

"Why not?" she said.

"Last person I invited in gave me this."

I pointed to the Mohawk of scar tissue bisecting my skull.

She tried on a smile. It didn't fit.

"You really don't trust me?" she said.

I said nothing.

She said, "Not everyone is out to kill you, you know."

I didn't reply.

Kiira said, "Most people in Gunflint Cove think you're a bit of a hero now. Susan would be dead if you hadn't found her."

It was still weird to hear her called Susan. When I'd been looking for her, her name had been Karla.

"This time you killed people that deserved it," she continued.

"Not sure they'd agree with you."

She laughed. Or tried to. The movement made her wince. I said nothing. I watched her and I waited. She'd get to it. After a time she pulled in a careful breath, set her jaw, and crunched the rest of the way toward me through the snow. When she got close her hand slid behind her back. Behind the door frame my fingers closed around the handle of my sledgehammer. No such thing as too careful when your last girlfriend put a bullet in your head. I watched her hand closely. It came back holding an envelope. She offered it to me. Tentatively. Like offering meat to a bear. I let go of the hammer, but didn't take the envelope.

"Four days ago," she said, "I woke up and found this under my pillow. Someone put it there while I was asleep. I want you to find out who it was and beat them to death."

I almost laughed. Then I saw her eyes. Fear. By the gallon. Enough for her to risk her life coming here. I took the envelope. No stamp. No name. I flipped it over. It hadn't been licked. I opened the flap and pulled out a folded piece of paper. Opened it up. In the middle were two typed lines:

Your haunting begins in three days.

xkq6zwgst3366vvgvhfx81.tor

I looked at Kiira.

"Someone's trying to scare me," she said.

"No shit."

The muscles in her jaw tightened.

"They came into my room, Einarr. While I was asleep."

"Security cameras?" I said.

She shook her head.

"Get some."

She breathed in and out. Trying to keep a lid on the panic.

"You have any idea what that code is?"

She jabbed a finger at the paper, grimacing. I looked at the code. Shook my head.

"Dot T O R stands for 'the onion router,'" she said.

"What the fuck is that?"

"It's a software program used to access the dark web."

I'd heard of the dark web. Just.

"I downloaded it," she said. "It's basically a web browser. Like Chrome or Safari. Except with TOR there's no search function. Turns out the dark web is just the part of the internet not indexed by search engines. So you can't search for what you want. You need an exact darkweb address to get anywhere."

I eyed the jumbled line of text.

"And this is an exact darkweb address?"

She nodded.

"To what?" I said.

She reached into her pocket and pulled out her iPhone. Handed it to me.

"That's a photo of the webpage the code led to," she said. "Lucky I got it. The page deleted itself not long after."

The webpage was very simple. Black background. Red text. No images.

It looked like this:

THE LABYRINTH

Depth 1 - Death threat: $5,000 USD
Depth 2 - Beating: $20,000 USD
Depth 3 - Kidnapping: $50,000 USD
Depth 4 - Rape: $100,000 USD
Depth 5 - Grievous bodily harm: $200,000 USD
Depth 6 - Deprivation of hearing: $300,000 USD
Depth 7 - Deprivation of vision: $400,000 USD
Depth 8 - Paralyzation: $500,000 USD
Depth 9 - Severe torture to death: $1,000,000 USD
Depth 10 - ???: $10,000,000 USD

Allow 3-7 days for stalk of victim. No refunds. The Descent will be carried out by any means necessary.

"Each price was a buy now link," said Kiira. "Cryptocurrency only. All sales final."

I looked at her.

"Looks like a scam."

"I thought the same thing," she said.

She unzipped her snowsuit and pulled up her shirt. I saw now why she was wincing. Her entire stomach was a purple-black bruise.

"I came here from the hospital," she said. "My death threat came yesterday. Exactly three days after the letter."

2

I pulled the truck off the Gunflint Trail at a faded wooden sign reading Hegseth Logging Company, since 1916. It wasn't yet five o'clock, but it'd been full dark for over an hour. The night was clear. But Minnesota cold. The dashboard thermometer read negative twelve and the brutal wind ripping off Lake Superior told me it was another night that would kill you quick if you weren't prepared.

"Remind me again what we're doing here?" said Gow as I eased onto the rutted track.

"A guy leapt out from behind a truck in the IGA parking lot and sucker punched Kiira in the stomach," I said. "While she was doubled over on the ground he told her, 'You're going to die soon, cunt.'"

Gow raised an eyebrow. The truck clawed its way into the pines.

"What'd this prick look like?" said Gow.

"Wore a balaclava," I said, glancing over at him.

Once upon a time, Gow had been hired to kill me. He'd come out of the woods behind my cabin wearing a balaclava and a Colt .45. Now I'd trust him with my life. Funny how that works.

"Okay," said Gow. "Anything else?"

"He was big."

"How big?"

"Big big," I said. "Not quite my height, but wider. And strong. Kiira said he looked like an NFL player. One punch to the gut put her in the hospital. She's still pissing blood."

"Sounds like Mykal," said Gow.

"That's not his name anymore," I said.

"What?"

"He's been initiated. Goes by Makwa now. Ojibwe for bear."

"Fitting," said Gow. "You like him for it?"

I shook my head.

"Why not?"

I said, "Now that he's Wendigo, Makwa won't fart lest Moosejaw OKs it. And Moosejaw knows Kiira's a friend of mine. He wouldn't do it."

"You sure?"

"He knows I'd kill him."

Gow weighed that with his head.

"Fair enough."

"Besides," I said. "Kiira said the guy was white."

Gow snickered.

"Ok. So why here?"

"No one else in Gunflint Cove fits the description," I said. "So unless the guy was hired from Duluth or The Cities, that leaves . . . "

"The logging camp," said Gow, looking out the windshield.

We rounded a corner and came to a gate. It was locked by thick chain and padlock.

"Looks like they're closed for the night," said Gow.

"They live on camp right?" I said.

"Yeah," said Gow. "Three hundred blokes. What you Americans like to call a sausage fest."

I checked the dashboard clock.

"So three hundred dudes lock themselves in at night,

eight hours before bars close?"

Gow raised a skeptical eyebrow.

"Maybe they like their beauty sleep," he said.

We shared a look, then opened our doors. I grabbed my sledgehammer from the backseat and walked up to the gate. We couldn't see the camp from here, just more trees, but through the frozen air came the thump of pounding bass.

"A concert?" said Gow.

I shrugged.

Gow said, "Isn't that a VIP pass I see in your hand?"

I swung the hammer down and obliterated the padlock. I pulled out the chain and walked back the gate, then we climbed back into the truck and headed in. I kept the headlights off and drove slow. The tire chains clawed the hard-pack. We rounded a corner and the trees opened up on a large open space filled with parked cars, mostly beat-up pick-ups like mine. Up ahead was the big mill. The lights were on and the music was pumping from inside. I could even make out the song.

"*Raining Blood,*" I said.

Gow raised an eyebrow.

I said, "Think Slayer flew in for a private concert for three hundred plaid-shirt jackasses locked in a barn?"

"I'm skeptical," said Gow.

I parked the truck at the back of the lot and we got out. I let Gow lead. He's ex-British SAS. Infiltration expert. I couldn't sneak up on Hellen Keller. Trying my best to stay low and quiet, I followed Gow, ducking from truck to truck. When we got to the end of the lot he held up a hand and peeked beneath a rusted bumper. I waited.

"One guy at the main door freezing his bollocks off," Gow whispered. "No weapons visible. But my guess is he's got something behind that pallet. Thoughts?"

"The usual," I said.

I stood up and headed straight for the guy. Gow stayed

hidden. I was about a third of the way across the open space between the last truck and the mill door when the guy noticed me.

"Hey!" he said, putting a hand behind the pallet and pulling out a pump-action shotgun. Looked liked a Mossberg, but I couldn't be sure from this distance. "Get the fuck out of here! Private function."

I kept walking.

"You hard of fucking hearing asshole!" the guy said. "I said get the fu—"

His eyes went wide. He'd recognized me. I kept walking. He hadn't racked a shell yet. By the time he realized his error I was on him. I grabbed the end of the single-barrel and yanked, pitching the guy forward into my left fist. He went down and now I had the gun. I cracked it, jacked the shell he'd forgotten and tossed the gun aside. Then I unsheathed my sledgehammer and rested the cold steel on his forehead.

"I'm sorry I'm sorry I'm sorry!" he said. He had his eyes squeezed shut and he was crying a little bit. "I didn't know it was you, Sledge! I swear!"

"What's the big party?" I said.

He peeked open an eye and glanced up at me. He was trembling.

"You d-don't know?" he said.

I ground the gnarled steel into his face. Let him feel the weight of it. He whimpered a bit, then said, "The fight man! The fight!"

"Dogs?" I said.

He shook his head.

"No, man. People. Bare knuckle. No holds barred."

"Why the secrecy?" I said.

"Marx is fighting," said the guy.

"Who the fuck is Marx?"

"Marx runs this place," he said. "Scariest fucking guy you've ever seen. He's training for some underground fighting tournament or something. No rules, man. Scary shit. Last time he killed a guy."

Hmmm.

"Why isn't he in jail?" I said.

The guy said nothing. He was looking real nervous.

"Cover up," I said.

It wasn't a question. The guy's eyes opened a little wider. He looked from me, to hammer, and back. Then nodded once fast.

"What story he got you shovelling?" I said.

"L-logging accident," said the guy. "Don't say I told you! Please! Marx broke a guy's legs with the back of an axe at breakfast last week. To show us what happens if we squeal. He's ramping up security. No one allowed in unless they live on camp."

"What's Marx look like?" I said.

"He's a fucking monster, man," said the guy. "Not quite as tall as you, but way more jacked. Never seen someone hit so hard in my fucking life. He killed that guy with one punch. Dropped on top of him and punched his head into the concrete. Skull cracked open like an egg."

"Who's he fighting tonight?" I said.

"Some guy named Homik," he said. "Poor fucker's in for a world of hurt."

"We'll see about that," I said.

3

I walked in the front door of the mill holding the hammer. Inside it was *loud*. Three hundred drunk assholes screaming at the top of their lungs over pounding death metal. Every eye in the place was glued to an illuminated square of concrete in the center of the cavernous space. A chain-link fence encircled the fighting square with coils of razor wire strung along the top. Cute. Inside the cage an enormous guy was holding another guy by the hair and punching him repeatedly in the face. With each punch the crowd's bloodlust intensified.

I walked up to the nearest drunk asshole and tapped him on the shoulder. He snapped his bearded head at me, angry to be distracted from the impending knockout. He found himself looking into the face of my sledgehammer.

"That Marx?" I said, pointing a thumb toward the cage.

The guy craned his neck to look up at me. His eyes went wide with recognition. He opened his mouth, but nothing came out. He blinked a couple times, then settled on nodding.

"Thanks," I said.

I shouldered my way through the crowd, inducing angry scowls from the burly lumberjacks that dissipated the moment they saw me and the hammer. I got to the cage and stopped. The cage door was locked with a padlock. More affect, like the razor wire. Once upon a time I'd done this kind of thing for real. This was play acting.

I reached out and tested the lock. It was indeed locked. Inside the cage, Marx had Homik in a headlock and was punching him in the face over and over again. Homik was a mess. Up close he looked to be about half Marx's size. He was way past being able to defend himself, if he'd ever been able to in the first place. Marx clearly didn't give a shit.

I reared the hammer back and swung violently down. The lock exploded. The music stopped and whole place went quiet. I opened the gate and stepped inside the cage.

"What the fuck do you think you're doing?" said Marx.

He was still holding Homik by the neck. I set my hammer down, head first, in a corner of the cage.

"I heard there was a fight going on," I said, turning to Marx. "Turns out I was mistaken."

Marx let go of Homik's head. Homik collapsed to the concrete and didn't move. I took off my trench coat and threw it on top of the sledgehammer.

"What the fuck's that supposed to mean?" said Marx.

Now that I was up close, I got a good look at him. He was big alright. Maybe six-seven, with the exaggerated traps and over-wide delts of a heavy steroid abuser. One of his pupils was slightly larger than the other, which told me anabolics weren't the only thing flying his kite.

"Heard you wanna try the real thing," I said, motioning to the cage. "Yet here you are beating on some shmuck you outweigh by eighty pounds."

Marx's jaw clenched. Homik had made it to his hands and knees and was crawling toward the exit, dripping a trail of blood from his ruined face. I waited until he cleared the gate, then levelled my gaze at Marx.

"Doesn't matter who's in front of me," he said, throwing back his massive shoulders and flexing his traps. "They all end up in the same place."

He pointed down.

I felt kinda bad for him. He was like that guy at the YMCA who thinks he can take Brian Scalabrine one-on-one. But I wasn't Brian Scalabrine.

"Whoa," I said, holding up my palms. "I had no idea what a tough guy you were. I bet you could cold cock a blond chick at the grocery store."

The lesser-dilated of Marx's pupils widened a little.

Gotcha.

I walked up and threw a left jab at his nose. He grinned and dodged his head. While his eyes were on my fist I front-kicked his right kneecap. His knee hyper-extended with a nasty crack and he screamed and bent at the waist to clutch his shattered joint and ran face-first into my rising right fist. The collision was catastrophic. He went down to the concrete and bled.

"Who hired your dumb ass?" I said.

"Aaaaahhh!" he said. His voice came out funny because of all the blood gushing from his broken face.

I kicked him in the shattered knee and he rolled onto his back and put one hand down as if to protect himself and another up to shield his face and I kicked him in the side of the head. He howled.

"Who hired you?" I said.

"I don't know!" he screamed.

I stomped his stomach.

"Who hired you?"

"Stop please stop!"

I kicked him in the knee again.

"Who hired you?"

"I don't know I swear!" he screamed. "My leg!"

"You'll be fine," I said. "Who hired you?"

"I don't know!"

"Tell me or I'll hurt you for real."

That got his attention. This wasn't for real?

"I don't know!" he yelped. "It was my first descent! I just got in a few weeks ago!"

"In to what?" I said.

"The Labyrinth!" he said.

"What the fuck is The Labyrinth?"

"It's . . . I don't know!" he said. "It's on the darkweb. You need a code. It's real man. The money's real!"

"Wet work?" I said.

I wasn't sure if he knew what I meant, but he nodded quickly, gasping in hard, fast spurts.

"How do you get in?" I said.

"They find you."

"How?"

"I got a code," he said quickly, bracing for more pain. "In a letter."

"Who gave you the letter?"

"Found it in my truck," he said. "On the seat when I came back from the bar. I thought it was a hoax, but the money's real man! Five g's, straight to my account. Got the cash out the same day!"

"Who pays?"

"I don't know! It's anonymous man! Bitcoin! Fuck my leg man I need a hospital!"

I kicked him again just for the fun of it. He started crying.

"This code," I said. "It targeted Kiira specifically?"

He nodded, sobbing and moaning and holding his broken leg.

"You followed her?" I said.

He shook his head.

"Website said she'd be at the supermarket on Monday between one and three."

I thought about that.

"Five grand to punch her in the stomach?" I said.

Marx shook his head.

"For a death threat."

"So the punch was extra?" I said, placing the heel of my boot on the side of his face and forcing his head to the side.

He began to scream in earnest.

"NOO!" he said. "NO PLEASE NO! I'M SORRY I'M SORRY OH GOD PLEASE NO GOD PLEASE NO!"

"When you get out of the hospital," I said, "report directly to me. Or I'll hunt you down and fucking kill you."

He tried to nod but I'd already buckled his mandible. I left him there screaming.

"Subtle," said Gow as I and my hammer ducked out of the cage.

The nearest spectators stumbled backward over each other at my approach. I levelled my gaze at them, daring one or ten or fifty to try me. All three hundred lumberjacks fled, stampeding for the exit.

I smiled.

"Why do you think they call me Sledge?"

4

Kiira's house was tucked in the trees half-way up Gunflint Mountain. Although the word mountain is a bit of misnomer, the elevation afforded her a hell of a view. I was sitting on the couch in front of the big bay window drinking coffee and gazing out over Gunflint Cove and the endless expanse of Lake Superior.

"You found the guy?" said Kiira. "In less than a day?"

She was on the other end of the couch sipping a cup of tea. I've never understood how people can drink that shit with a straight face, but she appeared undaunted. She had on black yoga pants and a white She-Ra t-shirt and a pair of thick woollen socks. I was trying to decipher exactly what she had on beneath the t-shirt without getting caught. It was a game I was unlikely to win, yet I remained steadfast.

"Yeah," I said.

Kiira's cat hopped up on the couch and nuzzled my arm. I scratched him behind the ears. He closed his eyes and purred. Kiira looked confused.

"I've never seen him do that before," she said. "He hates people."

"He's a cat," I said. "You're beneath him."

"He can sense a fellow predator."

"That, or he likes being scratched behind the ears."

Kiira smirked and sipped her tea. I had some coffee.

"How's writing?" I said. "Murder anyone today?"

She waffled her hand back and forth.

"I'm treading water at the moment. Still have no idea who the killer is."

I raised an eyebrow.

"Aren't you the writer?"

She shrugged.

"I never know what really happened until the end," she said. "I write myself into a corner on purpose, then spend the next six months figuring out how to get myself out of it. If I don't know whodunnit, then the reader can't either."

"Clever."

She shrugged.

"Pays the bills."

You've probably seen a couple of her books on Netflix. I drank some more coffee. Kiira's face turned serious.

"How'd you find him?" she said.

"Process of elimination."

"Who was it?"

"Guy named Marx."

"Marx Hegseth?" she said. "I should have known."

"You know him?"

She shook her head.

"Heard of him. The Hegseth's have lived in the area since forever. Family run business. Marx is one of the kids. Last I heard he was off on a football scholarship at the U. I guess he's back. Can't believe how big he's got."

"College football's forced labor," I said. "Day one he'd have been given a syringe with the option to shove it in his ass or never see the field. Unfortunately, the 'roids had him thinking he was a proper tough guy."

"He wasn't?"

I shook my head.

"No. He was a moron. He's not behind this."

"So who is?"

"No idea. Marx appears to have gotten himself into an online hitman network on the darkweb."

Kiira opened her eyes a littler wider.

"So the site's legit?" she said.

"It appears so. Marx got five k to threaten your life. Paid in Bitcoin. You know anything about the darkweb, or cryptocurrency?"

She shook her head.

"Not really. I've got a friend who'll know. I'll give him a call."

"A friend?" I said.

She rolled her eyes.

"Not that kind. No need to intimidate him."

I tipped the last few drops of my coffee into my open mouth and made to get up.

"No," she said. "Stay there. I've never seen Noir curl up on someone like that."

She made my coffee and brought it back. The cat was still asleep in my lap.

"So we still know nothing?" she said.

"No," I said. "We know a little more than we did."

"Like what?"

"We know someone is targeting you specifically. No way Marx put that letter under your pillow. He's too much of an oaf."

"Doesn't mean the person who delivered the letter is behind it either," she said.

"No, it doesn't. But we know someone's following you."

"How?"

"They knew you went to the supermarket on the same day each week. They told Marx where to find you."

Kiira looked at me with wide eyes.

"Einarr, that's not fucking funny. Why would someone do this to me?"

"I don't know," I said. "I'm not looking at motive."

"Why not?"

"No point. You've undoubtedly pissed off a lot of people basing your books on real crimes. You have millions of readers. Any one of them could have it in for you."

"But you said it's local," she said.

"Doesn't mean they live locally. Just that they've hired locally."

"You're not helping, Einarr."

"My point is, why they're doing what they're doing doesn't matter. What matters is how they're doing it. I focus on means."

"So how are they doing it?"

"No fucking clue," I said. "I don't know shit about the darkweb. Or cryptocurrency. Or any of it. I just know some asshole wants to hurt you. Or, more specifically, scare you and hurt you. He wants you afraid."

"Again, not helping," she said.

I shrugged.

"I want to find this fucker and cut his balls off," she said.

"As do I."

"So what next?"

"We wait."

"For what?"

"For the next asshole in The Labyrinth to show up."

Kiira's eyes bugged.

"*What*?"

For the first time she looked genuinely afraid.

"Which is why I'll be staying here," I said. "From now on, wherever you go, I, or someone I trust, goes with you."

She put a hand to her chest and pulled in a deep breath. I finally saw for certain what I'd suspected all along: she wasn't wearing a bra. She looked at me, followed my eyes, and shook her head in mock disgust.

Damn it. *Caught!*

5

Later that night, Kiira said, "You're on the couch."

We'd spent the evening in separate armchairs near the fire, reading. I'd been looking forward to bedtime for the last three hours. I tried my best not to look crestfallen.

"Oh don't pout," she said. "After you fuck you hibernate like a grizzly bear. Can't have that. I need you alert and angry."

I growled.

"That'a boy," she said, patting me on the chest.

She brought out a blanket and a pillow and said goodnight. Upstairs I heard the shower run for a while and tried not to think about her in it and failed. Afterward I heard her moving around for a bit and then everything went quiet and I was alone in the dark, waiting.

I didn't have to wait long.

Just after midnight, there came a knock on the door. I was up and to the door in ten strides. I threw back the deadbolt, ripped the door open and threw out a front kick. If someone had been behind the door they would have been obliterated. Too bad nobody was there. I stumbled out into the cold night feeling like a jackass.

Then, upstairs, Kiira screamed.

I spun and sprinted through the house. Kiira's piercing

shriek was cut short, as if someone had slapped a hand over her mouth. I blasted up the stairs and down the hall and through the door and found her up against the wall with wide open eyes and a gloved hand across her mouth. A guy in a white balaclava stood behind her. He had a knife to her throat.

I kept my hands out in front of me where he could see them but didn't stop moving forward.

"I'll cut her fucking throat!" the guy said.

"No you won't," I said, taking one last step. Eight feet separated us now. Far enough for him to feel safe. Close enough for him not to be.

"You're getting 20k to beat her," I said. "Not kill her."

The guy's head titled to the side, just a fraction, but it was enough to tell me I'd got it right.

"Listen carefully," I said. "I'm sure you're a scary guy. Maybe you've done this kind of thing before. But I can promise you two things. One, I'm much better at this that you are. Two, if you don't put that knife down right now, I will kill you."

A moment passed. I looked straight into his eyes. He looked back, saw what he needed to see, and lowered the knife.

"Kick it to me," I said.

He dropped the knife and his eyes went down with it and I used that moment to lunge forward and push his off button. My knuckles tapped the point of his chin, jolting his sinus. His legs gave out and Kiira leapt away with a yelp. I pointed to the door behind me and she skirted toward it. Without needing to be told, she flicked on the light.

The guy was already regaining consciousness. He blinked a few times. It took a moment for his eyes to focus and when they did they found me standing over him, one foot on each arm. I leaned down and yanked off his balaclava. He was Ojibwe. Maybe twenty-five years old. Young, but with a hardness in his eyes.

"You're one of Moosejaw's," I said.

"Fuck you."

I slapped him across the face with my open hand. It stung and it was humiliating and it woke him right up. He clenched his jaw and fought against me, trying to free his arms. I slapped him again, harder. He stopped fighting. He was breathing hard through his nose, trying to control his anger.

"You're blooded," I said. "*Majii Manidoo*."

That stopped him. He squinted up at me, suspicious.

"How do you know that?" he said.

"I know a lot of things," I said. "Who'd you kill?"

He breathed through his nose some more. Shook his head.

"Tell me," I said, digging my weight into his arms. He breathed in and out. I slapped him again. "Tell me."

He glared at me and I looked right back until he looked away.

"Who did you kill?" I said.

I saw his eyes go far away. Eventually, he breathed, "A man."

"In the Boundary Waters?"

He nodded. Moosejaw and his Wendigo control the unguarded border between the US and Canada known as the Boundary Waters. This kid was one of them. Silent assassins that know the land. Shadows that murder in the night.

"How'd you do it?" I said.

"*Waabishkiiwed* make so much noise," he said. "Wake the whole forrest. He was like a blind man. He never even saw me."

"How'd you do it?" I said again.

He breathed for a moment.

"Drowned him," he said.

"Did he fight? At the end?"

He nodded slowly.

"Did you watch it?" I said. "Did you take his spirit?"

The young Ojibwe said nothing. He breathed in and out, unable to meet my gaze. His eyes were wet.

"How often does he visit you?" I said.

His mouth began to quiver. He squeezed his eyes shut. A tear spilled down his cheek, leaving a glistening trail.

"Does Moosejaw know you're here?" I said.

He opened his eyes again. I saw fear there now. He shook his head. His eyes were wide. Moosejaw wasn't stupid. He knew Kiira was off limits. Which meant this kid was already dead if Moosejaw found out about this.

"What's your name?" I said.

"Mikwam."

"What's that mean in Ojibwe?"

"Ice," he said.

"How did you discover The Labyrinth, Mikwam?"

His eyes widened.

"Are you in it too?"

I shook my head.

"How do you know about it?" he said.

"As I said, I know a lot of things. Where did you find your code?"

"Someone texted me a link. Unknown number."

He paused.

"They knew," he said.

"Knew what?"

"His name."

"The guy you killed?"

He nodded.

I thought about that.

"Any idea how they knew?" I said.

He shook his head.

I took a step back and considered him. He'd forgotten to be afraid of me.

"I'm going to throw you out the window now," I said.
The fear came back.

6

We were in one of the parlours of Maldonado's main mansion. I was sitting on a gold-plated Harow Skull Chair with a thousand bucks of single malt in my hand. Kiira paced the room with her third Russo-Baltique martini. Gow was standing at the door, on duty, near enough to be part of the conversation.

"Someone's on her," I said. "And has been for a while."

"At least a week," said Gow.

I nodded.

"They knew her habits. The layout of her house. Where she keeps the spare key."

"You hadn't noticed anything?" Gow said to Kiira.

"No," she said. "But I wasn't looking."

"Gunflint Cove is small," he said. "See anyone you don't know lately?"

She bit her lip, then shrugged.

"It's a tourist town. The cabins up the trail are booked out all year round. I'm always seeing strangers up here."

"Anyone on foot near your house?" I said. "Maybe walking a dog? Pushing a stroller? Both good covers."

She shook her head.

"Not that I can remember."

"Thoughts?" I said, turning to Gow.

He tilted his head.

"What I want to know is how they got the name of who Mikwam killed."

"That's been bothering me too," I said.

"Why?" said Kiira.

"The Wendigo aren't just a gang," I said. "They consider themselves incarnations of the Wendigo. Evil spirits. The vengeance of the wilderness. All their murders are attributed to the land. Every time you hear of a hiker going missing, or someone's found frozen solid in the woods, there's a high chance the Wendigo are behind it. Who they kill, and how they do it, is their most closely guarded secret. That's how Mikwam knew the darkweb site was legit. They knew his deepest darkest secret."

Gow rubbed his chin.

"Points to it being another Wendigo," he said.

I nodded.

"I think I'm going to have to pay Moosejaw a visit." I said.

Kiira's eyes widened. Moosejaw's lair was hidden deep inside the Boundary Waters. It wasn't the kind of place you paid a social visit. It was the kind of place you went to die.

"If it's one of his guys that's spilling secrets," I said. "He'll want to know. And if it is, Moosejaw will solve the problem for us."

Gow smiled.

"See that," he said. "We're getting somewhere."

There came a beat of silence. Then Maldonado said, "I think not."

All three of us stopped and turned our heads. Maldonado had been in the corner of the room, facing the window, practicing his Muay Boran forms. He hadn't said a word in twenty minutes. You'd have thought he wasn't listening. And been a fool to do so.

"All of you, put your hand in your pocket," he said.

Like robots, we all did. Mine had nothing in it.

"Our friend Einarr here is unique in today's world," he said. "He's one of the last few who isn't bugged."

I looked at Gow, puzzled. He pulled his right hand from his pocket. It held his phone.

"Very good Gowain," said Maldonado. "What you're holding is your very own, personalized bugging device."

"You think they can actually spy on us?" said Kiira.

Maldonado smiled.

"Who's they?" I said.

Maldonado focused his gaze on me, eyes ablaze with their usual challenge. Remember how I told you Gow was sent to kill me? Maldonado gave the order. We settled our differences the old fashioned way, by me stabbing him in the throat with my shattered radius.

"Spyware companies," said Maldonado.

He floated to a nearby side table and opened a Macbook. He turned the screen toward Kiira. She threw a hand to her mouth.

"You fucking asshole!" she said.

I moved to get a better angle on the screen. When I saw what was on it, I laughed. Kiira's face was flushed. I'm not sure I'd ever seen her so embarrassed.

"Care to relive?" said Maldonado, his finger hovering over the play icon.

"Sure," I said, grinning.

"Don't you fucking dare!" said Kiira.

"We put on a pretty good show," I said, shrugging.

"That's not the fucking point," said Kiira. "That video was private. I had it locked away in an encrypted app."

"You seem to have misunderstood," said Maldonado. "For a modest six-figure fee, any number of companies will sell complete access to your phone. Military-grade spyware. All your calls, messages, passwords, photos, videos . . . everything will be forwarded, live. Anything the device's microphone can hear or its camera can see is recorded and uploaded. Instantly. Complete access to your entire life."

"What's a fucking password for?" Kiira said.

"In the end, very little," said Maldonado. "It's eloquently nasty software. One could spy on the entire world's population if one so desired. Think on that for a moment."

Kiira swore under her breath then skulled the rest of her martini.

"Delete it," she said. "Now."

Maldonado smiled.

"But of course," he said. "I was merely making a point."

Kiira poured herself another three inches of Russo-Baltique.

"So you're saying whoever did this had access to Mikwam's phone?" I said. "That's how they knew who he'd killed?"

Maldonado shrugged.

"I believe it's a strong possibility."

"How do we know it wasn't you?" I said.

Maldonado smiled at me. I didn't smile back.

"You'll have to trust me," he said. "Why else would I give you that information?"

I didn't trust him. But Gow did. And I trusted Gow.

"So you'll help me?" I said.

Maldonado measured me with his eyes. He pulled in a slow breath through his nose. Let it out.

"Yes," he said. "I will help you."

"Good," I said. "Here's what I need."

I told him. Afterward, he smiled.

"That's very you."

"So you'll get it for me?" I said.

"For you, anything."

7

My truck bounced and jolted down the narrow track, chains clawing for purchase in the powdery snow. Pine branches scraped and squealed across the sides of the truck. It was just on three o'clock, but already the light was fading. Snow fell steadily against the windshield. The track narrowed. I was nearing the end of the line. Five minutes later the track emptied out into a snowy clearing, just large enough to turn the truck around with the help of both winches.

I kept the engine running and the heater on and ran a quick inventory. I had on three layers of merino beneath a gore-tex shell, gloves, and balaclava, all in winter flecktarn. My backpack held three days worth of dry food, a 2L vacuum flask of water, two lighters, a flint, multi-tool, hunting knife, a thermal blanket, a set of dry clothing, and a film canister of cotton balls dipped in vaseline which had saved my life the last time I'd tried this.

I turned off the truck and climbed out. It was already well below zero and getting colder fast. I walked to the back of the truck, sat on the open tailgate, and clipped on my snowshoes. I locked the truck and hid the key high in a tree. Then set off.

I made my way due north by dead reckoning. In front of me was nothing but a million square acres of interconnected lakes, rivers and dense arboreal forrest. The Boundary Waters. The largest unguarded border between countries in the world.

I trudged through the pines. Darkness set in. Snow continued to fall. I'd been walking for just over an hour when I heard it. A crunch of snow. I stopped and peered through the trees. The beam of my headlamp discovered nothing.

"I'm here to speak with Moosejaw," I said in a clear voice. "Tell him Einarr Laukkanen wishes to sit with him."

I listened intently. I didn't hear another sound. I kept walking. Ten minutes later I heard it again. This time behind me. I stopped.

"Well done," I said, turning. "I didn't hear you until now."

A Wendigo stepped out from behind a pine into the beam of my headlamp. He wore a similar outfit to mine, except for the suppressed Sig Sauger MCX Rattler in his hands.

I put my hands up and smiled. I knew he wasn't the one to worry about. There'd be at least two more flanking me on either side, their suppressed Sigs beaded on my center mass.

"Moosejaw will see you," said the guy I could see. "Turn around. Keep your hands above your head. I'll direct you."

I did as I was told. He wound me through the trees for another thirty minutes. I was now totally lost. It was getting very cold. Finally, we got there.

The *waginagon* was hidden in the the center of a thick copse of pine. As we stepped out into the center clearing I saw that there were indeed two other Wendigo flanking me. I hadn't heard them once. They kept their cheeks to their rifles until I'd crossed the clearing and ducked through shelter's hide door.

Inside the *waginagon* it was very warm. A fire crackled in the center of the earthen floor, smoke wafting out the hole at the top of the dome. Makwa stood to my right. Too close for either of our liking. He hadn't shrunk any. He nodded to my backpack. I took it off and handed it to him. He took it in one meaty palm set it on the floor behind him. I took off my jacket and showed him my knives and lack of hammer. He took the knives and nodded. I stamped my feet and unclipped my snow shoes and leaned them against the wall of the shelter. My eyes adjusted to the gloom. Noodin stood on the far side of the room, opposite the fire. His 9mm was unholstered in his right hand and pointed at the ground. He could place a bullet in either eye before I could blink. Moosejaw sat at the fire, cross-legged, smoking from a long wooden pipe. I approached slowly, keeping my hands low at my sides.

I sat. Moosejaw stared into the fire, said nothing. He pulled from the pipe and offered it to me. I took a hit. The smoke was harsh and gave me an instant head rush. I handed back the pipe, then blew my smoke into the fire. Other than to use the pipe, Moosejaw sat perfectly still, his eyes never leaving the flames.

"I see you transported a new rifle shipment," I said. "Suppressed Rattlers. Very nice. Maldonado would have paid a fortune for those."

Moosejaw said nothing. Which was his way of affirmation. We sat and smoked for a while.

"Tell me about Mikwam," said Moosejaw. His voice was deep and reverberating.

I told him everything I knew. Which wasn't much. I apologised for throwing Mikwam out a window, but said he deserved worse. Moosejaw nodded very slightly. Which told me Mikwam was dead.

"Whoever's behind this knew who he'd blooded," I said. "How is that possible?"

Moosejaw said nothing. This time his silence meant, "I don't know."

"When you find out," I said. "I'd like to know."

A silent agreement passed between us.

I said, "I would also like the identity of anyone you run across the border, in either direction, until the perpetrator is found."

Moosejaw said nothing. That was a big ask. The Wendigo are deathly strict about their anonymity protocols. Moosejaw sat completely still for a long time, watching the flames. Finally, I caught an almost imperceptible nod of his head.

I said my thanks, then stood and headed out to face the elements.

8

Kiira and I had been holed up in my cabin for nearly a week. It had snowed lightly but steadily for the last three days and we were buried again. Kiira'd spent most of the time writing. I'd been training and keeping the fire going and trying unsuccessfully to come up with a plan. I'd yet to see her naked.

Then, this morning, calamity.

"What is it?" said Kiira, seeing my face.

"We're out of coffee," I said, crushing the empty bag in my fist.

She let her head loll back and let out a satisfied sigh.

"Thank fuck. We can go into town."

"No," I said.

"Yes."

"It's not safe."

"Einarr," she said, "I need to get back online. I have six thousand words to back up. It's giving me anxiety. And I know what you Norsemen are like without coffee. You should see your face right now. You look like you could murder someone."

She wasn't far off.

"Please," said Kiira. "We'll be careful."

I thought about it.

"I don't like it," I said.

"Please."

I let out a breath.

"Fine. But you do exactly as I say. No questions."

We made the trek to my garage. Even with the plow, chains and winch it was a bitch getting out to the road. Highway 61 was slightly better. It had been salted overnight, but there were already three fresh inches on top. I took it slow. The roads improved as we neared town. I pulled the truck over at My Sister's Place and got out. Kiira frowned.

"What are you doing?"

"You're going to drive in alone," I said, pulling up the collar of my jacket. "Park at the far end of the Java Moose parking lot, near the big oak tree. Count to a hundred, then get out. Walk in. Don't run. Don't look around. Once you're inside, buy me twenty pounds of dark roast."

Kiira opened her mouth to say something. I held up a hand.

"I said no questions."

She did as she was told. By the time she exited the truck I was in position along the marina. The panel van was easy to spot. Parked at the end of Superior Street right where it joins Highway 61. From there it had a good view all the way down town's main thoroughfare. The snow around the van was unbroken, which meant it had been there overnight. But the circle of clean black pavement below the tailpipe gave it away. They'd needed the heater.

Kiira made her way across the Java Moose parking lot. She cut quite the figure. She went inside. Eight minutes later she exited with a large paper bag under each arm. Twenty pounds is a lot of coffee. The van's engine turned over. The front wheels pivoted away from the curb. I ducked out from behind a Ford Explorer and walked up beside the van. I watched the driver's reflection in the big side mirror. He wore a black baseball cap pulled down low over dirty blond hair and sunglasses. Sunglasses in Minnesota in January. He noticed me just as I reared back my fist and punched a hole through the driver's side window.

Punching through a car window is not easy. Not unless you've put in some work on your technique. I had. I grabbed the guy by the throat and yanked his head out the hole my fist had made. I uppercutted him in the chin with my left and his head snapped around and he was out, head lolling down the side of the van.

The first bullet blasted a second hole through the glass. If the window hadn't spider-webbed when I punched it, the guy in the passenger seat might have got me. As it was, his view was obscured.

I ducked and spun and got behind the back wheel. A second bullet came out through the van's side panel. Low and at an angle. It cut a furrow through the snow six inches from my feet. I chanced a quick glance at Kiira. She was still making her way to the truck. She hadn't heard a thing. The gun was suppressed. A bad sign.

I tried to think but it was happening fast. The scar along my scalp and the hole in my thigh should tell you all you need to know about my skills at dodging bullets. I'm a big target. And I'm not fast.

I heard the passenger door open on the far side of the van. I ducked down and peered beneath it. Snow blocked most of the view, but I saw feet come down and skirt toward the back bumper. Keeping my head as low as my six-ten frame allowed, I grabbed a fistful of snow and ducked around the back end of the van. I made it to the edge of the back bumper and waited for the gun to appear. When he did, I realised I was dead. The guy was good. He hadn't edged along the side of the van as I'd hoped. He'd heard me coming and backed away through the calf-deep snow, toward the sidewalk. He side-stepped into view eight feet from me. He held the silenced handgun firmly in a gloved right hand, his left hand bracing his wrist. It was impossible for him to miss. I had nowhere to hide.

I threw the snowball underhanded. Flinching is an instinct. It happens automatically. He blinked and dodged his head to the side and took a fractional step back, all to avoid a harmless snowball. He didn't anticipate the curb beneath the snow. His heel clipped and his eyes went wide and he stumbled and fired and I was on him.

I took out my rage and mortal terror on his upturned screaming face.

9

"Einarr!" said Kiira. "What the fuck is going on!"

We were in my truck heading north out of town on Highway 61. It was snowing again. Visibility was bad. Kiira'd just watched me bind two unconscious men with duct tape and throw them into the bed of the truck. I was breathing fast, still jacked on adrenaline.

"Einarr," said Kiira. "Talk to me!"

"They're here for you," I said. "Grab job."

"*What?*"

"Kidnapping," I said. "The next item on the list. You're supposed to be in the back of that panel van."

Kiira's eyes went very wide.

"How'd you know they'd be there?" she said.

"I guessed," I said. "Java Moose is another one of your routines. Like the supermarket."

Her jaw fell open. Then her face got hard.

"You used me as bait."

"Yeah," I said. "I thought you knew that."

"You motherfucker."

"Sorry. I figured them for amateurs."

"They weren't?"

I shook my head.

"The second guy had a silenced MK-23. They don't sell

those at Target."

"What's that mean?"

"They were pros," I said. "At least the grab guy was. He had training. He got the bead on me pretty slick. I should have another hole in me."

"Why don't you?"

"I threw a snowball at him."

Kiira's eyes went even wider. I gave her a grin. I pulled the truck into the IGA parking lot and parked at the back, out of sight of the highway. I fished out my wallet from the center console and handed Kiira a wad of cash.

"Grab a cart," I said. "Buy four plastic buckets. The kind you use to mop the floor. The bigger the better. And four five-gallon water bottles. The big ones you invert on top of a water cooler. Know the ones I mean?"

She nodded, eyes still bugging with panic.

"If anyone asks, say it's for work," I said. "Go now. Be quick."

She went. I kept the engine running, hoping the vibration would keep the guys in back lulled to sleep. Ten minutes later Kiira was back pushing a cart. She'd gotten the correct stuff. I helped her transfer it to the back seat and we drove off, heading north.

"Where are we going?" said Kiira.

"Someplace we can talk," I said. "In private."

Kiira looked at me.

"What are you going to do with them?"

"That depends on them," I said.

"What are the buckets for? And the water?"

"You'll see."

We were silent awhile. I kept an eye on the rearview mirror. Visibility had worsened, which was ideal, but I needed to get off the road. I didn't feel like explaining to Sheriff Colson why I had two bound and gagged bodies in the trunk. I kept driving. The whole time I felt Kiira glancing over at me. She wanted to say something, but was scared to say it. I waited.

"Why aren't you afraid?" she said. "Someone just tried to kill you."

I nodded.

"They got closer than I liked."

"So why aren't you freaking out?" she said.

"Who says I'm not?"

"Are you?"

I thought about it.

"I'm replaying it," I said. "In my head. I wasn't at my best. I underestimated the second guy, which was stupid. He was the grab guy. The more difficult job. So of the two, he'd have the most experience. I should have expected that. The other guy was just the driver. I should have gone up the passenger side of the van, taken the other guy out first."

"So you screwed up?"

I nodded.

"But you're not afraid?" she said.

"I think I am," I said. "On some level."

"There are different levels?"

"Of course," I said. "Some fear is necessary. It's a survival mechanism. Keeps you alert, weary. Someone without any fear at all is dangerous, but not in a good way. I've known guys like that. They're reckless. They end up dead pretty quick. And they endanger others. But the opposite of that is too much fear. And that isn't good either. It paralyses you. Ever woken up in the middle of the night and thought someone was in the house and been completely unable to move?"

"Yes," she said. "Recently. It's horrible."

"That's too much fear. That's letting the fear control you."

"How do you overcome it?"

"Same as anything. Practice. And preparation. My grandfather spent the last fifteen years of his life training me for this kind of thing. I've had a lot reps."

She was quiet a moment.

"In The Pit?" she said.

I said nothing.

"Were you afraid in there?" she said.

I didn't want to talk about it. But I thought, maybe, it could help her.

"I was very afraid," I said. "One week before each fight they told us who we would face. You're fighting him. We all knew each other. We trained together. They put us all in the same block of cells, so we could talk to each other at night. That was all on purpose. They wanted us to get to know each other, so when we had to kill each other, it was that much worse."

Kiira looked aghast.

"How could you do it?" she said. "How could you kill another prisoner? For the entertainment of others?"

I took my time answering. It was very hard to talk about. Even now.

"I didn't have a choice," I said. "No, that's not exactly true. Some of the guys gave up. They made the choice to die, rather than kill. Others went insane. They loved the killing. It's what gave their life meaning. It's what they were best at. But the sick fucks running the show didn't like it when the fights were uneven. When one guy gave up. It wasn't a good spectacle for the paying customers. So they put a stop to it."

"How?"

I looked at her. The look said, *Sure you want to know?*

She swallowed. Then met my eye.

"If someone gave up," I said. "They'd stop the fight. A big alarm would go off and they'd come in with guns and restrain us. Then they'd give the spectators a show with the guy who'd quit. Something to bet on. Usually, it involved dogs. Sometimes, a hungry bear."

Kiira put a hand over her mouth.

"So I didn't really have a choice," I said. "It was survival. I had to trick myself. In The Pit, I wasn't fighting the other guy, I was staying alive another day. In order to escape. That was my only focus. To get out and get to the fucks who were behind the whole sick enterprise, make them pay with their lives."

"And you did," she said. "In the end."

"You're god damn right."

She was quiet after that. I wasn't sure I'd helped. We made it to the res without being pulled over. We were on federal land now. The Sheriff couldn't touch us. Twenty minutes later we were bumping along the same unmarked track I'd used to visit Moosejaw. A thump came from the back of the truck. Then another. Then a wild thrashing accompanied by muffled screams. Kiira looked at me with wide open eyes.

"They're awake."

10

"Most people don't understand how cold a Minnesota winter is," I said.

I was standing in the clearing at the end of the unmarked track. Kiira was in the truck with the engine running, trying not to look. The two guys from the van were each duct taped to a birch tree. Their mouths were gagged. The driver was a fattish guy with thinning blond hair. He whimpered a lot. The other guy was stocky and hard with a short-cropped military haircut. The moment I pulled him from the truck he'd tried to headbutt me. I'd had to hurt him quite a bit to get him up on the tree.

"Even Minnesotans forget," I said, "that in January it's colder outside than it is inside your freezer."

The fat guy was struggling to breath through his snot-filled nose. I knelt down in front of him and untied his shoes and took them off one at a time and then peeled off his socks. He began to scream and thrash behind the duct tape so I punched him in the gut. He tried to double over but the tape held him up. I watched to make sure he didn't vomit behind the duct tape and asphyxiate himself. He stopped thrashing, but kept moaning. His breathing wasn't getting any better.

I picked up one of the kitchen buckets from the stack

beside me and looped it under his left foot, then did the same with a second bucket and his right. He started breathing very fast. I stood and stepped out of the way before too much snot got on me. I ran some more duct tape around his lower legs to secure them tighter to the tree. Now he was standing with a bare foot in each bucket. I stood up and looked him in the eye. He was in the throws of a full-blown panic attack.

"The standard freezer temperature is zero degrees Fahrenheit," I said. "That's due to Van't-Hoff's equation. Rate of reaction doubles for every ten degree increase in temperature. The colder the freezer, the longer fruit and vegetables will keep their vitamin content, but too cold and they get freezer burn. So zero degrees it is."

Fat Guy cried some more and tried not to choke to death on his own snot. I walked over to the stocky guy. He was breathing just fine. He watched me with hard eyes. Rather than deal with him again, I sucker punched him in the liver. His core was hard as a two-by-four and he tried to swallow it, but there's no swallowing a good liver shot. Not when I throw it. As he wheezed through the agony I knelt down in front of him and did the same thing to his feet with the other two buckets.

I walked back to my truck and hefted all four water cooler bottles out of the back seat. I carried them, two in each arm, over to the two men and let them drop to the snow. Fatty started screaming behind his gag again.

"The thing is," I said, "it's colder than that out here. According to my truck dashboard, the current temperature is negative seventeen Fahrenheit, plus wind chill. That's pretty damn cold. As I'm sure your feet are telling you."

I picked up one of the bottles and pulled the plastic ring to open the seal, then thumbed off the cap. A little water sloshed out onto the snow. It froze instantly. I walked up to the fat guy and emptied all five gallons into one of his buckets. The excess water sloshed over the sides, melting the snow around it slightly before freezing solid. The fat guy screamed and sobbed and choked on his nose snot. I filled the other bucket with a second bottle. Then I did the same to both of the stocky guy's buckets. He stayed pretty calm, which I gave him credit for.

"Here's the deal," I said when I was done. "At this temperature and wind chill, it'll take about an hour for those buckets to freeze solid. Answer me truthfully, and you can walk out of here. Take too long, and you'll have ten pound ice blocks for feet. You won't be walking anywhere. Ever again."

The fat guy started hyper-ventilating in earnest. He was going to die if I didn't do something. I walked up to him and slid the end of my hunting knife beneath the duct tape encircling his face. I slit it open and and yanked it off his mouth. He sucked in a huge lungful of air then blurted, "I don't know nothing I swear! Jake paid me five grand to drive! Said he was grabbing someone. I didn't ask who or why or nothin'! That's all I know I swear to God!"

"What's your name?" I said.

"Mikey!" he said. "Don't kill me I swear to god it was Jake's idea he asked me to drive I don't know nothing I swear to God I don't kno—"

I slapped the duct tape over his mouth again. Mikey kept screaming. I walked over to Jake. I cut his duct tape and freed his mouth.

"Hi Jake," I said.

He shot a furious look over at Mikey, who bowed his head in dishonor.

"You're in The Labyrinth," I said.

That made him look at me.

"Fifty k for kidnapping," I said.

"Fuck you," he said.

I shrugged and turned and walked back toward my truck.

Mikey started screaming behind his duct tape. I was about half way there when Jake spoke again.

"Fifty k to grab her. I don't know anything else. That's how it works."

I turned and walked back toward him.

"They tell you where she'd be?" I said.

He looked at me. I waited. You could almost hear the water in the buckets freezing.

"The website said she got coffee each morning at a place called Java Moose," he said. "We been there watching for three days. Fucking Mikey is a piece of shit. Can't go three minutes without having to take a leak. Should never had brought him."

Mikey's head hung a bit lower.

"They have something on you?" I said to Jake.

He paused. I turned and headed toward the truck.

"Yeah," he said. "They got me."

I turned back.

"How?"

"I was in the Navy," he said. "SEALs. Well, almost. Pissed through BUDs. Failed the psych. Fucking yes sir no sir bullshit. Got DD'd not long after. Whoever got in touch with me knew all about it. Stuff nobody's supposed to know. So I figured they were military. Black ops. Real hush hush."

"What'd they say to do with her once you grabbed her?" I said.

"They didn't," he said. "Just had to kidnap her. Plan was to keep her until the money came through, then drop her. I figured it for a test. See if I was capable of handling an asset."

"Where were you planning on keeping her?" I said.

He breathed in and out.

"Duffy's," he said.

"Who's Duffy?"

"Guy I get most of my work from."

"Duffy the guy gave you the MK-23?"

Jake nodded.

"Where can I find him?"

"Works out of a bar in Duluth. The Dockside Tavern."

He had a thin smile on his face when he said it. He couldn't wait for me to go see Duffy. Duffy would show me.

"You know anyone else in The Labyrinth?" I said.

Jake shrugged. I waited.

"One guy," he said.

"What's his name?"

"Don't know. People call him Wraith."

"How you know him?"

"He does wet work for Duffy. Real slick. Scary motherfucker."

I couldn't think of anything else to ask, so I turned and walked back to the truck.

"Hey!" said Jake. "You said if we talked you'd let us walk out of here!"

"That's not up to me," I said.

I assumed a few Wendigo were within earshot. If not, the wolves would be here soon enough.

11

The Dockside Tavern was, aptly enough, opposite the docks, about a mile south of the Lift Bridge. It was a rusted shithole smack dab in the middle of an industrial area. There was a Range Rover parked on the street out front that stuck out like dog's balls. I pulled up behind it and headed inside.

The interior was exactly as shitty as expected. There was a pool table with a rip in the felt and a few wooden tables with odd chairs. A grimy bar stretched across the back wall with a handful of cheap bottles gathering dust behind it. There was a door at the far end past the tables. It was closed. Two guys were sitting in two of the odd chairs. When they saw me, they got up.

"Who the fuck are y- . . . *Sledge Laukkanen*?" said the smaller of the two guys. His hair was thinning on top and he was trying to make up for it with with a bad mullet. It wasn't working.

"I'm here to see Duffy," I said. "Jake sent me."

"Jake?" Mullet said. "He's out on a job for a few days."

"Job's over. Jake and Mikey won't be back."

The bigger of the two guys took a step forward. He had a wide bald head and very little neck.

"What you mean they won't be back?" No Neck said.

"They got cold feet," I said.

No Neck glowered at me. He was trying his best to look scary.

"Jake's been here a long time," he said. "Done plenty of work. He wouldn't just quit."

"Never said he did," I said.

"Then what exactly are you saying?"

"I'm saying Duffy needs to find some better guys."

The door behind the tables opened and a man walked out. Like the Range Rover outside, his double-breasted suit was glaringly out of place in this shithole. He had long dark hair tied at the back, very white teeth, and eyes that didn't smile.

"You Duffy?" I said.

"How can I help you?" he said.

"Tell me about The Wraith."

No Neck and Mullet exchanged a look. Duffy said nothing, but his eyes flickered.

"I'm going to need his name and address," I said. "Give it to me now and I'll only hurt you a little."

Duffy laughed and showed his teeth. No Neck and Mullet exchanged another look. While we'd been talking I'd been slowly edging forward, a few inches at a time. Almost imperceptibly. I was now less than six feet from the two of them. They'd both just realised it.

"You two," said Duffy, "show Mr. Laukkanen out."

I was pretty sure Mullet had a piece, because his first move was to reach behind his back, but by the time he did I'd punched him in the throat. He went down choking and I turned my attention to No Neck who came in low with his chin tucked behind his left shoulder and his fists up. I dropped an elbow down in an arc toward the top of his head and he put his forearms up to block which opened up his face for my rising knee. I heard bone buckle and he went down in a heap and I went back to Mullet who was still bent over choking. I hammered the second knuckle of my right middle finger into the base of his skull right where it connects to the spine and he lay down next to No Neck and stayed still.

I looked at Duffy. He opened his eyes wide and nodded, impressed.

"You're right. I need to hire some better guys."

He turned and walked back through the door into the next room. I followed. The door led to a small office with a desk and a grimy window looking out at a rusted corrugated iron wall. Duffy was behind the desk with a silenced MK-23 in his hand.

"You buy those direct from Maldonado?" I said.

That threw him a bit.

"What do you want?" he said.

"Your guy Jake was part of a darkweb group called The Labyrinth. You know anything about it?"

Duffy looked confused.

"What the hell's a darkweb group?"

"Indeed," I said.

Duffy held the gun on me. I'm not a fan of guns. So cheap. I really wanted the thing Maldonado was making for me, but it wasn't ready yet.

"Someone's terrorizing a friend of mine," I said. "They hired Jake to grab her. He planned on keeping her here until the money came through."

"I don't know anything about it," said Duffy.

Either he was telling the truth or he was so used to lying it came out like truth.

"So you're telling me one of your guys was going to hide a woman at your place for days without your say so?" I said. "That the kind of ship you run around here?"

Duffy's face darkened.

"Is it?" I said.

"No," he said. "It's not. But like I said, I didn't know anything about it."

I looked at him. He smiled. I pulled out one of the plastic

chairs in front of the desk and sat down. This seemed to give Duffy confidence. He was on my level now. And he had the gun.

"Tell me about The Wraith," I said, leaning back in my chair and resting a foot on the front of the desk.

Duffy shook his head back and forth, still smiling.

"What if I say please?" I said.

"Same answer."

I planted my back foot, the one still flat on the floor, and kicked the desk over top of him. It was a big heavy thing. A good three hundred pounds of solid oak. It was on him before he could fire the MK-23 and I was up and leaning over the top and slamming a fist down hard into his face and ripping the pistol from his hand. I tossed the gun behind me and leaned my weight on top of the desk and let all five hundred and fifty pounds press down on his ribcage.

"Tell me about The Wraith," I said.

Duffy told.

12

"Is it ready yet?" I said.

I was in Maldonado's library. Vaulted mahogany ceiling. Stone fireplace. Spiral staircase to get at the upper shelves. You get the idea. Gow was standing at the door. Kiira was safely tucked away on the estate in one of the other mansions. Gow'd put Rupert and Ajax on her around the clock. For the moment, she was safer than the president.

"It's barely been a week," said Maldonado.

"So?"

"So what you've asked for is cutting edge," he said. "A prototype. The materials are extremely difficult to synthesize, not to mention extremely costly. And you require a very large quantity. Then there's the craftsmanship. This has never been done before. It will take time."

"How much?" I said.

Maldonado breathed through his nose. No one rushed him. Not even me.

"Hard to say. But trust me when I tell you the world's best material engineers are at my disposal. It will be ready when it's ready."

I growled.

"Tell me about Duffy."

"Sounds like you got him talking quite effectively," said

Maldonado.

"Humor me."

Maldonado smiled thinly. He rarely bequeathed information about his business dealings.

"Duffy runs most of Duluth," he said.

"Define 'runs.'"

"Drugs, prostitution, guns," said Maldonado. "They all pass through him. And he takes his cut. He's got a crew that runs security, and a deal with the foreman at the docks. Gets his product in from Canada through Moosejaw, then out on the ore ships through the Lawrence Seaway."

"If he's got his own supply, why'd he buy from you?" I said.

"Someone along the chain tried holding out. He needed a show of force. For which he paid a hefty sum."

"I'm sure," I said. "Know anything about a guy called The Wraith? Does Duffy's wet work. Supposed to be real slick."

"Hmm," said Maldonado, tapping his chin. "Can't say for sure. Sounds ominous."

Gow shuffled his feet from his spot next to the door. I raised an eyebrow at him.

"I know him," he said.

"How?"

"The MK drop. Duffy had five guys there. The guy that did the talking sounds like Jake. There was a fat guy, real jittery, sounds like Mikey, some muscle, and a shooter."

"No Neck and Mullet," I said.

Gow nodded.

"And the fifth guy?" I said.

"Never saw his face," said Gow. "Stayed at the back. Overseeing. Gave me a bad feeling."

"Ex-military?"

Gow shrugged.

"Ex . . . something."

"Description," I said.

"Average height. Lean build. Had the look."

I ran a hand down my beard and stared at the fire a while.

"They're getting better," I said.

Gow nodded.

"Money's escalating. Bigger money buys better guys."

Something was still bothering me, but I couldn't quite place what it was.

"How's he getting the dirt?" I said. "He knew who Mikwam killed, and got access to Jake's psych. That information isn't lying on the ground."

Gow put his palms to the ceiling and shrugged.

"I already answered that," said Maldonado.

"Phones?" I said.

Maldonado said nothing.

"Then why hand deliver a letter?" I said. "If the guy's a tech guru, setting up dark web sites, hacking phones, why put his neck in the noose?"

Maldonado smiled.

"I believe you know the answer to that one."

I waited.

Gow said, "He wants us to know exactly how good he is."

I thought about that for a while.

"What about this Wraith?" I said. "How good do you think he is?"

"Good enough," Gow said.

"Plan?" I said.

"We could use Kiira as bait again."

I shook my head.

"You know what's next on the list."

Gow nodded slowly.

"Rape."

Our eyes met.

"Time to hunt," I said.

13

I was sitting at the bar in the Manitou eating a plate of walleye tacos and washing it down with Deer Brand. For a secret bar that only admits locals, the place was packed. Shane was holding court for a couple guys watching the Timberwolves' game.

"No fucking way you were better than Schilling, Sledge!" gasped Shane. He was gawping incredulously at the flat screen above the bar, palms on his head. ESPN had just released their list of the top seventy-five NBA players of all-time. They had me at 21. One in front of Shawn Schilling.

"He won three MVPs!" yelped Shane. "What'd you win? A couple measly rebounding titles?"

"Ten," I said. "But who's counting?"

"No one!" said Shane. "It's a travesty."

"I agree."

"You . . . wait . . . what?"

"I agree. Whoever wrote the list is full of shit. I shouldn't even be on it."

Shane stared at me with his mouth open, looking disappointed. He wanted the argument.

"But . . ."

"Shawn got me into the league," I said. "He hired the lawyers, made the big stink in the media. Without him I'd still be in prison. He was a superstar. I was just out there to protect him. Whoever wrote that list is an asshole trying to rile up dumbasses like you. And it's working."

Shane frowned, opened his mouth to say something, thought better of it, then said, "Where you been anyway? Haven't see you in weeks."

"Been busy," I said.

"With?"

"A problem."

"Anything I can help with?"

"As a matter of fact . . . "

This was, of course, why I was here.

"You know the owners of all the tourist cabins, I assume? The tucked away ones up the trail?"

"Sledge, I run the town bar," said Shane. "I know everyone."

"Can you get in touch with them? Discreetly?"

Shane raised an eyebrow.

"Sure. Why?"

"I need names and descriptions of all their current guests," I said.

Shane frowned.

"I'm not sure that's legal. What am I supposed to say when they ask why?"

"Drop my name," I said.

"That'll work," said Shane. "Who are you looking for?"

"It's best if you don't know. But Shane, listen to me."

I waited until he met my eyes.

"This is for real," I said. "Understand?"

I'm pretty sure he did.

14

"We don't even know it's him," said Gow.

We were laying prone in a snow hide taking turns watching the cabin through a pair of ATN PS31-3W dual night and thermal vision goggles. It was nearly four a.m. The night was bitter cold, but we were dressed properly and out of the wind and the air trapped between the snow and our bodies afforded us some insulation. Still, I wouldn't call it cozy.

"Guy named McKnight owns the place," I said between a mouthful of snow. "Last one in a line of four. Nothing out back but trees until you hit Deer Yard Lake a couple miles north. No egress in that direction. McKnight said it's a single male occupant. Called ahead yesterday afternoon on a private number. Gave a name of Bill Johnson. Paid cash. McKnight hasn't seen him other than a nod through the car window as he pulled off the highway and dropped the cash in the mailbox."

"Could be him," said Gow. He was also chewing snow. "Could also be some schmuck with five kids and a nagging bitch of a wife in need of a weekend of peace and quiet."

"If it is," I said, "he's in for a fucking surprise."

Gow turned his head. A balaclava hid his face, but I could feel his expression.

"What?" I said.

"You gotten any better at being quiet?"

"What do you think?"

"I think you couldn't sneak up on a corpse."

"Your point?"

"You know my point," said Gow.

"Are you saying if this guy's as good as we expect, attempting a sneak attack on his fortified position is tactically unsound?"

"That is, indeed, what I am saying."

"And yet here we are," I said.

Gow shook his head.

"And yet here we are."

"Time?" I said.

Gow checked his watch.

"4:01."

"Cold?" I said.

"Oh no, not at all," said Gow, eating another clump of snow. "If you'd brought scotch, I could use my bollocks for ice cubes."

"My grandfather could lay in one of these for weeks on end," I said. "All for a single shot at a high-value target."

"I'm not your grandfather," said Gow.

"Neither."

I rose to a crouch, crumbling the hide. The sky was clear and the moonlight reflecting off the snow made it easy to see. I was dressed head to toe in winter flecktarn, so from this distance I'd be hard to spot unless he had thermal on me, in which case I was fucked.

"Now?" mouthed Gow.

I shrugged.

"Fuck it," I said. "I'm bored."

I crept forward, attempting to sneak from tree to tree, but there was no real point. None of the birch trunks were wide enough to hide me, and at my quietest I made more noise than a grizzly bear in a swarm of hornets. I got to the edge of the trees, pulled in one quick breath, then broke across the clearing for the front wall of the cabin. I kept my head low and skirted as fast as my legs would carry me, high-stepping through the unbroken snow. If The Wraith was watching between the curtains, now would be a great time to put a bullet in me. I got to the front wall of the cabin with no new holes.

I stood with my back to the log wall next to the door and listened. I heard nothing other than my own breathing and the thump of blood in my ears. I pulled my sledgehammer from its sheath on my back and unclipped my Olight Warrior X tactical flashlight from my belt. There are times when my disdain for firearms really seems idiotic. This was one of those times. I put the flashlight between my teeth and gripped the neck of the sledge in my left hand and the bottom of the handle with my right and widened my stance and swung the flat of the hammer into the door like a battering ram. The door exploded inward and I barrelled in after it.

I was hoping the last thing The Wraith expected was for a giant barbarian to stomp straight up to the front door and bash it in with a hammer. I dove in the low and rolled to the center of the room, coming up on one knee. I had my flashlight in one hand and the sledge in the other and I flicked on the high-powered beam and swung the sledgehammer around in a wide horizontal arc paralleling the floor. Anyone within an eight foot perimeter was going to eat an eyeful of blinding LED and forty pounds of hardened steel.

As I spun I scanned the cabin's interior, checking corners and other possible hiding spots. The cabin's main room was comprised of a pot bellied stove and chimney, a wooden table, a small couch, and a kitchenet along the back wall. No one was in it. At the back an open door led to a toilet and sink, also empty, and a ladder climbed to a lofted sleeping area in the apex of the roof. I rolled again toward the back of the room and came up to my knee facing back toward the door. Gow was already in behind me, suppressed Rattler at his shoulder.

"Loft!" I yelled.

Gow swung his rifle upward and scanned the ceiling with the rifle's muzzle-mounted flashlight.

"Clear!" he yelled.

That's when a shape slipped through the front door of the cabin and placed a silenced MK-23 on the back of Gow's head.

"Took you long enough," said The Wraith.

15

"You didn't seriously think that would work?" said The Wraith.

Behind his white balaclava I sensed a cocksure smirk.

"Barging in the front door with a hammer?" he said. "Honestly? That was your play?"

Gow and I said nothing. We eyed each other through the darkness, trying to silently communicate some semblance of a plan. Gow's hands were in the air. I was still down on one knee, my sledgehammer clutched to my chest. Any sudden movement from either of us and I had no doubt The Wraith would put a bullet straight through Gow's face.

"I didn't figure you two for complete amateurs," said The Wraith. "Not when I saw the size of this behemoth barreling toward the door. But breaching a fortified location without a gun? Honestly that goes beyond mere idiocy, into the realm of insanity."

Gow and I said nothing.

"And what on earth was that ridiculous pirouette manoeuvre?" said The Wraith. The smirk in his voice widened even further. "Spinning around on one knee with a flashlight? Did you genuinely expect that to work?"

The Wraith let out a condescending snort, which turned into a sniff. He smelled the air. Once. Twice. Then he began to choke. He dropped the gun and his hands went to his throat but never quite made it. Before they got there his legs gave out and he went down to the floor, convulsing.

Gow gave me a thumbs up.

Unbeknownst to the asshole dying on the floor, as I'd rolled into the room I'd broken open a vial of oxalonitrile, also known as Cyanogen. A colorless NFPA Level 4 gas with an LC50 toxicity of 0.06 parts per million. It interrupts the electron transport chain inside your mitochondria, preventing your cells from producing energy. That's a complicated way of saying it's really nasty shit. The tiniest whiff will knock you unconscious instantly.

My ridiculous pirouette had stirred the stale air in the enclosed space, increasing the heavy Cyanogen molecules' rate of diffusion into The Wraith's nostrils. Gow and I had been holding our breath for the last few minutes, waiting for it to hit. Now we had to get The Wraith's convulsing body out into the open before he inhaled a lethal dose, without inhaling any ourselves.

Clenching every muscle in my face to keep the air out, I sheathed my hammer and grabbed The Wraith's booted feet while Gow hefted him beneath the armpits. Together we shuffled out the door with the body. We rounded the side of the cabin, lungs shrieking for air. We got to the back and into the slicing wind. We dropped The Wraith and I looked at Gow and held up ten fingers. I dropped them one at a time, counting down. I faced my nostrils into the wind in case a few molecules of Cyanogen had been caught in my nose hairs. Finally I dropped my last finger and Gow and I opened our mouths and gasped deep lungfuls of glorious air.

Gow offered his knuckles, which I bumped. I chucked him a roll of duct tape from the pocket of my jacket.

"Where on earth do you get that shite?" said Gow, as together we hog tied The Wraith's hands and feet.

"High school chem lab," I said.

"You can mail order it?"

"No," I said. "You gotta make it. *Breaking Bad* sucked, but it wasn't wrong about the chem teacher bit. You can make pretty much anything if you know what you're doing. The base reaction is just methane and ammonia in oxygen with a platinum catalyst. Methane comes out of the taps and you can buy ammonia at IGA. That gets you hydrogen cyanide. React the HCN with sodium hydroxide, a chemistry class staple, and you got aqueous potassium cyanide. Then it's a simple reaction with Copper(II) sulfate, another staple, and you got yourself some Cyanogen. I can get you more by the end of the week. With nail polish."

Gow raised an eyebrow, then shook his head. With The Wraith gagged and hog tied we hefted him once again and started the long trudge through the snow to the truck. We'd parked just off the highway about a quarter mile from McKnight's driveway and worked our way up the hill through the woods to scope out the cabin.

"How long until someone can go in there?" said Gow, nodding back toward the cabin.

"Day or two to be safe," I said. "Be quicker if you want to go back in and open a couple windows."

"No thanks."

"I'll let McKnight know," I said. "I got 10k cash to pay for the door and the favor."

"Would you look at that," said Gow.

"What?"

"Sledge Laukkanen, gone soft?"

We dropped the The Wraith at the top of the hill. He'd stopped convulsing, but his breath was coming in fits and starts. His energy system was still rebooting. I checked his pulse. It was there, rapid but weak.

"Think he'll make it?" said Gow.

I shrugged, then put a boot on The Wraith's back and

shoved him down the hill. He flipped and flopped like a dead deer, ricocheting hard off a birch tree before somersaulting the rest of the way down.

"Well, there goes that theory," said Gow.

I looked at him.

"Sledge Laukkanen, still an arsehole."

16

I'd just finished my sixth set of pinch-grip pull-ups on the ceiling beams of my garage when The Wraith came to. We'd stripped him to his underwear and bound him to a chair in the middle of the concrete floor. He jerked awake as if from a bad dream, blinked a few times, then puked on himself. Gow picked up a bucket of water and doused him. The Wraith yelped and spat and spluttered, then puked again. Gow doused him with a second bucket then headed over to the sink to refill.

"Wha' . . . appen'?" slurred The Wraith, his chin on his chest.

"You inhaled a nearly lethal does of Cyanogen," I said. "What you're experiencing now is the worst headache of your life along with severe nausea. Both of which will persist for the next three to four days unless you take these."

I pointed to a nearby chair which held a small glass vial of amyl nitrate and IV bags of sodium nitrite and theosulfate, all of which I'd mixed in the high school chem lab. The Wraith tried lifting his head. The motion made him puke again. Gow doused him with a re-filled bucket.

"Whether I administer them or not is entirely up to you," I said. "Without the antidote, your mitochondrial system will sustain permanent damage. Climbing a set of stairs will feel like scaling Everest for the rest of your relatively short life."

"You . . ." murmured the Wraith. "How?"

"How did I know you weren't in the cabin?" I said.

The Wraith bobbed his head the tiniest bit, then dry wretched. Gow doused him again and headed back to the sink.

"You're not used to hiding in the cold," I said. "You buried yourself pretty well, but you didn't put snow in your mouth. Every time you exhaled it lit up on thermal like a strobe light."

The Wraith shook his head, which brought on another bout of nausea. Gow doused him again.

"Please . . . stop," said The Wraith.

"Wraith's a cute little nickname," I said. "How'd you get it?"

"Call sign," he mumbled. "I was . . . Force Recon."

"What's the name on your phone bill?" I said.

"Jarek," he said. "Kowalski."

"What's a Force Recon Marine doing in Duluth working for a shithead like Duffy?" said Gow.

"My mom got sick," Jarek said. He was talking a little easier now. "Got out. Hardship Discharge. First six months or so were fine. Then money got tight. Needed cash to foot mom's bills. What else was I gonna do? I have a certain skill set, but it's no use at Home Depot. So I went looking for work. Found Duffy."

"When did you join The Labyrinth?" I said.

Jarek tried to look up again and another bout of nausea wracked his abdomen. He was all out of puke. Gow witheld the water this time.

"Few months ago," said Jarek, when he was through wretching.

"You got a name for me?" I said.

Jarek shook his head. And convulsed again.

When he could speak, he said, "I get an email. Sometimes

a text. Different address or number every time."

"A darkweb code?" I said.

He nodded.

"Tell me how it works."

"I check the site," he said. "It's got a link to the money. Money's real. It's got another link to the next job. I do it. Money appears in my account. I have no idea who's behind it."

I pulled back the chair containing the drugs. Jarek saw me do it and breathed out. I looked at Gow. He tilted his head back and forth, considering, then nodded once. He believed him.

"How many jobs have you done for them?" I said.

Jarek lifted his head. It stayed upright a full five seconds before he vomited bile again. Then he said, "I'm Depth 4."

I frowned.

"What's that mean?"

Jarek kept his chin on his chest this time.

"There's a ranking system," he said. "When you check the site, it tells you your current score and rank. You start at Depth 1 of The Labyrinth."

"An example being a death threat on a woman in a supermarket parking lot?" said Gow.

Jarek tilted his head and wretched.

"Yeah," he said once he'd regained his breath. "A death threat is involved. I had to do some tail work. Basic intel gathering."

"On Kiira?" I said.

Jarek shook his head.

"No. Some football player at UMD," said Jarek.

Gow and I exchanged a look.

"Describe him," I said.

"Big motherfucker," said Jarek. "Like six-eight, three-fifty. Hard into the gear. With the right training he'd be a monster, but I suspect he's a complete moron."

"His name is Marx Hegseth," I said.

Jarek tried raising his head and wretched again. Afterward, he said, "You know him?"

I nodded.

"He killed a guy in an underground cage fight," I said. "I assume that's what they had on him. The Labyrinth hired him to threaten the same woman you were hired to grab. Didn't work out too well for him, either."

Jarek nodded. "He'd be Depth 1."

"Not anymore," I said. "Let me guess, your buddy Jake, the SEAL washout, was Depth 3."

Jarek took a moment to reply.

"They sent Jake after her too?" he said.

I nodded.

Jarek went silent again. I let it come to him.

"They're sending someone from each Depth," he said. "All for the same woman."

"Indeed," I said. "Which begs the question. Who's Depth 5?"

Jarek didn't reply.

"If you can't give us a name," I said. "You're not getting the antidote."

Jarek pulled in a breath through his nose. Let it out. Nodded. He knew the score.

"I don't know anyone else in The Labyrinth," he said. "But . . . I know there's exactly a hundred people in it."

"How?" said Gow.

"Everyone is ranked," he said, "You start at a hundred and work your way up, or I should say down, deeper into The Labyrinth. My current Labyrinth rank is 59 out of 100. Depth 4. If this Descent would have been successful, I'd descend to Depth 5. Depth 5 jobs pay two-hundred k. Grievous bodily harm. But I was unsuccessful. My ranking's gonna drop. And I suspect there'll be some sort of punishment."

"Any idea what that might be?" I said.

Jarek shook his head.

"My guess," he said. "They'll send a Depth 4 or 5 for my mother."

"How deep does it go?" I said.

Jarek shrugged.

"Depth 10 I think."

"Let me guess," I said. "The top ten guys."

Jarek shook his head, swallowing back spew.

"There's only one guy at Depth 10," he said. "The Final Boss, they call him. Rank 1."

"Who is it?" I said.

Jarek shrugged.

"No idea," he said. "They have a name printed at the bottom, but it's in Russian or some shit."

I looked at Gow. He raised an eyebrow.

"You got a picture of it?" I said.

Jarek nodded.

"On my phone," he said.

I looked at Gow. He nodded. If it was on his phone, Maldonado would have it. I looked back at Jarek.

"I'm really sorry," I said, looking down. "That's not enough."

Jarek blinked a couple times, then let out a long breath through his nose. He seemed to relax in on himself. He didn't beg. Death was, after all, his chosen profession. Finally, he lifted his head, managing to control the nausea one final time, and said, "You sure it's her they're after?"

That one hit me right between the eyes.

"What do you mean?" I said.

"They're sending a guy from each Depth," he said. "All for the same target."

"So?"

"Sounds to me like they know she's protected," he said.

I looked at Gow. He was looking right back. We both

turned to Jarek.

He smiled up at me, weakly, and said:

"Sounds to me like they're after you."

17

Kiira was staying in a suite on the top floor of Maldonado's second largest mansion. If you're picturing the penthouse at the Four Seasons, aim higher. The bathroom alone was three times the size of my cabin. Kiira and I were in the master bedroom drinking coffee and eyeing each other.

"I'm so over this, Einarr," she said.

She was still in bed, half-tucked under million thread count Egyptian cotton bedsheets. I was in a chair near a window checking out the billion dollar view of Lake Superior.

"Yeah," I said, sipping coffee. "Must be tough staying in this shit hole."

Kiira didn't smile.

"Don't be an asshole," she said. "There're enough of them waiting in line to kill me."

"Yeah," I said. "About that."

Kiira's coffee cup paused an inch in front her mouth.

"What?" she said.

"We caught the fourth guy," I said.

"And by caught, you mean killed," she said.

I shook my head. Kiira took a sip of coffee, frowning.

"You let him go?" she said.

"Yes," I said. "But he won't be troubling you anymore. In

fact, he might be useful."

"You made friends with him?" said Kiira.

"Not exactly."

Kiira let out an exasperated sigh.

"Is this like you and Gow?" she said. "Some macho bullshit where once you've tried to kill each other you pass some sort of test?"

"It's not disimilar," I said.

"I'll ignore the double negative," said Kiira, her face hard.

"Like Gow," I said, "he was simply hired to do a job."

Kiira's jaw clenched.

"A job?" she said. "That's what I am now? A fucking job?"

I sighed.

"Hear me out," I said. "I'll admit the job he was hired to do wasn't nice. It takes a certain kind of guy to do that sort of thing in the first place, regardless of the money involved. But you have to remember, this is a man with a very particular skill set. The government invested tens of millions of dollars into him to turn him into a world-class weapon. Then he has to re-enter normal society and suddenly those skills are useless. He can't get a job at fucking Home Depot. You hear what I'm saying? What's a guy like that supposed to do when someone waves serious cash in his face?"

"Take it to rape an innocent woman," said Kiira, nonplussed.

"He didn't know if you were innocent, or not," I said.

"Would he have cared if he did?" said Kiira.

I let out a breath through my nose.

"Probably not," I said. "Like I said, he's a weapon. He's paid not to care."

"So that's it?" she said. "He gets a free pass?"

"He gets severe cyanide poisoning," I said. "Take my word for it, that's not a free pass. And he could be useful. He's on the inside of this thing, and now he owes me his life."

Kiira eyed me over her coffee cup.

"You think you can trust him now?" she said.

"I don't need to trust him," I said. "I just need to be able to use him. He's already given us some useful information."

I explained to her about the ranking system.

"So you're telling me the guys coming next are going to be even better?" she said. "But you have no idea who they are, or when they'll be coming?"

"Correct," I said.

"Gee Einarr," said Kiira, casting aside her empty coffee cup. "That's really fucking great. Thank you so much."

"He also made another interesting point," I said.

Kiira eyed me, suspicious.

"I'm listening," she said.

"Maybe it's not you they're after," I said.

Kiira blinked a couple times.

"What are you talking about?" she said. "Every one of them has admitted that I was their target."

"Correct," I said. "But whoever's behind this has been one step ahead of us the entire time. They knew your habits. Your tendencies."

"So?"

"So it follows that they also knew your associates."

A pause.

"Your point?" she said.

"It's fair to assume they would have known exactly what you would do once you were threatened."

Kiira stared at me, her eyes slitted.

"You think they're after you?" she said.

I shrugged.

"The letter had no name on it," I said.

"It was under my pillow," Kiira said. "They snuck into my fucking bedroom, Einarr."

"Which they knew would make you run straight to me," I said. "And I'm hard to get to. There aren't many people I'd let get as close. No one, in fact."

Kiira closed her eyes and pinched the bridge of her nose.

"Well that's just fucking great, Einarr," she said, opening her eyes. "Really fucking great. I'm so glad I know you."

"It's not all bad," I said. "If it really is me they're after, you just need to stay here until I can deal with the rest of these assholes one by one."

"Yeah, that's amazing news," said Kiira.

"And if we're right," I said. "For the first time, we're one step ahead of them. You can look into it from this side. Figure out who, locally, might want to hurt me."

"Where to fucking start?" she said. "I thought you said you don't care about motive."

"I don't," I said. "Motive's your bag. You told me yourself. You write yourself into a corner, then figure out who did it. So . . . do that."

"Fuck you, Einarr," she said. "I mean that with all my heart."

I smiled.

"That'a girl."

18

Later that same day Gow and I were in Maldonado's training facility doing some light sparring. If I ever turn into the sort of asshole who refers to my home gym as a "training facility," you have my permission to shoot me, but in Maldonado's case the description was apt. He had enough weight in there to sink an ore ship, along with every imaginable piece of martial arts training equipment money could buy. Gow and I were repping out some disarming techniques with the rubber handguns when the intercom buzzed.

"Sledge," came Rupert's voice from somewhere in the ceiling. "There's a big motherfucker at the gate says he needs to see you right away."

Rupert was one of Gow's guys, currently on perimeter detail. Gow tapped my shoulder and nodded to a wall-mounted monitor that had just flicked on with a feed from the front gate. Sitting behind the wheel of an enormous Chevy pick-up truck, in startlingly clear 4K detail, was Marx Hegseth. The camera zoomed in on his face. Marx looked like absolute shit. Two black eyes owled the sides of a white cast holding together his shattered nose. His lips were splayed over a network of gleaming metal wires.

"His jaw's wired shut," said Gow.

"Can you hear me, Rupe?" I said.

"Loud and clear," said Rupert. "Should I let him in or tell him to fuck off? Mr. Maldonado said your call."

"Bring him to the training facility," I said.

"Roger that."

On screen, the camera zoomed out. The gate swung open and Marx rolled onto the estate. The feed switched from camera to camera as the Chevy climbed the winding drive and arrived at the double front doors of the main mansion. Clancy and Ajax met Marx outside the truck, guns drawn. Marx came out with wide eyes and hands up. Ajax ordered him against the truck and patted him down. Marx wasn't carrying.

I looked at Gow. He was watching his guys work. They escorted Marx through the front door and across the foyer to the elevator. All three got in. The camera switched to a high shot inside the elevator. Marx didn't move a muscle on the way down. The MK-23 muzzle pressed to his ribs probably had something to do with it. The elevator dinged on our end and the doors slid open. Gow and I were there waiting. When Marx saw me, his eyes bugged even wider. I watched him relive our first encounter.

"Leave him," said Gow. "I'll let you know where to dump the body when Sledge is finished with him."

Marx's eyes nearly popped out of his head. I forced myself to keep a straight face. I almost felt bad for the guy. Until recently, the big lug had imagined himself quite the tough guy.

Clancy and Ajax shoved Marx roughly from the elevator and let the doors slide shut behind him. Marx glanced nervously over his shoulder, then back to me and Gow. He'd realized, quite suddenly, that he was alone with us and in a very bad spot.

"Plea'," he said between locked teeth. "I don' wan' any 'rouble."

I stepped forward. Marx leapt back as if bitten and hit the elevator doors and got a second fright. He looked like a cornered three-hundred pound mouse.

"You shaid to repor' t'you when I had shomethin'," he said quickly.

I said nothing. Made sure not to blink.

"I got a . . . a figh'," Marx said, his voice teetering on the edge of panic. "Tonigh'."

He was breathing in and out loudly between his teeth, trying to control the panic and not doing a very good job of it.

"You got a code?" I said.

He nodded, eyes wide.

"What'd the darweb site say?"

He squeezed his eyes shut and tried to hold it together and let out a whining cry.

"I didn' know it wa' like thish!" he cried.

"Like what?" I said.

"Ish . . . ish fucked up, man!" said Marx.

"Explain," I said.

"I—I'm shupposed to show up at a GPSh location," said Marx. "There'll be a bottle of gash there. I'm supposed to pu' on the mashk and inhale the gash."

I looked at Gow. He raised his eyebrows. Marx's panicked breathing increased in pace.

"And then what?" I said.

"How the fu' should'I know!" whined Marx, his panic starting to overflow.

"Walk me through it," I said. "How did you get in this deep?"

"I don' fucking know!" cried Marx. "I got a broken fucking jaw and a broken fucking noshe and I can barely walk and I'm going to fucking die man! Help me! If I don't show up they'll fucking kill shomeone face to me! Tha'sh wha' they shaid. They'll shend a Depsh 5 for someone closhe to me! I shouldn' never have done thish! I shouldn' have clicked tha' fucking link!"

Marx dropped to his knees and started sobbing in earnest. I took the time to do some light stretches. Marx sobbed and sobbed. I did some more stretches. Finally, the crying slowed. Marx breathed in and out a bit, then looked up at me. A three-hundred-and-fifty pound puddle.

"What link?" I said.

Marx sniffed and blinked a couple times.

"Wha'?" he said.

"You said you never should never have clicked the link," I said. "What link?"

Marx sniffled a moment, then said, "There's a lisht. We're all ranked man. I'sh like a fuckin' game!"

"Tell me about the game," I said.

Marx sniffled. "A' firsh I wash the lowesh rank. Depsh 1. 100 ou' of a 100. Then I did my firsh job. Threa'en the wri'er chick. The money came through and my rank wen' up to 85. There wash a link to my nexsh job. Beating. But then you came in and . . . and I failed! Sho now there'sh a punishmen'!"

"The link," I said.

Marx nodded and started crying again.

"What'd the link say?"

Marx sniffled and blinked back his tears.

"I'sh a Death Matsh," he said.

He broke down crying again. Gow and I exchanged another look. I stretched some more and waited for Marx to cry himself out.

Eventually, he said, "If I win, I deshend, b-but if I loshe . . . or if I don't show . . ."

Marx started sobbing again.

"I see," I said. "You got any idea who you'll be fighting?"

Marx shook his head, snot dribbling from his nose onto the rubber floor mats.

"A-all they told me wash hish level," he said, between sobs. "Depsh 4. Rape."

19

Marx's GPS location turned out to be an abandoned truck stop off an old two-lane highway in the middle of nowhere, half-way between Embarrass and Ely. I arrived just on 8 p.m., the time designated on Marx's darkweb site. It was full dark, no stars, and very, very cold.

The truck stop was buried in a good three feet of hard-packed snow, and fucking eerie. Most of the windows of the old building were boarded over, but there were enough darkened gaps to make me real nervous. Out back, a dilapidated car wash made an ideal sniper hide.

I found the gas bottle and mask behind the middle deisel pump beneath the awning, exactly where Marx said it would be. The olive green bottle reminded me of those you see on NFL sidelines pumping oxygen into obese linemen. I picked it up. It was very cold. I wondered if they'd calculated how much the change in temperature would effect the bottle's pressure. I guessed not. Not that it mattered. I unscrewed the valve and emptied the bottle's contents into the freezing wind. Then I pulled up my jacket collar, leaned against the rusted pump, and waited.

They had me under surveillance. Of that, I had no doubt. At this temperature, if Marx had been stupid enough to actually inhale the gas and knock himself unconscious, he'd have maybe twenty minutes before he froze to death. They knew I was here. And they were stationed not too far away. My guess: they had an SUV parked on a side road less than ten miles up the highway in either direction and were watching on a wireless camera feed. I had a quick look around, but there was no point looking for the camera now. Even if I found it and disabled it, it's job was already done.

Sure enough, eight minutes later, headlights appeared on the desolate highway.

"Let's fuckin' do this," I said to the wind.

The SUV slowed and pulled off the road a hundred feet from the truck stop. There it sat, idling. I stood up under the awning and waited. If they planned on shooting me, now was the time.

But they wouldn't.

If Wraith was right, and I figured he was, whoever was behind this shitshow was after me specifically. If so, they didn't want me shot dead in the boondocks where no one would find me until spring. They'd put in too much effort already. They wanted to haunt me. They wanted me in the game. Inside The Labyrinth. Which meant whoever was in that car had been given strict instructions to take me in alive.

I didn't envy their task.

"Come on, ladies!" I shouted through the frozen night air. "It's fucking cold out here! Let's get this over with!"

The SUV idled. A few minutes passed. Then I heard the transmission shift, and the SUV eased forward.

I wondered if there were three guys in there, or four. They would have learned from last time that two wasn't enough. Three was logical. A driver, a gun, and some muscle. Four was smarter. Driver, gun, two guys to subdue me. Which meant they planned on incapacitating me and stashing me in the back.

Good luck.

I walked out into the road and marched straight up the

center line toward the SUV. It was a good call. As the SUV closed in I heard the electric buzz of the window going down and in the glare of the headlights saw the guy in the passenger seat lean his head and arm out the window and aim a gun at me. If I'd been on the side of the road he wouldn't have had to lean out. I sprinted forward and dove head-first at the ground, came up out of a roll and dove again. I heard the shot and the tinkle of breaking glass to my left. Tranq dart.

It takes roughly five seconds to reload a tranq gun. I heard commotion in the front seat as the shooter scrambled to reload the dart, by which time the SUV had stopped and I'd made it to the front bumper and ducked beneath the hood. Without pausing to catch my breath I dropped to the ground and rolled onto my back and reached under the truck and pulled myself fast beneath it as if climbing a greasy metal ladder. I popped up behind the rear licence plate.

Had they heard me? Only one way to find out.

I scampered low around the passenger side. The passenger window was still down. I watched the side mirror. The guy inside saw me. The gun came out the window with a tranq dart loaded, but now I was behind him and he didn't have the angle. The guy shifted in his seat and his arm came all the way out and I stood and pulled his arm into my hip and yanked back hard. His elbow dislocated and I heard his humorous fracture with a muffled crack.

The guy screamed and the tranq gun dropped and I dropped and caught it before it hit the ground. The door behind me opened and I saw hands come up and I stood up on my tiptoes and brought the butt of the gun down hard on the shaggy head I found there. My freakish height is good like that. The guy dropped and I figured he was out of the way for the time being.

The opposite rear door opened and a big bald guy got out. They'd brought four after all. Smart. This one, however, was stupid enough to glance at me over the top of the SUV, which gave me plenty of time to shoot him in the face with the tranq dart. His hand went to his cheek and he stumbled back and yanked out the dart and looked at it for a second and then his eyes rolled back into his head and he fell straight back.

That left the driver.

If he'd been smart he would have cranked the SUV into drive and peeled off to fight another day. Instead, he opened his door and got out and went for his gun which he had stashed somewhere under his jacket. He was still fumbling with his lapel when my elbow fell from the sky like a meteor and obliterated his face. He went down and I stood on top of each arm, pinning them to the road. He thrashed and bucked while I reached down with both hands and strangled him.

Once he'd stopped bucking I turned to the guy with the broken arm, still sitting in the passenger seat. The only guy still alive and conscious. He was clearly in a lot of pain. I left the driver lying dead in the road and walked around the front of the SUV and pulled open the passenger door. The guy with the broken arm shied away, as if to shrink in to the seat crack.

Which is when I made my mistake.

20

The guy had dark hair and three day's growth of black beard and hard eyes that weren't used to being afraid. His right arm hung oddly in his jacket and appeared to have an extra joint above the elbow. His face was white, his forehead beaded with sweat. His breath came in labored gasps. He appeared completely incapacitated by the pain, which is why I leaned in confidently and nearly took a knife in the eye.

The blade came up fast and I dodged but not enough and it bit deep into the bone of my right eye socket and scraped along the side of my skull. The guy struck with his weak hand and had aimed for a small, moving target. My eyeball. If he'd gone for my throat or heart or gut I'd have been in real bad shape. The guy reared back and tried again but I was ready this time, and fucking pissed. Gow and I had been training disarming techniques that very morning for fuck's sake.

I parried the second stab with my forearm and grabbed his wrist and yanked it out of the car and slammed the door until bone crunched and knife dropped to the road. Then I opened the door and stood over the guy, bleeding and furious.

"Who hired you?" I snarled.

I couldn't see out of my right eye.

"Fuck you," said the guy in an eastern European accent.

"Wrong answer," I said.

I grabbed the wrist of his broken dislocated arm and jerked it up and down as if snapping a towel. He let out an ear-piercing shriek and clutched at his shoulder.

"That jog your memory?" I said.

He shook his head, momentarily unable to speak.

"I know nothing," he groaned when he could. I almost believed him. These guys were street labor. They wouldn't know much.

Then, to my left, movement. I snapped my head around. The guy I'd brained with the butt of the tranq gun had regained consciousness. He lay on his stomach on the road shaking his head and blinking. I walked up and stood over top of him. I looked back at guy in the car to make sure he was watching. He was. The guy beneath me put his palms to the pavement to push himself up. I raised my boot. The guy in the car's eyes went wide and he called out in Russian.

The guy underneath me looked up just as I stomped down. Skull crunched under heel. The guy spasmed beneath my boot. I raised my foot again. The guy in front seat looked at me with wide eyes.

"Still nothing?" I said to him.

He looked down at his friend, who was in a real bad way, then back to me.

"Fuck you," he said. This time, he smiled.

I stomped down. Harder. The guy on the road stopped spasming. I walked back to the guy in the SUV and placed my hand on his right wrist again.

"Okay okay okay!" he said, shrinking back. He couldn't move his right arm at all. I closed my fingers around his wrist.

"The drop!" he said.

"What about it?" I said.

"I know where it is," he said.

"Give me the address," I said.

He shook his head. I gave his arm another yank. When he could speak again, he said, "I can show you."

"Tell me," I said, squeezing his wrist with the full force of my grip. Bones creaked. "Or I'll rip this arm off and beat you to death with it. I've done it before."

"If you kill me," he groaned, "you'll never find it."

I torqued the guy's arm once more then walked to the back of the SUV and opened the hatch. Inside I found a box of zip ties and a roll of duct tape, along with a black canvas bag I assumed was meant to be used as a hood. I headed back to the front seat and yanked the guy out by his bad arm and zip tied his wrists behind his back. He was less than enthused by the manoever. Then I shoved him into the footwell behind the front seats.

"Stay down and shut the fuck up or the arm's coming off," I said.

I hefted the other three bodies from the road and chucked them in the ditch. The guy I'd tranq'd was still out. He'd most likely freeze to death before he woke up. I wasn't too worried about it.

I got behind the wheel of the SUV and adjusted the seat, then checked my face in the rearview mirror. I wasn't looking great. Blood painted the entire right side of my head. Bone gleamed within a splayed five-inch gash. Good news: my eyeball was intact.

Using the knife I'd recovered from the road I cut a swath of fabric off the black bag and pressed it to the gash. It stung like a motherfucker. I encircled my head in duct tape, fixing the fabric to the wound, and checked my handiwork in the mirror. I looked like a guy who'd just had his face cut in half.

"Okay," I said, looking back into the foot well. "Where to?"

It took us just over an hour to get there. An abandoned

iron ore processing plant just outside of Mork Lakes. I remembered it. In the early 90's the local taconite mine had dried up and the town of Mork Lakes had died alongside it. Nowadays the derelict sprawl of rusted iron buildings, broken conveyor belts, and steel connecting tunnels looked like the bad future from *Terminator 2*. I drove up to the rusted chain link gate and stopped the truck.

"What happens now?" I said.

The guy in the back had passed out a couple times along the way until I yanked his arm to ask for directions. I did so again.

"Follow the road to the train tracks," he gasped.

The perimeter road hadn't been plowed, but a truck had driven it recently. I followed the tire tracks through the snow until we bumped over a set of train tracks. There, a single set of footprints connected a gap in the perimeter fence to the nearest building of the abandoned refinery. Someone had been dropped off, and not too long ago. I looked back at the guy.

"We were supposed to leave you inside," he said.

"Leave me?" I said, pointing at my chest.

The guy's eyes widened. He'd just fucked up. So this was about me.

"I'm supposed to wake up inside that building?" I said.

The guy nodded. He was not in a good way.

"And what exactly do they have planned for me in there?" I said.

The guy attempted a grin.

"You don't want to know," he said, showing me his bloody teeth.

I punched the grin off his face, then turned off the engine and stepped out into the cold. I left the door open.

"If you can walk," I said, looking in at the guy, "you're free to go. If you're still here when I get back, I'll kill you."

The guy lifted his head to look at me.

"What makes you think you're coming back?" he said with a bloody grin.

"Call it a hunch," I said, and started walking.

21

I followed the footprints through calf-deep snow toward the refinery proper. The place was an infiltration nightmare. A hundred broken windows grinned from towering walls of rusted iron. There were two main buildings connected by a rising zig-zag of tunnels and broken conveyor belts, any of which could have held a shooter. Soon I was hemmed in on all sides.

The footprints led to an iron sliding door at the base of the right-hand building. I tried the handle. Locked. I looked down. The footprints had definitely entered here. I craned my neck, searching the rusted surface of the building. I found the first camera fifteen feet up. A semicircle of infrared lights grinning down evilly at me. I waved. Time passed. Whoever controlled the gate discussed with their superior what to do next. They hadn't expected me to arrive conscious. I took off my jacket and did a slow twirl with my arms up to show I was unarmed. Another minute or two passed, then I heard the click of an electromagnetic lock. I tried the door again. It rolled back on squeaking iron wheels.

Beyond the door: darkness.

Was I really going in there? At the moment, it didn't seem like the best idea. I let out a deep breath, looked around one last time, then stepped inside. The moment I ducked through the door it pulled shut behind me. I spun and tried for a handle but the inside of the door was smooth iron. I went for the gap but before I could get my fingers to it the door slammed shut and the lock re-engaged.

Fuck.

"Should'a seen that one comin'," I said aloud, turning back to face the darkness.

With the door shut, I couldn't see a damn thing. I closed my eyes and counted to ten. When I looked again the ghostly light from the broken windows shone along a stretch of pale concrete littered with scraps of broken machinery and crumbling pavement. Beyond that, a towering maze of pipes and vents, interlaced with narrow metal stairwells and catwalks, stretched off into the darkness.

I shook my head.

"A fucking labyrinth," I said. "Get it."

I glanced around more carefully. From where I stood, I counted ten more infrared cameras leering at me from the darkness. I imagined a hundred more mounted to every nook and cranny within the sprawling steel maze. I had an audience. I wondered how much they'd paid for a ticket.

"So what now?" I called loudly.

Except, I knew. There was someone else in here with me. Someone at Depth 4 of the Labyrinth. Waiting . . .

"I know you're there," I said.

No sound came from the darkness. But I could feel him. Watching.

"Come on out," I said. "Fight like a man."

Silence.

"Figures," I said. "You're only a Depth 4."

More silence. I looked at the maze of pipes. I really didn't want to go in there. I stood there in the silence. Then . . . a gentle clang of steel on steel. Whoever was in there had tapped a pipe. The reverberation made it impossible to pinpoint his location. Clever. He was in there . . .

somewhere. Fucking with me.

"OK asshole," I said. "Here's the deal. If I have to come in there and find you, I'm going to make you wish you were never born. Come out now, and I'll make it quick."

I waited. Listening. From deep within the maze, came an evil chuckle. The sound seemed to emanate from multiple places at once. It took me a moment to figure it out. He was laughing into a vent, the sound echoing and reverberating through the maze of pipes.

"Cute," I said. "What's your name?"

Silence. Then . . . an omnipresent voice whispered, "Skinpeeler."

"You've got to be fucking kidding me," I said.

Silence. Then the freak referring to himself as Skinpeeler chuckled once more. I let out a long breath through my nose.

"Have it your way," I said.

I searched the littered concrete floor for something that might be useful. I settled on a two foot length of rebar jutting from a chunk of broken concrete. I broke it out of the concrete and hefted it. It made a decent sledge. Heavy and gnarled on top, yet short enough to swing in close quarters. And only someone with my forearm strength could wield it effectively. It wouldn't be an issue if he got his hands on it. Unless the prick was my size.

Brandishing my new hammer, I strode to the base of the nearest metal stairwell and peered up into the darkness. I spotted more infrared grins. I imagined the assholes behind their computer screens, watching gleefully as two men hunted each other. I wanted to murder them all, but that would have to wait.

I started up the stairwell, making enough noise to alert the entire building. I had no real plan. I didn't know the deal with weapons. Had Skinpeeler been allowed to bring one in? Or was it finders keepers? I probably should have asked. With a name like Skinpeeler, I figured him for a blade guy.

He'd be hiding somewhere, waiting for me to get close so he could stick me with something sharp.

"I'm coming for you motherfucker," I growled, hammering my mace onto steel.

No reply.

I plunged into the maze. The catwalks were narrow. Pipes and steel girders jutted down low overhead, forcing me into a crouch. I inched forward, sledge first, stabbing the jagged shard of concrete into darkened nooks and crannies as they appeared. The only source of light emanated from the evil red grins of the infrared cameras. I didn't dare smash them or I'd be blind. Let 'em watch, I thought. Whoever was running this shitshow was about to see exactly who they were fucking with.

Choosing a path at random, I delved deeper into the labyrinth, swinging my club around blind corners and up darkened stairwells, making a lot of noise. A big blundering idiot with no idea where he was going or what he was doing.

In the end, I never saw him coming.

22

Skinpeeler was quiet, clever, and fast. A deadly combination. And he picked the perfect spot for an ambush.

I'd climbed six sets of the narrow steel stairs by then, which, to be fair, was fucking stupid. I should've waited him out down low. Made him come to me out in the open. But fuck it. I was cold and tired and the cut across my face stung like a motherfucker and the simple fact is, I hate waiting. To kill me, he had to get close, and when he got within arms reach . . . well, I liked my chances against anyone. Even six stories up in a fucking maze.

The catwalk I'd been following emptied out into an open space high up in the rafters. Off to my right, an infrared camera grinned from an I-beam supporting the corrugated iron roof, illuminating a criss-crossed intersection of catwalks. I paused. Below my feet yawned inky blackness. I imagined a fall to the jagged, junk-covered floor sixty feet below. No surviving that. Up ahead, at the intersection, three pathways led off into darkness. Left. Right. Straight ahead.

Yeah. Fuck that.

The smart move was to turn back, but as I said, patience has never been a virtue of mine. And I knew he was close. I could feel him. I'd been hunted before. I knew that sudden lack of noise. The silence of held breath and tensed muscle.

He was up ahead, along one of those pathways. I was certain of it.

I didn't want him to know I'd sensed him, so I kept up the oblivious act and strode confidently into the intersection.

That's when I made him.

He was along the right-hand pathway. Again, I can't tell you exactly how I knew. But I knew. I spun and lunged, stabbing my hammer into the darkened space in which he was hiding.

He was there all right. But my hammer didn't connect.

Because the fucker was *above me.*

I later realized he'd been hiding behind the infrared camera, clinging to the inside of the ceiling rafter I-beam. I lunged right beneath him. And never saw the blade. I felt a sharp stab down through my jacket into the meat of my trapezius. I immediately let go of my legs and fell along with it. The move saved my life. If I'd stayed standing, he would have stabbed straight down between my clavicle and first rib, into my heart from above. An expertly aimed kill strike. As it was, I fell and twisted and my butt slammed into the steel walkway and I felt the blade rip down my back.

Skinpeeler had taken his shot.

Lying on my side in a tangle of legs I swung my hammer up and over my head and felt it come down hard on something soft. Skinpeeler let out an anguished scream. I scrambled up to my knees and felt him do the same and saw the blade—a long pointed scrap of steel—coming at me fast, but my hammer was already on it's way down again. He got me a fraction of a second before I got him, the blade piercing my gut. Then the high velocity mass of the hammer obliterated his collar bone and he went down with a scream and I heard the blade clatter across the diamond-holed steel and skip off the edge into darkness. There was a long silence before it struck the littered floor.

I had no way of knowing what other surprises Skinpeeler

had in store, so without pausing I pounded my hammer into each of his knees, one after the other. Bam. Bam. Skinpeeler sat up fast, howling over his shattered patellas.

"STOP!" he screamed. "ENOUGH! ENOUGH!"

I punched him hard in the face, then stood over him, brandishing my hammer, bleeding bad.

"You done trying to kill me, motherfucker?" I growled.

He sucked in a breath through his teeth, nodded. His legs were broken, and he wasn't moving his right arm, but he'd survive.

I, on the other hand . . .

I stepped back and put a palm to my gut, felt blood pulse, then arched my shoulder blades. Pain seared down my back. I was not in a good way. I felt hot blood sheeting down my lower back, soaking into my underwear. I needed to pressurize both wounds, quickly, or I was going to bleed out.

"You got a kit?" I said, looking at Skinpeeler.

The stabbing prick was still in too much pain to speak. Let him live in it. I stepped over him and patted him down quickly, eating jolts of pain across my back and gut. Skinpeeler was much smaller than I'd anticipated. A slight guy. Wiry. With narrow shoulders and waist. All bone and sinew. A climber. Which explained how I'd missed him in the I-beam. He was dressed in all black. Lightweight pants and a dry-fit hoodie along with a pair of climbing shoes and black rubber gloves I assumed improved his grip. No first-aid kit. I loosened his belt and ripped it from his waist, then stood back and slipped off my trench coat and pulled off my own belt. I looped the belts together into one long strap. My trench was nearly in half. I ripped it the rest of the way.

"Feel like giving me a hand, Asspeeler?" I grunted.

He tried spitting back a reply, but the pain was too much.

"Fine," I said. "Be that way."

Holding the end of one sleeve, I tossed a coat-half over my shoulder and grabbed it at my waist, then fished it back-

and-forth as if drying my back with a towel until I found the line of the laceration. I followed the coat with the double belt and cinched it at the buckle vertically across my sternum, squeezing the jacket into the long wound. It was less than pleasant. Then I picked up the other coat half and tied it tight around my waist, pressurising the stab wound.

I'd just bought myself a little more time, but I was still in a bad spot. I turned to Asspeeler. He was still writhing on the floor. I leaned down and pulled off his balaclava. He was Asian. Hmong, at a guess. Maybe twenty-five. Maybe forty. In the eerie red light of the camera I met his eyes. He looked liked the kind of guy who would happily stab me in the back, and had before.

"What's your name?" I said.

He breathed in and out.

"Che," he said.

"How many times you done this, Che?" I said.

"A few," he said.

"One of us has to die?" I said.

He nodded.

"What happens if I leave you here?" I said. "Alive."

His eyes went very wide and he started shaking his head fast.

"No," he breathed. "Please no."

23

"What did you do with him after that?" said Kiira, her voice slightly muffled behind a surgical mask.

It was six a.m. and I was lying facedown on an operating table in Maldonado's on-site medical clinic. I hadn't slept. Code Barnes, Maldonado's live-in surgeon, had just finished sewing me up. Gow was at the door, ever vigilant.

"Threw him off the catwalk," I said between gritted teeth. The local was wearing off. And I'd refused any hard stuff.

Kiira balked.

"You should see what he landed on," I said between clenched teeth. "Poor fucker got an ass full of steel."

Kiira's eyes popped wide. I tried shrugging, but the two foot millipede of sutures along my spine turned it into a wince.

"I hope it hurts," said Kiira. She was angry. "That's barbaric, Einarr."

I rolled my eyes. My quick fall had really saved my ass. Or rather, my back. That, and the bony ridges of my spinous processes, which had shielded me from any major tissue damage. But I was out of action for a while. Less than ideal when someone wants you dead on TV.

Kiira wasn't finished.

"I can't believe you," she said, shaking her head "That

was so fucking stupid."

I glared at her from the table, hoping she might get the message.

She didn't.

"How many people have you murdered so far?" she said. "You nearly fucking bled to death. And all for . . . what exactly?"

Now that the local was gone, the pain had really sunk its teeth in, and with it, came my old friend, rage. Still, that doesn't excuse what I said.

"Maybe next time they send someone," I growled, "I'll let 'em rape you."

Bit harsh. In my defense, I had two hundred stitches in my back, face, and gut, and no pain meds. Kiira's eyes went wide and her mouth fell open. A shocked silence followed. I looked to Gow for help, but he just pinched the bridge of his nose and shook his head ruefully. Thanks buddy. I tried to offer Kiira my hand, but another rip of pain froze me in place.

I opened my mouth, but didn't know what to say.

"Don't even try," said Kiira, stopping me with her palm. "You fucking sicken me."

She spun and stomped toward the door. I let her go a couple steps, then said, "I found out plenty."

She grabbed the door handle and yanked it open, then paused. She didn't turn around. She waited. She didn't need to say, *This better be fucking good.*

"Che was more scared of them than he was of me," I said.

Kiira craned her neck to look at me, her face splayed with incredulity.

"So what?" she snapped.

"There was a couple hundred grand of equipment in that shed," I said. "Automated locks. Wireless infrared cameras. The whole thing beamed straight to the darkweb, I assume. Live. Something that well-organized takes planning. A team of people. Both on-site and online. Weeks of prep. We're talking major infrastructure. And in any business, the higher you climb, the more dirty secrets you unearth. Che knew enough about the people behind this thing to be very, very afraid."

Kiira let out a breath through her nose. Her hand came off the door and it swung back shut.

"How does any of that help us?" she said, turning to face me.

"We know the score," I said. "They're well-organised, well-funded, and have plenty of man power. This goes a lot deeper than we originally thought."

"No shit," said Kiira.

She stared at me for a moment, making a decision, then let out a breath and pulled a manila envelope from inside her jacket. Reluctantly, she walked back to the bed.

"While you were out being a reckless fucking meataxe," she said. "I did some actual detective work."

She opened the envelope and pulled out a stack of papers. There was a headshot paper-clipped to the top corner of the front page. My head shot.

"The CIA has a file on you," said Kiira.

I frowned.

"How'd you get that?" I said.

Kiira glanced at Gow.

"Pulled in a favor," he said. "A big one."

"You never told me you worked for the CIA," Kiira said, eyeing me.

I looked at Gow. He shrugged.

"I didn't," I said. "Not officially."

She raised an eyebrow.

"Well this says you did," she said, glancing down at the file. She folded back the first page. "'After his escape from the maximum-security Russian gulag known as The Pit, Einarr Laukkanen installed himself as a deep-cover operative under the guise of a professional basketball player for Euroleague club CSKA Moscow, where he proceeded to infiltrate and dismantle the mafia-run gulag system from the inside, assassinating . . . [six names redacted].'"

I blinked a couple times, looked at Gow.

"They took credit for it?" I said between my teeth.

Gow closed his eyes and nodded. I turned back to Kiira, my face a thundercloud.

"Read," I said.

"On February 18th, 2001, you were kidnapped from Reeves County Detention Complex in Pecos, Texas," Kiira began, "and falsely imprisoned in a secret maximum security gulag in northern Siberia."

"Kidnapped my ass," I said. "That slimy cunt, Hemmingson, sold me to the highest bidder."

"Hemmingson?" she said. "The warden?"

I nodded. Kiira opened her mouth, but nothing came out.

"Doesn't matter," I said. "He's dead. Keep going."

"The Gulag was barbaric. Government funded, but run by the mob."

"In Russia, those words are synonymous," I said.

"Prisoners were basically meat in a grinder," she continued. "They bought or kidnapped the worst of the worst from across the globe. The more violent and psychotic, the better. No one got out alive."

She paused. I said nothing.

"The way to earn special privileges," she said, "was to fight in The Pit. But it wasn't voluntary."

As if I needed reminding.

"The Gulag was designed around The Pit, it's main source of income," Kiira said. "Pit fighters were revered within the prison. Modern day gladiators provided with luxury accomodation, training facilities, coaches. And women. Pit fights were performed in front of a live and very exclusive audience. Ticket prices ranged into the millions, bets were even larger. Identities of the spectators were a very tightly held secret, but rumors abound. Pit fights . . . were to the death."

She lowered the file and looked at me. I said nothing. There wasn't anything to say.

"During your five years of imprisonment, you fought in The Pit one hundred and thirty-three times. The most fights in the history of the gulag, by a wide margin. You became a legend. The most feared man in a world occupied solely by the world's most violent criminals. And then, on October 31st, 2006 . . . you escaped."

She set down the file and met my eyes. They'd gotten most of it right. How, I had no idea. I'd never told anyone.

"I assume you have a point?" I said.

Kiira eyed me.

"Does the name Viktor Taktarov ring a bell?" she said.

It did, of course.

"He's dead too," I said.

Kiira nodded.

"He's the reason you were in there," she said. "Payback. For what your grandfather did in the Winter War."

I said nothing.

"Your grandfather recorded more confirmed kills in a single conflict than anyone in human history," said Kiira. "Most notably, one Viktor Taktarov, Senior. Commanding General of the invading Soviet forces."

I hated hearing my grandfather's life read to me like a fucking history book.

"Would you please get to the fucking point," I said.

Kiira pursed her lips.

"Do you remember Taktarov's nickname within the Red Army?" she said.

I did, of course. Taktarov was a psychotically brutal commander, fond of throwing POWs into pits with live bears for the amusement of his soldiers, among other delights.

They called him The Juggernaut.

Kiira held up a piece of paper. On it was a screen shot of The Labyrinth website stolen from Wraith's phone. As he'd mentioned, at the lowest Depth, there was a single name:

джаггернаут

"Dzhaggernaut."

24

I spent the next few days holed up in Maldonado's clinic, healing. Kiira came in each day, asking more questions. It went great. The first two days ended with her calling me a barbaric cunt and storming out. The third day she slapped me across the face and said she never wanted to see me again. On the other hand, it was a total waste of time. So on the fourth morning, against Code's orders, I climbed behind the wheel of my truck and headed straight to the Manitou. Nothing beer can't fix.

"Jesus H. Tapdancing Christ," said Shane, by way of greeting.

It was nine a.m. The place was empty.

"Beer," I said, easing atop a stool.

"Do I dare ask?" said Shane, eyeing my split-open face as he poured a Lift Bridge Irish Coffee Stout.

I skulled the meaty beer in three gulps and slid the glass back to the tap.

"I'll take that as a no," said Shane, pouring me a second pint.

I drank. Shane disappeared into the kitchen for awhile. Eventually he emerged with a steaming cauldron of clam and oyster chowder, two loaves of freshly baked bread, and half a pound of garlic butter.

"Eat," he said.

I ate. Shane poured stout.

"I take it you heard about the mayor," he said.

I shoved a slice of thickly buttered bread into my mouth and shook my head.

Shane eyed me over the tap.

"He's gone missing," he said.

Still chewing, I raised an eyebrow. I'd yet to meet the new mayor, but he was big news around town. One of those shaggy vegan elites you get nowadays. I believe the term is woke. He'd moved up from the Cities on a righteous mission to save the Boundary Waters from taconite mining. He was young, single, and charismatic, with a million instagram followers to prove it. People around here loved him.

"Sheriff was in here last night," said Shane. "Let it slip."

"What happened?" I said.

"Mayor didn't show up for a photo-op yesterday," said Shane. "Which, if you know the mayor, is very out of character."

Yesterday was Monday.

"Where's he live?" I said.

Shane said, "Up on Poplar Lake. One of those uber-cabins across from The Ugly Baby."

"How'd he get himself one of those?" I wondered. "He's young, right?"

"Thirty-two," said Shane.

I raised my eyebrows.

"Kombucha sales must be skyrocketing," I said.

Shane snickered.

"Sheriff checked the house?" I said.

Shane nodded. "No signs of forced entry. Suitcases still there. Prius still parked in the garage."

"Hmm," I said.

"Sheriff thinks he might've gone on a hike."

I frowned.

"In this cold?" I said.

"He grew up in Minnetonka," said Shane, by way of explanation.

At least a couple times every winter some dumbass from downstate underestimated the cold and froze to death in the woods. Darwinian, if you ask me. We were past due this year.

"They're searching the trails up near his house," said Shane. "But you know what it's like. Needle in a thousand haystacks."

"If he's in the woods," I said. "There's nothing left to find."

Shane questioned me with an eyebrow.

"Wolves need a huge amount of calories to survive this cold," I said. "They'll eat bones and all."

Shane's eyes widened.

"It's scary you know that," he said.

I drank my beer.

"If they don't find some sign of him today," said Shane. "Ken's gonna have to call The Cities. You know how that'll chap his ass."

I did. Once upon a time, Sheriff Ken Colson had been Unit Commander of Homicide in Minneapolis. Now he was a jaded, small-town Sheriff so deep in Maldonado's pocket he couldn't see out.

"Maybe I'll head up there," I said, smirking. "Give him a hand."

"Yeah," said Shane. "He'll love that."

I finished my beer, thanked Shane for the food, and left. Outside, it was still the middle of winter in northern Minnesota. The blinking time and temperature sign at Wells Fargo said minus twenty-one. If the mayor was out there, he was very much dead. I stomped through the dirty snow to my truck.

And stopped dead.

There, in the salt grime on the driver's side door, someone had written:

xkznz
sv6686
rt44z

25

"Someone's here," said Gow. "In town."

We were standing in front of Maldonado's mansion, staring at the side of my truck.

"We knew that already," I said. "The letter under Kiira's pillow."

"Someone could have been paid to do that," said Gow.

"Someone could have been paid to do this," I said, nodding at the scrawl on the truck door.

"I take it you didn't spot the guy?" said Gow.

I shook my head.

"I was at the Manitou, talking to Shane."

"CCTV?" said Gow.

"It's Gunflint Cove," I said. "Not New York."

"It's still possible. I'll look into it. If there's a camera, we can access it."

"Yeah," I said, under my breath. "About that."

Gow looked at me out of the corner of his eye.

"What?" he said.

"Mayor's missing," I said.

Gow's eyes widened a fraction.

"Convenient," I said. "For a guy eyeing the taconite under the Boundary Waters."

"Maldonado?" said Gow, barely moving his mouth.

I said nothing.

Gow let out a breath.

"You do it?" I said, eyeing him.

Gow shook his head a fraction of an inch.

"You'd tell me if you did?" I said.

Gow met my eye.

"I like to think so," he said.

"So do I."

We looked at the truck some more.

"They were on you right away," said Gow. "How?"

"No idea," I said. "Get Rupert to check the truck. Maybe they slipped a tracker on it when I was parked at the truck stop."

Gow spoke into his ear piece. We stared some more.

"Lot of money being thrown around," I said. "And a lot of time. Not many can afford both."

"Who wants you that bad?" said Gow.

"Who doesn't?"

We stared at the door some more.

"Another darkweb code?" said Gow.

"Time to find out," I said.

Gow pulled out his phone and took a photo of the door, then we went to find Kiira. She was in her room. From the look she gave me as I ducked through the door it was clear she was still repulsed by me. Gow showed her the photo. Her eyes widened. A clue! She flipped open her Macbook and, with Gow and I watching over her shoulder, clicked a purple icon at the bottom of the screen. A window popped open. Tor | Browser, it read at the top. The o in Tor was in the shape of an onion. The softward ran through its diagnostics, then, just like that, we were on the darkweb.

Reading off Gow's phone screen, Kiira typed xkznzsv6686rt44z.tor into the address bar and pressed return.

After a second's churning, a website popped up.

"Fuck me sideways," breathed Kiira.

The entire page was dedicated to me. It reminded me of my old player profile page on NBA.com, if it had been written by a gaming nerd. The page's background was black. Along the right side of the page was a red-bordered photo. A screen shot from one of the infrared cameras inside the abandoned ore refinery. It showed my white-green outline looming over Skinpeeler's prostrate form, the concrete hammer a black outline in my hands, merging with the cold background. You couldn't see any details of my face, but it was recognisably me. Below the image, red font on black, was a list of stats:

VICTIM PROFILE
Code Name: Sledge
Height: 6'10"
Weight: 266 lbs
Labyrinth Depth: 5
Labyrinth Rank: 44 of 100
Labyrinth Souls: +9,750
Career earnings: $525,000 USD

Power Grid
Toughness: 5/8
Strength: 6/8
Speed: 1/8
Fighting Skill: 2/8
Intelligence: 1/8
Cunning: 2/8

Depths Descended
1 - Death Threat (rank 86-100, bounty $5000 USD, +250 souls)
2 - Beating (rank 71-85, bounty $20,000 USD, +500 souls)
3 - Kidnapping (rank 61-70, bounty $50,000 USD, +1000 souls)

4 - Rape (rank 51-60, bounty $100,000 USD, +2,000 souls)

5 - Grievous Bodily Harm (rank 41-50, bounty $200,000 USD, +3,000 souls)

.

.

.

.

10 - Final Boss: джаггернаут (rank 1, bounty ?, +? souls)

Bonus Kills - 3 (bounty $50,000 USD x 3, +1000 souls x 3)

"You've got to be fucking kidding me," I said.

The three of us stared at the screen a while.

Kiira said, "Intelligence score looks about right."

Gow snorted.

"What is this shit?" I said. "A fuckin' video game?"

Kiira clicked the career earnings link. It led to a page called cryptocash.com. It showed an account with a balance of $525,000 USD. Kiira clicked the withdrawal icon. It asked for a bank account number.

"You got a safe account?" I asked her.

"Sure."

"Type it in," I said.

She did so, then pressed send. We waited five minutes then she checked a banking website.

"Holy shit," she said.

The account showed a deposit of $525,000 USD from Cryptocash LLC.

"Fuck me," I said.

Kiira looked back to the screen with newfound interest.

"Who did you rape?" she said.

I looked at Gow. We came to it at the same moment.

"Skinpeeler," said Gow. "Arseful of steel."

Kiira shook her head, letting out a long breath through her nose. Gow and I turned back to the screen.

Below the stats were two hyper-links:

Indemnity

Descent (Depth 6)

Kiira clicked the Indemnity link. A new page appeared. An embedded video took up most of the screen. The still was blurred. Kiira clicked the central play icon. The video started.

I stood in the middle of the desolate highway outside the abandoned truck stop, strandling the guy I'd brained with the butt of the tranq gun. The guy in the passenger seat, the one who'd directed me to the ore refinery, must have had a bodycam on him, because the video was from his perspective, sitting inside the SUV. The guy lying on the road was slowly coming to. I raised my boot. The guy behind the camera yelled out in Russian. This time I understood what he said:

"You sure about that?"

The guy on the ground looked up.

Kiira gasped.

"No!" she said, throwing a hand over her mouth.

From this angle I saw that the guy below my boot didn't understand what the guy in the car had just said. He wasn't Russian. They didn't know each other. In fact, I thought I recognized him.

On screen, I stomped down hard. It was a grisly watch.

"NO!" screamed Kiira.

I raised my foot again above the now-twitching body.

"NOOOOO!" Kiira shrieked. "NO! NOOOOOO!"

I stomped down the second time, crushing the guy's skull. Kiira flew from her chair, hands over her mouth, screaming incoherently.

I looked at Gow.

"Well," he said. "At least we know what happened to the mayor."

26

Fuck me. I'd murdered the mayor.

The Labyrinth assholes had set me up. And now they had me on Murder One. If that video got out, my life was over. And my dumb ass hadn't even thought to wear a mask.

Kiira handled it as well as you'd expect. Which is to say, not. She knew the guy. She's written a few human interest pieces on him in the Times, promoting his positive vegan vibe. He'd been trying to get in her pants for the last year, but she didn't see it that way. She liked him.

I went over and tried talking to her. As if I had any fucking idea what to say. She recoiled.

"DON'T EVER COME NEAR ME AGAIN!" she screamed, her tear-streaked face exploding into a rictus of revulsion. She reared back and slapped me. I let her, hoping it would help let some of it out. She screamed again, then turned and streaked from the room, slamming the door behind her, leaving Gow and I in startling silence.

"So," said Gow, "going well then."

"One a scale of one to ten," I said, eyeing him, "what's my general level of fucked?"

Gow weighed his head back and forth.

"Thirty."

"That's helpful," I said. "Thanks."

"You asked."

"So what now?" I said.

"We might as well have a look," said Gow, nodding to the laptop screen.

I sat down at the desk.

Back on the main page I found this blurb:

Congratulations on your successful Descent of Depth 5 of The Labyrinth. Your Depth 5 Descent—Grievous Bodily Harm to Mayor Todd Trusdale—was successful. Your Depth 5 Bounty of $200,000 USD and +3000 souls has been transferred to your account, and can be accessed via your Victim Profile page. In addition, you earned a third kill bonus of $50,000 USD and +1000 souls for the unsolicited murder of the target. Excellent work, your players will be delighted.

Your first Descent into Depth 6 of The Labyrinth awaits you. Please follow the link below.

Good luck on your next Descent.

"Motherfuckers," I said.

"Pretty much," said Gow, reading over my shoulder.

I sat there for a moment, staring at the screen.

"Go on," said Gow. "Get it over with."

I scrolled down to **Descent (Depth 6)** and clicked. A new page popped up. We read it.

"Ouch," said Gow.

It was far worse than I'd expected, which was saying something, since I'd expected chainsaw sodomy.

"Isn't she . . . ?" said Gow, pointing to the name of the target.

I nodded.

"She is," I said.

"Oh," said Gow. "Fuck me."

Back in college, during an NCAA Tournament game

broadcast on international television, I nearly killed legendary York University head basketball coach, Xavier Child, with a single punch to the side of the head. I did so in defense of my opponent, York University star Shawn Schilling. I was sentenced to five years in Texas state prison for aggravated assault with a deadly weapon. My fist. I never made it that far. Viktor Taktarov Jr, The Juggernaut's son, saw footage of the punch online, realized who I was, more specifically who my grandfather was, and paid a king's ransom for my capture and enslavement inside his fucked up death-prison in Siberia.

Six years later, after I escaped The Pit, I was still facing jail time in the U.S. It was Shawn Schilling, now a bonafide NBA superstar and president of the NBA Players Association, who kept me out of jail and got me a job as his enforcer on the Detroit Pistons. Hence my ten-year NBA career.

Shawn's black. I'm white. He's from inner city Minneapolis. I'm from the snow. Yet, we worked. We were best friends for a long time. Won two Championships together. Then Shawn got traded to the Timberwolves to be the saviour of a dying franchise. He did it too, dragging them all way from the bottom of the standings to the NBA Finals.

Where he faced-off against me.

I assume you know the rest. Shawn destroyed me in Game 1, which we lost by forty-seven, still an NBA Finals record for futility. He had twenty-one in the first eight minutes of Game 2, before going up for the fatal dunk attempt.

And . . . yeah.

What can I say? It was a cheap shot. I knew there was danger in it. But I didn't mean to hurt him. Not as bad as I did, anyway. Shawn came down with his right leg fully extended. His knee bent ninety degrees the wrong way. His series, his season, and nearly his career, were over.

We went on to win the Championship. All it cost, was a friendship.

Luckily for Shawn, while he was out of the game recuperating from his devastating injury, he had the full love and support of his beautiful, mega-talented wife. A woman so famous she's referred to by only a single name: Ariana.

Yeah, *the* Ariana.

The world-renowned pop-singing sensation.

My target.

27

Shawn's sprawling Lake Minnetonka estate was less than twenty miles from the south Minneapolis tenement block where he grew up, but it might as well have been on another planet. Prince had Paisley Park. The 3M guy had Bella Vista. Shawn had titled his uber-mega-mansion Hooper's Heaven. It was a hell of a place.

I climbed out of the SUV, back aching from the five-hour drive, and trudged across the dressed stone driveway to the mansion's arched front doors. I rang the orange, basketball-shaped doorbell, my pulse a couple BPM higher than I cared to admit.

Shawn and I hadn't spoken in over ten years. Since the day after the injury. Our last conversation hadn't gone well.

"Yo," said Shawn's voice from the other side of the door. "Who dis?"

"Really?" I said. "You answer your own fucking door?"

A pause.

"Who dis?" he said again.

"You don't recognize my voice?" I said. "After all those O boards I fed you?"

Shawn burst out laughing. A lock clicked and the door started to pull open.

"Motherfucker, don't play that shit!" said Shawn. "That

crazy ass cracker ain't about to come down here and show his . . ."

Shawn's smiling face appeared in the gap. Then he saw who it was and his eyes went wide for an instant, then hard, then he tried slamming the door in my face. The door didn't budge. I'd done the old cop trick and stuck my boot in the gap the moment he'd pulled it open.

"'Fuck you doin' here, nigga?" said Shawn, slamming the door against my boot to no avail.

"You know I wouldn't be here unless it was important," I said. "Let me in."

"Ain't nothing important enough to let yo motherfuckin' ass in!" he said. "Get the fuck on motherfucker!"

I didn't move.

"What about Ariana?" I said. "She important enough?"

At the mention of his wife's name, Shawn ripped the door open, which I'd been waiting for. I pushed in fast before he'd realized his mistake. Now we were chest to chest. Or should I say, chest to sternum. There are few people in the world whom I have to look up to. Shawn was one of them. He tried stepping back, but I'd clamped the wing of his iliac crest between my thumb and forefingers.

"Motherfucker get off me!" he said.

"No."

He'd forgotten about my grip strength, which was funny, since I'd used the same trick on him the first time we'd played each other back in college. He hadn't liked it then, and he didn't like it now.

"Get the fuck off me nigga!" he said, swinging down hard with his left arm.

Our forearms clashed. Shawn yelped and clutched his wrist. He'd forgotten about my hardened bones as well.

Using my thumb as a fulcrum, I tilted Shawn's pelvis to the anterior and lifted upward, forcing his legs straight. Until he dislodged my grip, I had complete control of his center of gravity. I steered his seven-foot-three frame backward into the cavernous foyer of Hooper's Heaven.

Most of the kids Shawn grew up with were dead. Casualties of the three C's: crips, cops, and crack. Roughly in equal measure. Those that weren't were alive mainly due to Shawn's money and influence. He'd signed his first Nike deal at eighteen. Since then he'd turned himself into a billion dollar brand. He employed literally hundreds of family members and friends, funded inner-city basketball programs across the country, built schools, sent thousands of underprivileged kids to college each year, the list goes on. He was, quite simply, the most beloved sports figure in America. Hell, maybe the world. And basketball was the reason behind all of it. Shawn loved the game with a reverence bordering on zealotry, and his home was a reflection of that love.

Now recall that I was the guy who took it from him.

Yeah.

High over our heads an exquisitely detailed mural, reminiscent of the Sistine Chapel, sprawled across the domed ceiling. In place of religious dudes it showed basketball greats executing their signature moves. In the center of the room were four regulation NBA basketball hoops, each facing one of the cardinal directions. The north court was inlaid with the blue and orange of Washburn high school, where Shawn had starred from 6th to 12th grade. South: York's blue and white. East: the Piston's teal and crimson. West: the Timberwolves' navy and forest green. Racks of basketballs in each team's colors were built into the walls. I knew all this without looking. Once upon a time, I'd helped with the design.

I marched Shawn through Washburn, beneath the hoop chandelier, and into Blue Demon territory. There, Shawn tried a new tactic: a right hook to the face. I caught it in mid-air and ground his knuckles together.

"Aaaah! Motherfucker stop!" he yelped.

"Don't start something we'll both regret," I said.

"You the one started this shit motherfucker!" seethed Shawn, shaking his hand. He tried a left. The better punch, since I couldn't deflect it without releasing his hip. I turned my head and took his knuckles on my frontal bone, the hardest section of my battle-hardened skeleton. I heard something snap. Most likely a metacarpus. Shawn yanked his hand back, crying out in pain.

"Aimed too high," I said. "Kidney shot was the go."

"You broke my hand motherfucker!" he said. "Get the fuck outta here 'fore I call the cops!"

We finally made it through York, under an archway, and into a room with furniture. I steered Shawn to an L-shaped suede couch and shoved him backward. He fell butt-first onto the chaize.

"Did you just threaten to call the cops on me?" I said, standing over him.

"Fuck you motherfucker!"

I furrowed my brow.

"Imagine what Dejontay would say," I said.

That one got him. As I figured it might. He tried sitting up fast but I shoved him back down.

"Say my brother's name again and I'll fucking kill you!" he said, seething.

"No you won't," I said.

"Fuck you!"

"First of all," I said, "you need better security. No fucking way should I be able to walk up to your front door. For starters a perimeter fence, vertical bar, ten feet minimum, spiked finials if you don't want razor wire. Then a gate rated to withstand a high-speed truck. Cameras. Motion-sensed, night vision, fed straight to both your phone and that of your head of security. Speaking of which, where the fuck is everyone?"

The Shawn I knew had an entourage at least fifty deep suckling on him at all times.

"None of them mu'fuckers live here no mo'," he said.

I raised an eyebrow.

"Trouble in Heaven?"

"Fuck you," he said.

"Let me guess: the wife."

Once again, at the mention of his wife, Shawn's face darkened. I could tell from his expression that I'd nailed it.

"I wouldn't want those leeches hanging around either," I said.

"Fuck you."

"She here?" I said.

"I ain't letting you near her," spat Shawn.

"So she is here," I said. "Good."

Shawn swore under his breath.

"Fuck you want with her?" he said.

I nearly said, *Someone's paying me three-hundred grand to deafen her*.

Instead I went with, "I need to see her. *Now*."

"No fucking way," he said.

"Listen," I said. "Either you take me, or I take you. It's up to you."

Shawn glared up at me. I waited.

Finally, he said, "Aight, motherfucker. But I ain't lettin' you in a room with her alone."

I slipped my hand behind my back. The number eleven surgical scalpel I'd brought along for the job was still there. I smiled down at Shawn.

"Probably for the best," I said.

28

MINNEAPOLIS STAR TRIBUNE
DEAFENED!

Pop sensation Ariana in critical condition after brutal home invasion.

Friday, February 17th, 2022 | by Bridgett Sansovere

Pop mega-star Ariana, 37, was in the recording studio of her Lake Minnetonka home late Thursday night when an as-yet-unknown assailant viciously attacked her, leaving her permanently deafened in both ears. Ariana's husband, NBA-legend Shawn Schilling, was found unconscious inside the home, bound to a toilet in a nearby bathroom.

The assailant is thought to have entered the home through the front door, which sustained no damage, leading detectives to believe that the attacker was known to the Schillings.

The pop-sensation was found unconscious, blindfolded and restrained, with severe trauma to the head. Early medical reports state the assailant specifically targeted the singer's ears, using a sharp, bladed weapon, to surgically remove them.

"It's pretty clear the intent was to deafen her," says one

medical professional close to the scene. "The wounds are consistent with someone who knew anatomy. All four auditory nerves clusters were severed, and most of the ear tissue itself was removed. This was clearly a targeted attack. She's very lucky to be alive, currently, and we're doing the best we can to keep her that way."

Ariana regained consciousness only momentarily, but was sedated soon after. She has been moved to a private medical facility where she is in intensive care. As of the time of this reporting, Shawn Schilling has yet to release a statement regarding the attack. Again, it is believed that the Schillings may have known the identity of the assailant when they let him or her into their home.

The police ask for anyone close to the case who may have information regarding the identity of the assailant to please notify their local police department.

29

Handcuffed to a fuckin' toilet?" said Shawn. "For real? How long you think that bullshit gonna work?"

We were on our way back to Gunflint Cove in a burner Chevy Silverado Gow had organized. I'd dumped the SUV inside one of Maldonado's warehouses, where one of his guys would give it a full scrub down. It was four-thirty a.m. Shawn was crammed into the passenger seat next to me, Ariana in the back by herself. I couldn't see her face in the darkness, but her ramrod posture told me the can of coke I'd given her for the shock hadn't done shit.

"Until someone talks," I said.

Shawn muttered something under his breath. I looked over at him. His knees were up near his chin and even with the seat cranked all the way back his scalp scraped the ceiling as he looked over at me.

"What?" he said.

"How long you think your dumbass homeboys can keep their mouths shut?" I said.

"Fuck you," said Shawn. "I told 'em exactly what you said to tell 'em."

"Which was?"

"The shit they gonna hear on the news ain't true. Everyone gonna be asking about it. But they best keep they ass quiet. *For real* quiet."

"And how did they respond?" I said.

"They was cool. Dayshawn wanted to know what he could do to help."

I rolled my eyes. "Don't tell me you're still paying that lazy prick to play video games in your basement all day."

"Motherfucker you ignorant," said Shawn. "Dayshawn a smart motherfucker. Got my socials running slick as fuck. Got more followers than Lebron and Steph combined."

I heard Ariana shift in the backseat. I once again got the impression she shared my disapproval of Shawn's homeboys. I smirked.

"Fuck you," said Shawn. "Don't judge me, motherfucker. You the one brought this bullshit down on us. In case you hadn't noticed, we was doing just fine until your cracker-ass showed up."

"Always the racist," I said.

"Fuck you nigga," he said.

I shook my head.

"Last time I checked, someone hired me to deafen your wife," I said. "I wouldn't say you're doing too great at the moment."

"And who's fucking fault is that?" said Shawn. "Who the fuck hired you?"

I didn't reply. He had me there. I glanced in the rearview mirror.

"You okay?" I said to Ariana.

"Don't talk to her," said Shawn.

I looked at him. He was serious. I shook my head and turned my eyes back to the road. We drove in silence for a while. Every couple of miles the dash thermometer dropped another degree.

Then Ariana said, "Who would do this to me?"

It got real quiet for a second. I could feel both Shawn and Ariana's eyes on me. I let out a breath through my nose.

"I don't know," I said.

I glanced in the rearview mirror at her.

"What are you going to do?" she said.

"I'm gonna find the fucker," I said. "But until then, you two need to stay out of sight. You're the most recognisable couple in America. No one, and I mean no one, can know where you are. That means no phones. No calls. No internet. No social media. Nothing. Understand?"

I saw Ariana nod.

"Motherfucker, we get it," said Shawn.

"You sure?" I said, eyeing him. "Because if Dayshawn or one of these other fucking idiots lets this shit out, people are going to die. Is that clear?"

I eyed him.

"Yes, motherfucker," he said. "We get it. Some crazy fuck out there wants to hurt my wife. This shit as real as it fucking gets."

"Correct," I said. "So you need to hang tight while I sort it out. 'Aight?"

Shawn let out an exacerbated sigh, swearing under his breath. We were quiet for a while.

"You've done this before," Ariana said.

It wasn't a question.

I glanced at her in the rearview mirror. Nodded.

"You're good at it," she said.

I said nothing.

"At hunting men," she said.

I didn't reply.

"And that's why they're hunting you," she said.

I glanced into the rearview mirror again. She was perceptive.

"I suppose that's one way of looking at it," I said.

Shawn let out a puff of air and shook his head against the ceiling leather again.

"How the fuck you got us into this shit?" he said. "This is

my life. Our life. Why we dealing with your shit? What we got to do with any of this?"

I didn't know what to do with that one, so I left it alone.

"Listen," I said. "Someone's after me. I don't know who it is, but they have the time, money and inclination to really hurt me. They want to haunt me, before they kill me. And they're doing that by targeting the people closest to me."

"Motherfucker, we ain't close to you," said Shawn. "Ariana never even seen yo white ass before."

"Didn't know she wanted to," I said. "I can show her when we get there. Bit difficult while driving."

Ariana snorted.

"Fuck you," said Shawn, but I saw him suppress a grin.

Something in the air broke. I let out a laugh.

"It's good to see you," I said.

Shawn eyed me.

"I mean that," I said. "I'm sorry about the circumstances. But . . . I've missed you."

"Shawn shook his head, let out a breath.

"You're a fucking dick," he said.

"I know," I said.

"You best sort this shit out," he said. "Right fuckin' quick. We got lives motherfucker. *Important* lives."

"Relax," I said. "I'll do all the heavy lifting and you can take the credit at the end. Just like the old days."

"Motherfucker don't even start," said Shawn.

The mood was lighter now. I saw Ariana relax into her seat, her adrenaline finally petering out. She'd crash hard now.

But before she did, she had one more question.

"What if they find you first?" she said.

Like I said. Perceptive.

30

Ariana was so mega-famous it was startling to see her in the flesh. Imagine waking up and finding Beyonce at your breakfast bar, nibbling an omelete. That's what it was like. To make it more surreal, Kiira was there too, sharing a plate with the pop megastar, the two of them laughing uproariously at something I didn't catch.

"I see you two've met," I said, pouring myself a mug of coffee from the Moccamaster next to the enormous bay window overlooking the lake.

I'd grabbed a few hours sleep and felt slightly less dead than I had the night before, but not by much.

"Speak of the devil," said Kiira.

She and Ariana glanced at each other and shared a snicker.

"I'm glad you both can find the humor in your current predicament," I said.

"No thanks to you," said Ariana.

I wasn't going near that one this early in the morning.

"Where's Shawn?" I said.

"Still asleep," said Ariana.

"Good," I said. "I imagine he needs it."

Both women looked at me now, their laughter gone.

Kiira said, "We've been discussing the case."

I tried extremely hard to suppress my eye roll. The results were inconclusive.

"So," said Ariana. "What's the plan?"

I sipped my coffee.

Kiira and Ariana looked sideways at each other.

"See what I mean?" said Kiira.

"Mmmhmmm," said Ariana, looking me up and down. "Reminds me of Shawn. Must be a male thing."

"You still have ears," I said flatly.

This was not how I'd wanted to wake up.

"Yet you have absolutely no idea who wants to take them," said Kiira.

I rubbed the sleep out of my eyes. Let a breath out through my nose.

"I'm working on it," I said.

"No," said Kiira. "You're not."

My face hardened.

"You're just waiting for them to try to kill you," said Kiira.

I pulled a breath in and out. Stay calm, Einarr. The sleep deprivation didn't help.

"Everyone's a tough guy until they meet a real one," I said between gritted teeth. "Let 'em come."

Kiira and Ariana shared another sideways glance. I felt an almost irresistible urge to to palm the back of their skulls and clap. Hero that I am, I abstained.

"Einarr, whoever's behind this had been two steps ahead of you the entire time," said Kiira. "They're playing you. Waiting for them to make the next move plays right into their hands. *Again*."

"And what would you have me do?" I growled.

Kiira smiled.

"Relax sugar," said Ariana, her voice butter and honey. "You got two super-fly sugar-mammas here with you. We gotchu baby."

I yawned, letting the eye roll free this time. Ariana's face transformed.

"Don't you dare eye roll me motherfucker," she said, her voice a knife. She jabbed her finger at me. "You must'a forgot who you sittin' with."

I suppose I had.

"Now you listen motherfucker, and you listen good," said Ariana.

I smiled, but I'll admit, I was listening.

"Whoever's after you has someone local," she said. "We know this because of the letter under Kiira's pillow, how quickly they became aware that you'd foiled their kidnapping plan with the guys in the van, and the code written in the dirt on your truck door."

I crinkled my brow, glanced at Kiira. She smiled. The two of them made quite the pair.

"So," said Ariana. "All you got to do is find the local connection. Then do what you do best."

"Which is?" I said.

"Beat the shit out of them until they give you what you want," said Kiira.

"That easy, huh?" I said.

"Nothing's easy, sugar," said Ariana. "Any woman'll tell you that."

"I had Gow check for security footage of the guy who wrote on my truck," I said. "There're only two online webcams in Gunflint Cove. One overlooking the harbour. One at the Trading Post. Nothing on 'em. He sent Clancy to ask around. No one saw anything. So that's a dead end."

"Doesn't matter," said Kiira.

"Oh no?" I said.

"No," she said.

"Please enlighten me."

"There're only so many people it can be," said Ariana. "Think about it. Who in town has the time, manpower, crooked morals, and a deep-loathing for you?"

I could think of quite a few, so I said nothing.

"We've narrowed it down to a list of prime suspects," said Kiira.

She picked up a yellow notepad that had been sitting between them on the breakfast bar, and held it out to me.

"Who's at the top of the list?" I said, reaching for it.

Kiira smiled.

Ariana said, "You ain't gonna like it, *sugar*."

31

She wasn't wrong.

There were few places on earth I enjoyed less than the Gunflint Country Law Enforcement Center. Last time I'd been in there Sheriff Colson tried to pin a murder on me. This time I *had* murdered someone. A couple someones. Yet here I was on another negative twenty degree day, standing beside the rear exit door, waiting for someone to spot me on the security camera.

St. Peter came out at three minutes past two. Shift's end.

"Hey Virgil," I said as the door swung shut, revealing me behind it.

St. Peter spun. As usual, his pants were so tight that if you weren't careful you'd catch an eyeful of nut hair. When he saw who it was, his face screwed into a rictus. St. Peter reviled me with a depth of depravity that would sicken Mengele. His hand went to his hip and he glanced quickly over each shoulder, making sure it wasn't an ambush, then took three steps back, trying to put distance between us. I kept exactly in step, keeping him within arm's reach.

"What the fuck do you want Laukkanen?" he said, unsnapping his Glock. He was smart enough to keep it in the holster. Last time he'd pulled a gun on me I'd tossed it in Lake Superior.

"How 'bout we fast forward this bit?" I said.

He backed up another step. I smiled and stepped with him.

"Fuck you," he said. "Get away from me."

"You can do better than that," I said.

He glared at me. His hand didn't leave the gun.

"What do you want?" he said.

"Just to talk," I said. "Couple questions regarding a couple things."

He furrowed his brow, as if that one was hard to compute.

"Don't get any closer," he said.

"Don't worry," I said. "Your pants are keeping me at bay."

"Still the funny guy."

"What's life without levity?"

"Huh?"

"You hire someone to kill me?" I said.

"What?" he said. "No."

He seemed genuinely confused, a look I'd seen on him often.

"Any idea who might have?" I said.

He looked around, as if the wind might have the answer.

"There's a hit out on you?" he said.

"Something like that."

He smiled and laughed silently to himself.

"Good," he said.

"Same guys who snatched the mayor," I said.

That got him.

"What do you know about that?" he said.

"More than you," I said.

"Tell me," he said. "Sheriff's blowing a gasget."

"No body yet?" I said.

St. Peter let a breath out through his nose and shook his head. They weren't going to find the body. After I stole the SUV to go fight Skinpeeler, Gow, Rupert, and Ajax had cleaned up the scene at the truck stop. They'd incinerated all four bodies at one of Maldonado's refineries that same night. They hadn't recognized the mayor because he'd had no face.

"Any idea who took him?" I said.

St. Peter studied me.

"Why do you think he was taken?" he said.

"Because the same asshole tried kidnapping Kiira Thorisdottir," I said. "And now they're after me. They got someone local. Feeding information on whereabouts, habits."

"And you thought it might be me?" said St. Peter.

I shrugged.

"You're local," I said. "And a fuckin' prick."

"Fuck you," he said.

"If the shoe fits," I said.

St. Peter shook his head. It was getting cold standing there in the parking lot. My ears burned. St. Peter's fingers would have lost much of their dexterity. I thought about taking his gun again, just for the hell of it.

"It's not me," said St. Peter. "But I hate to admit it. I think you're right."

"First time for everything," I said. "Why?"

"Mayor Trusdale's phone was still on the kitchen counter," said St. Peter. "Prick doesn't take a shit without that thing, let alone go on a hike. No way."

"So you'll keep an eye out for me?" I said.

St. Peter ran a hand over his chin. He was starting to shiver.

"Only so far as it helps in the investiagion," said St. Peter. "I don't give a fuck what happens to you."

"And here I thought we were becoming friends."

32

It took less than five hours for The Labyrinth to get to St. Peter. The media shitstorm surrounding Ariana's attack had reached fever pitch, with every news agency in the country leading with the story for the six o'clock news. So far, none of Ariana or Shawn's people appeared to have blabbed. But I figured it wouldn't be long before the major networks started throwing money around for an inside scoop. Once they did, I had little doubt one of Shawn's dumbass homeboys would buckle. Time was of the essence.

Shawn, Gow, and I were in front a wall-sized TV eating slabs of sous vide filet mignon when Rupert buzzed through the intercom.

"That prick St. Peter's here," he said. "Permission to shoot him and bury his body in the woods?"

Gow raised an eyebrow at me. I shook my head, albeit begrudgingly.

"Let him in," said Gow. "Second guest house."

"How many houses this motherfucker got?" said Shawn.

"Sixteen," said Gow. "On this property."

"God*dayum*."

We told Shawn to keep Ariana the fuck out of sight and headed over to the second guesthouse. Outside it was dark and cold as death. We found St. Peter in the living room, warming his hands over the fire. He didn't look happy.

"What the fuck you got me into, Laukkanen?" he said, by way of greeting.

"Hi Virgil," I said. "Long time no see."

"Fuck off," he said. "Who are they?"

"Who are who?" said Gow.

"Stop fucking around," he said. "The fuckers that sent the email."

He pulled a piece of paper from his pocket and handed it to Gow. Gow opened it up and had a look, then handed it to me.

Here's what it said:

This message is to be hand-delivered to the individual you met with in the back parking lot of the Gunflint County Law Enforcement Center at 2:03 p.m. today. Failure to do so with result in a Depth 5 Descent on someone close to you. Thank you very much.

d86jkxndl182nkhprd2k09

Gow and I exchanged a glance.

"You had a tail you dumb shit," said St. Peter.

I rolled my eyes.

"No, I didn't," I said.

"Well then how the fuck do you explain how they knew they exact time we met?" said St. Peter.

Good question.

"It wasn't a tail," I said.

"Then how the fuck did they know?"

I looked at Gow, silently asking him how much intel I should reveal. He shrugged. Thanks buddy. Big help.

"We don't know," I said. "Did you have your phone on you at the time?"

St. Peter furrowed his brow.

"Yeah," he said. "So?"

"We think they might be able to tap into phones," I said. "There are companies that can do it. For a price. Theoretically, they could be listening to us right now through that thing in your pocket."

St. Peter pulled his phone from his pocket and looked at it as if it were the face hugger from Alien.

"What am I supposed to do?" he said.

"Turn it off, take out the SIM card," said Gow.

"You fucking serious?" said St. Peter.

I stared at him. He shrugged, then held the button down on his phone until it turned off.

"How the fuck do I get the SIM card out?" he said.

Gow handed him a paperclip from his pocket and showed St. Peter where to insert it.

"Another possibility is security cameras," I said, once St. Peter's phone and SIM card were back in his pocket. "I assume you guys got CCTV on the back lot?"

"Of course," said St. Peter.

"So it's possible they tapped into it somehow."

St. Peter's eyes widened a fraction. It was dawning on him exactly what we were dealing with.

"Who are they?" he said.

"We don't know," I said. "Pricks call themselves The Labyrinth."

This time, St. Peter's eyes nearly bugged out of his head.

"You've heard of it?" said Gow.

St. Peter's mouth was slightly agape. He nodded slowly.

"Talk," I said.

For a while, St. Peter just stood there, shaking slightly.

"There's a video," he finally breathed, his voice fragile. "Got shared around the department a while back. Maybe a year ago. Sickest shit I've ever seen."

"Snuff?" said Gow.

St. Peter nodded. Cops were known for leaking

particularly nasty evidence between departments. Same thing happened with Kobe's helicopter crash.

"Describe it," I said.

St. Peter shook his head, eyes wide.

"Tell us," said Gow.

"I can't," he said.

"Try," I said, between my teeth.

St. Peter looked at me. I'd never seen him this scared. I waited. He closed his eyes, then let out a long, shaky breath.

"They . . . " he breathed. "There was this girl. She was tied up. Secured to this . . . rack. A guy in a mask had a blade. Long serrated thing. All rusty or bloody or some shit. Looked like disease. And . . ."

He let out a long breath and shook his head.

"What'd the guy do?" I said.

"He . . . you know."

"Fuck me," breathed Gow.

"It got worse," said St. Peter. "After he cut out her snatch . . . he pulled her guts out of the hole. While she was still alive. Screaming."

St. Peter stopped talking. He looked like he was going to be sick. Gow let out a low whistle.

"That's not even the worst part," said St. Peter, breathing deeply, his eyes on the floor.

Gow and I exchanged a glance. St. Peter shuddered, trying to rid himself of images he'd never be able to un-see. We waited for him to keep going. Eventually, he did.

"They forced her husband to watch," he said. "At least we assumed it was her husband, the way he was reacting. They had him strapped to the same sort of rack. Naked. Arms and legs spread out, dick and balls hanging through the steel bars. His eyes were pulled open by these hooks, so he couldn't look away. They forced him to watch what they did to his wife. We figured it was some sort of punishment for something he'd done."

"Jesus fucking Christ," said Gow.

"Sounds like some cartel shit," I said. "What's it gotta do with us?"

St. Peter looked at me. All the the color had drained from his face.

"After they were done with the woman, they started in on the guy," he said. "Same blade. Up his ass. While they were going at it, the camera went up close to his face and a voice said, 'Say it!' As they went to work, he started screaming. Words."

He stopped. The room was very quiet.

"What'd he scream?" I said.

St. Peter breathed in and out a few times, trying to calm his ragged breath. Then, with tears in his eyes, he breathed:

"'No one escapes The Labyrinth.'"

33

St. Peter didn't know the identity of the man or woman in the video. Up until now, The Labyrinth had been nothing more than a scary story circulating through the sheriff's department rumour mill. Another horror perpetrated by a cartel down in Central America somewhere. He agreed to make some calls to see what he could find out, but I was't holding my breath. If the video had been going around for a year already, that meant no one knew shit.

The moment he left, Gow and I headed up to Kiira's room to check the new code.

<u>VICTIM PROFILE</u>

Code Name: Sledge
Height: 6'10"
Weight: 266 lbs
Labyrinth Depth: 5
Labyrinth Rank: 50 of 100
Labyrinth Souls: +6,750
Career earnings: $525,000 USD

<u>Power Grid</u>

Toughness: 5/8
Strength: 7/8

Speed: 1/8
Fighting Skill: 3/8
Intelligence: 1/8
Cunning: 4/8

<u>Depths Descended</u>

1 - Death Threat (rank 86-100, bounty $5000 USD, +250 souls)

2 - Beating (rank 71-85, bounty $20,000 USD, +500 souls)

3 - Kidnapping (rank 61-70, bounty $50,000 USD, +1000 souls)

4 - Rape (rank 51-60, bounty $100,000 USD, +2,000 souls)

5 - Grievous Bodily Harm (rank 41-50, bounty $200,000 USD, +3,000 souls)

~~**6 - Deprivation of hearing (rank 31-40, bounty $300,000 USD, +4,000 souls)**~~

.

.

.

10 - Final Boss: джаггернаут (rank 1 of 100, bounty ?, +? souls)

Bonus Kills - 3 (bounty $50,000 USD x 3, +1000 souls x 3)

Penalties - 1 (bounty witheld, -3000 souls x 1)

"Your cunning score went up," said Kiira, frowning.

I nodded.

"The article in the paper," I said. "Guess they thought it was clever."

"What's the penalty for?" she said.

"Keep reading," said Gow.

Below the stats was a paragraph of text:

We are disappointed to confirm that your Depth 6 Labyrinth Descent—Deprivation of Hearing to the target,

Ariana—was unsuccessful. Your Depth 6 Bounty of $200,000 USD has been withheld, and a penalty of -3000 souls has been deducted. Your Labyrinth Rank has dropped to 50 of 100. You are still exploring Depth 5 of The Labyrinth. Failure to comply with your Death Match Summons will result in your Indemnity being released to the media, along with a Labyrinth Depth 6 attack on a friend or family member. Please follow the links below. Good luck on your next Descent.

Below the blurb were two links.

Indemnity

Death Match Summons

"Fucking cunts!" I said, slamming a heavy fist onto the desk. The wood bucked, rocketing Kiira's laptop off the side onto the hardwood floor. The three of us stared down at it.

"That about covers it," said Gow.

Kiira shot me a angry look and picked up the computer, opening it to check the screen.

"Get Shawn and Ariana in here," I snapped at Gow. "One of their fucking dumbass homies blabbed."

"Not necessarily," said Kiira, setting the laptop back on the desk. There was a dent in one corner of the brushed aluminum frame, but it appeared to still be in working order.

"How else would they fucking know we faked it?" I said.

Kiira shrugged.

"Does it matter?" she said. "They were always going to find out. It just happened a little sooner than we'd hoped. The question is, what sort of psychotic bullshit are they up to now?"

I leaned over the laptop and clicked the Indemnity link. It looked exactly the same as last time. A video of me murdering the mayor. Kiira turned away, unable to watch. Gow and I watched all the way to the end, making sure they hadn't added anything. They hadn't. But there was no doubt the fuckers still had my nuts over the coals. I cursed under my breath and clicked the Death Match Summons.

It was another black screen with red text:

Due to your failure to complete your Depth 6 Labyrinth Exploration, you have been Summoned to a Labyrinth Death Match. You will fight to the death on Friday, February 25th. The location of your Death Match will be released nearer to the date. Victory in this Death Match will descend you to Depth 6 of The Labyrinth and carries a Depth 6 bounty of $300,000 USD and +4000 souls. Defeat will result in your death. Failure to comply with this Death Match Summons will result in the immediate release of <u>Indemnity</u> to all major national and international media outlets, along with a Depth 6 attack on someone dear to you.

Good luck on your next Descent.

The room fell silent. I saw Gow and Kiira exchange a glance. Neither would meet my eye.

"Welp," I said, slamming the laptop shut. "Who's hungry?"

Kiira looked at me, incredulous.

"What are you going to do about this?" she said.

"Right now, I'm gonna eat a sandwich."

"Einarr, we need to make a plan. You can't go in there and fight again. It's suicide."

I shrugged.

"Unless we find these pricks before then, I'm gonna have to," I said. "They have me by the nuts with that fucking video. And we have no way of knowing who they'll target with the attack. It could be you. Your parents. Your sister's kid. Anyone. You willing to risk it?"

Kiira eyes went very wide.

"It's insane," she said. "You're playing right into their

hands. You can't go back in there."

"If you've got a better idea," I said. "I'm all ears."

34

Kiira did, in fact, have a better idea.

The set-up at the abandoned ore refinery must have taken weeks, so she reasoned The Labyrinth would be prepping another location in a similar fashion. All we had to do was find it.

Kiira got her tech-nerd "friend" on it, a guy named Deckert who'd masterminded the phone hacking spyware Maldonado had shown us. Deckert rang the next morning through some fancy end-to-end encrypted video software on Kiira's laptop. He looked exactly like a gaming nerd should. Unkempt greasy hair. Hipster glasses. Stained Deadpool t-shirt over skin so white it was nearly translucent. I reminded myself that this was the guy who could tune into your phone camera any time he pleased.

"Hi guys!" he chirped through Kiira's laptop screen.

We were in Kiira's room, drinking coffee. I'd just woken up from a fitful night's sleep. Unfortunately, it hadn't been with Kiira. When Deckert saw my face, his eyes opened wide.

"Holy shit!" he exclaimed. "Sledge Laukkanen! It's really you! The man, the myth, the legend!"

I clenched my jaw. Not one of these fucks.

"You got something for us, Deckert?" I said, rubbing sleep

from my eyes.

"I wouldn't be calling if I didn't!" he said with entirely too much enthusiasm for this time in the morning. "By the way, Sledge, do you mind if I call you Sledge? Or would you prefer Einarr The Mighty? Or Mr. Sledge Fucking Laukkanen, or King Sledge the-"

"Just give us the fucking information," I said.

"Stop," said Kiira, stabbing me with the corner of her eye. She smiled apologetically into the camera.

"Sorry Sledge," said Deckert, looking crestfallen. "I mean Einarr! I mean Mr. Laukkanen! I mean Barbarian King of Doom!"

I squeezed my eyes shut, pinching the bridge of my nose and letting out a low, growling breath.

"Uh, right," said Deckert, swallowing. "Sorry. Sorry. It's just, I can't believe it's really you. I mean, holy shit. The legend himself. The mighty Sledge! King of The Pit!"

I levelled my gaze at the camera. It took everything I had not to punch a hole through it.

"Sorry!" said Deckert. "I'll stop." He pulled in a slow breath, fanning himself with his hand. "So . . . where to start? I did some digging and found that the abandoned ore refinery and surrounding landholdings were purchased just over a year ago by a shell company called Unified LLC. Obviously, that's the type of name that tells you absolutely nothing about the company, which, of course, tells us everything we need to know."

Deckert paused, raising his eyebrows and grinning. I got the impression that he was one of these pricks who liked to make a big show out of being the smartest guy in the room. To prove my point, he didn't go on, instead waiting for Kiira or me to ask the obvious question.

"Get to the fucking point, Deckert," I said.

Deckert's smile faltered.

"Right, um, well," he said. "If there's one thing rich guys

are really really good at, it's making their money untraceable. Wouldn't wanna do anything so plebeian as pay taxes, you know what I'm saying?"

He stopped again, grinning. I growled.

"Right," said Deckert quickly. "So I did some more digging and discovered that Unified LLC is owned by a subsidiary named Frontier LLC, another one of those say-nothing names. Frontier LLC, in turn, is owned by a conglomerate of other shell companies, all of which have been set up anonymously using offshore accounts."

Deckert paused again. He didn't smile this time.

"So you got nothing," I said.

Deckert was starting to look nervous.

"Not necessarily," he said, holding up a finger. "Mr. Maldonado mentioned a wi-fi security camera with a smiling array of infrared lights?"

I furrowed an eyebrow.

"Yeah, so?"

"Here," said Deckert, tapping his keyboard. His camera feed was replaced by a screen-share of his desktop. The background said *Bloodborne*.

"Is this it?" he said, clicking open a webpage.

I recognized the camera immediately. I wouldn't admit it, but that evil red grin had been keeping me up at night.

"That's the one," I said.

Deckert's face reappeared on screen.

"Thought so," he grinned. "The Eufy Cam 6X. Nice rig. Twelve-month battery life on a single charge. 2560p HD with 4K HDR and an array of thirteen infrared LEDs. Range of a hundred feet in total darkness, all instantaneously uploaded to the cloud in real time."

He stopped and waited for applause.

"Get to the fucking point, Deckert," I said again.

"Right," said Deckert, his smile evaporating. "I, uh, contacted the manufacturer. All I had to do was drop Mr.

Maldonado's name and the guy happily sent me a list of their most valued customers."

Deckert paused again, giving us another eyebrow raise to go along with the groveling grin.

"I take it there's more?" said Kiira, annoyance creeping into her voice now.

"But of course," said Deckert, pausing again, completely oblivious to our growing animosity.

"Deckert," I said. "Stop fucking pausing or I'm gonna drive down there and shove this computer up your ass."

Deckert's eyes widened.

"You're just like I thought you'd be," he said, shaking his head in admiration. "Only scarier."

I let out a low growl.

"Right," said Deckert. "So, as it turns out, Frontier LLC, along with half a dozen other subsidiaries on the list of Frontier's shell conglomerates, purchased a large portion of Eufy's worldwide product last year."

I glanced at Kiira. She raised an eyebrow. Maybe this annoying fuck was onto something. Deckert must have sensed our interest, because he paused for an extra excruciating beat before the final reveal.

"After the merest hint that I might know someone willing to match or even succeed that volume of product," said Deckert. "The Eufy CEO kindly revealed the details of their most recent shipment: three hundred Eufy Cam 6X's, purchased by non-other than Frontier LLC, and shipped to an industrial warehouse in Elk River, out of which runs a business called DTS Companies, whose land holdings were purchased a year back by one Aeon LLC, which is, you guessed it, another subsidiary of Unified LLC."

"Son of a bitch," I growled.

"What?" said Deckert, looking hurt.

I shook my head ruefully.

"Deckert," I said, "I think you're growing on me."

35

DTS Companies' warehouse stood in the south-east corner of a forty acre industrial site on the outskirts of Elk River. From the satellite stills Deckert had sent through we estimated the rectangular structure at two hundred yards long and a hundred wide. We could see a series of loading docks along one long side and a small connected outer office building on the south end. The rest of the industrial site was an undulating expanse of dirt and gravel used for God-knows-what. The entire forty acres was surrounded by a perimeter fence of unknown height and, although it was hard to be sure from the stills, appeared to have a six-man security team walking its two-mile perimeter.

"That's some serious security for a company specialising in . . . industry analysis," said Gow, reading from a print-out of the DTS Companies' homepage that Deckert had sent through.

We were parked with the engine running in the back of a Super Target parking lot about five miles from the site. It was just after six p.m., dark as death and twice as cold.

"More of that bullshit business-speak that tells you nothing about the actual business," I said.

"Hell of a place to infiltrate," said Gow, eyeing the stills again. "All open space between the fence and the warehouse. No approach where they won't see you coming a mile away."

"Correct," I said.

"So you have some sort of plan?" said Gow, handing me the stills.

"Nope," I said.

"Of course not," he said, easing the truck out of the parking space and heading toward the exit. "Going with old faithful."

It took us eight minutes to get there. The perimeter fence was similar to what I'd advised Shawn to install. Ten vertical feet topped with four rows of outward-angling razor wire. The front gate was steel rebar on a recessed track. Enough to stop an SUV at sixty miles an hour. It was shut tight. There was a small guard house just inside the gate. It was unoccupied.

"Head left and take a right on Proctor," I said, reading from one of the stills.

Proctor Road ran the length of the west side of the industrial site. Gow dropped me off a hundred yards along, where a rise in the gravel blocked the view of the warehouse.

"You sure about this?" said Gow as I climbed from the SUV.

In place of an answer, I slammed shut the door.

As Gow's taillights receded down the road, I stomped through the crusted snow along the roadside until I reached the fence. The mesh was 6-gauge fencing wire. Thick steel used for high-security applications. Not ideal. I waited. It was very dark and very cold. The only illumination came from the orange sodium lights on the warehouse proper, which at the moment were hidden by the gravel berm on the far side of the fence.

It took eighty-seven seconds for the first security guard to come into view, and another twenty-three before he spotted me.

"Hey!" he said as he neared. "Hey you there!"

There wasn't much concern in his voice. Yet. I was safely on the wrong side of the 6-gauge fence, carrying no visible weapons. I didn't reply. The security guard kept coming.

"Hey, you deaf?" he said, closing in.

I said nothing.

The path of trampled snow the security team had been following ran parallel to the fence, twelve feet inside the inside the perimeter. Too far away. When the guy got level with me along the path he stopped and faced me. His body language inside his all-black tactical gear was casual. Probably due to the HK416 assault rifle in his hands. Almost as an afterthought, he aimed it at my head.

"Talk motherfucker," he said from behind the rifle scope. I couldn't be certain he had thermal, but bet on the worst. Behind that scope I'd be lit up like a christmas tree. I smiled and waved.

"You got any idea what you're guarding in there?" I said.

Behind the scope, I saw the guy's head tilt. He wore a black beanie which exactly matched the shade of his chunky, collar-length beard. I wondered if he dyed it.

"What's it to you?" said Black Beard.

Making no sudden movement, I pinched the hood of my jacket and pulled it backward, revealing my face and the serpentine scar bisecting my scalp. Black Beard lifted his head from his scope and took single step forward, squinting into the darkness. Then his eyes went wide. He lowered the rifle.

"*Sledge Laukkanen*?" he said.

I pulled my hood the rest of the way down and smiled.

"What the hell are you doing here?" said Black Beard.

His confusion appeared genuine.

I glanced over each shoulder, then leaned conspiratorially into the fence and said, very quietly, "You got any idea what's in that warehouse?"

Black Beard took another step forward. Eight feet from the fence now.

"No," he whispered, shaking his head. "They pay me to keep people out."

"You really don't know?" I said.

Beard shook his head.

"They also pay me not to give a fuck," he said.

"Aren't you curious?" I said, quieter, in my best conspiratorial air, which, granted, wouldn't be winning me any Oscars.

"Yeah," he said. "We all are."

"What needs twenty-four hour surveillance from a six-man team?" I said.

Black Beard shrugged, but almost unconsciously he took another step toward me. Six feet away now.

"We secure the perimeter," he said. "No one's allowed inside the warehouse. They were very clear about that."

"So you are curious," I whispered, leaning in closer.

Unconsciously, Black Beard took yet another step.

"You know?" he said.

I smiled.

"What's your best guess?" I said.

Black Beard looked over each shoulder, then took another step closer.

"The boys have been theorising," he said.

"I bet they have," I said. "What'd they come up with?"

"The usual. Guns, drugs, UFOs. So what is it?"

Again, I took a furtive look over each shoulder, then leaned in closer to the fence. Black Beard didn't bite.

"No one's taken a peak?" I whispered.

Black Beard shook his head.

"Cameras all over the fucking place," he said.

I nodded.

"The Eufy Cam 6X," I said. "4k, motion-sensing, night-vision at a hundred feet in complete darkness. All wirelessly zapped to the cloud in real-time. Someone's watching us. Right now."

"How the fuck do you know that?" said Black Beard, and this time he did lean in.

I glanced around again, and leaned in until my face was right up against the fence.

My mental count had reached a hundred. At a rough estimate, the next guy in the line would walk into view in less than sixty seconds.

Finally, Black Beard took another half step forward and leaned in, the point of his chin roughly half a foot beyond the 6-gauge wire. Still too far away. But I was out of time. I dug my boots into the gravel underneath the snow and unleashed a savage right fist into the center of the fence. 6-gauge is as thick as a number 2 pencil, but over a ten-foot span it does have some give. And I have a hell of a punch. The fence wire exploded inward. With each inch the elastic force pushing back on my fist doubled. Did I have the power? Black Beard flinched, leapt back, but not before the 6-gauge riding my knuckles tapped the point of his bearded chin. He dropped like a sack of rice.

I looked around. At a guess, I had less than thirty seconds before the next guy in line came along and shot me to shit.

36

Over the fence, or through it? That was the question. But not much of one. 6-gauge is way too thick to cut through fast, even if I'd had a bolt cutter stuffed down the back of my pants, which I didn't.

I squinted down the fence line into the darkness in the direction Black Beard had come. No movement yet. But the count in my head was getting perilously high. I looked up at the concertina of razor wire. It would quite happily cut me to ribbons if I tried scaling it the old fashioned way.

I reached up with both hands. My standing reach is nine feet on the dot. With a little hop I could grab the wire loops no problem, if I didn't mind shredded hands. I slipped off my jacket and put my back to the fence. My jacked was thick canvas anorak. Holding it by the waist, I tossed it overhead like a towel for the clothes line until it lay draped over the top of the razor coils. Then I leapt up and grabbed hold of two of the coils through the canvas and held on as I returned to earth. The razor wire, only 14-gauge, had much more play. The question was how strongly was it fixed to the top of the fence? Already I felt the edges of the square razors digging into my hands beneath the canvas. If I yanked they'd cut me to shit.

In the distance, I heard a crunch of snow. I squinted into

the dark. Fuck. There he was. Maybe a hundred meters off, heading straight this way. He hadn't spotted me or his unconscious buddy yet, but it was only a matter of seconds until he did.

Using my thumbs I bunched as much loose jacket beneath my palms as I could in two seconds, then slackened my knees and dropped my weight straight down. One, two, three, four concertinas of razor-wire ripped free off the top of the fence with a loud *twang*. My ass hit snow. Without checking to see if I was cut, or if the guy had heard me, I leapt to my feet, stomped atop the uncoiled razor wire with my boot, and scaled the now razor-free section of fence, dropping down on the far side beside the still-unconscious Black Beard.

I was in.

No sooner had I hit the ground than a voice broke the silent night air.

"Hey! You! Freeze!"

The sound of running footsteps. The new guy, dressed in the same black tactical gear and carrying the same HK416, loomed out of the darkness, sprinting straight at me.

"Help!" I said. "Get over here! He's hurt!"

I was hoping Sprinter was a moron and would run right up to me. He didn't. Instead he pulled up twenty feet away and leveled his HK at my center mass.

"Put your hands over your head and step away from the body!" he shouted.

I held out my palms forward in front of me, not over my head.

"Put the gun down," I said slowly.

"Put your hands on your fucking head!" shouted Sprinter. His breath was coming in quick bursts, causing the muzzle of his HK to waver back and forth. He hadn't done this before.

"I'm going to say it one more time," I said, my voice very

calm, as if I did this every day. "Put the gun down. This is your final warning."

"I have you dead to rights motherfucker!" said Sprinter. "Put your-"

I didn't let him finish. I'd waited until the HK barrel wavered two inches to the right, then dropped to my knees, snapping my hands onto the unconscious body beside me, grabbing hold of each side of Black Beard's kevlar body armor, and rolling left, pulling the body over the top of me. The first shots exploded into the night. Wide right, as I'd expected. I rolled once and came up onto my knees, yanking Black Beard's body up in front of me. I now had two layers of Level 3 tactical armor and a human torso between me and the HK.

The HK416 uses a 5.56 x 45mm NATO cartridge, the same one used to kill Osama Bin Laden. By design, the 60-grain lead core tends to yaw inside soft tissue and fragment at the crimping groove. That makes it very good at shredding people's guts, but very bad at penetrating all the way through an armored body.

Keeping my head ducked low behind Black Beard's shoulder blades, I charged.

Sprinter fired the HK. One, two, three, four quick rounds. I felt two of them shudder into Black Beard's center mass, maybe killing him. Neither penetrated all the way through.

I lifted my head and peeked over Black Beard's left shoulder. I was ten feet from Sprinter and closing fast. With a bellowing roar I shoved Black Beard's body forward. As I've said, flinching is involuntary. Sprinter yelped and dodged to his right to avoid Black Beard's flying body. He loosed another four rounds in my general direction. All flew wide. Two more sprinting steps and I leapt on top of him. We landed hard and I hammered three overhands into his face as fast as I could. Right. Left. Right. He was out after one, damn near dead after three. I grabbed his HK and tossed it over the far side of the fence.

Two down. But twelve shots fired.

The other four guards would be here fast.

37

I was reasonably fucked. Wide out in the open, with nowhere to hide. I probably should have kept the machine gun. The enormous warehouse loomed a hundred metres in the distance across an open expanse of gravel, lit up like a Christmas tree. The glaring orange sodium lamps decimated my night vision, making it impossible to see anything in the darkness to either side of the building.

Based on Black Beard and Sprinter, the security team appeared reasonably competent, albeit inexperienced in live-fire situations. I figured they'd be trained enough to approach in pairs, one tandem to each side of the warehouse, leapfrogging each other from cover. They'd stay hidden in the shadows just outside the reach of the warehouse lights, at ninety degrees to each other to avoid crossfire. At least that's what I would do. Out here in the open I was a sitting duck, but if I broke for the warehouse I'd be a rabbit under a spotlight.

What were my options?

I could hop back over the fence and grab the HK. There, I could lay in the ditch alongside Proctor and try to pick them off as they approached.

Fucking guns.

If you haven't guessed by now, firefights aren't my

speciality. I'm a big, lumbering target, and that shallow ditch provided little cover. Besides, automatic gunfire doesn't go unnoticed, even on the outskirts of bumblefuck nowhere. If the security guys didn't fill me with me with holes, the Elk River Sheriff's department surely would soon thereafter.

Maybe I should have thought this one through.

Up ahead, in the inky darkness to the left of the warehouse, I sensed eyes. The perception wasn't visual. Or even rational. But it was there, in my gut and bone, just as it had been in the refinery. Predators were closing in, momentarily too distant for a clean shot, but not for long.

Still, I stood there, frozen.

Then, the primitive part of me, the savage leviathan who controls my fight-or-flight response, took over. I dropped to a knee beside Black Beard's bullet-ridden corpse and, leaning low, snaked a hand up his back, beneath his body armor, and clamped my fingers over the nape of his neck. I hefted the body aside, uncovering Sprinter's newly disfigured face. He was still breathing, albeit barely. I rolled him over and clamped an arm beneath his armor in similar fashion. Then, with a guttural roar, I powered to my feet, yanking Black Beard and Sprinter up with me. I now held two human shields, one alive, one dead, attached to each forearm via kevlar stitching and my vice-like grip.

Roaring unintelligibly, I set off at a dead sprint, straight toward the warehouse. My animal brain had dumped so much adrenaline into my thighs I felt faster than Usain Bolt. Automatic gunfire erupted from the darkness on both sides of the warehouse, exactly where I'd anticipated.

Deltoids searing, I rotated my arms until Black Beard and Sprinter faced directly into the gunfire. Bullets pinged all around me, sending chips of gravel flying. Ninety yards from the warehouse, cutting across their line of sight, moving faster than a six-foot-ten behemoth carrying two grown men in full body armor should be able to move.

The warehouse loomed before me. Eighty yards away. Seventy. Sixty. Bullets pinged and thwacked all around me. They were spraying me with fire, but their inexperience was evident. They were panicking.

Sprinter picked that moment to wake up. His head jerked up and he peered around wildly, trying to find his bearings.

"WHAAAA?" he bellowed through his shattered jaw.

He kicked his legs, glanced down, found his feet dangling a foot off the ground. He craned his neck, glancing back over his shoulder with wide, terrified eyes. He saw me and started screaming.

"PUMEDOWWWWW!" he shrieked through his mangled jaw.

I met his eyes and laughed maniacally. A fleck of gravel thwacked into Sprinter's neck. He snapped his head around.

For the first time, he realized we were being shot at.

"STAAAAAW!" he screamed, frantically waving his arms over his head. "STAAAAAAAAAAW!"

Amazingly, the gunfire ceased. I didn't.

Thirty yards away. Twenty. I burst into the brightly lit patch of gravel beside the warehouse. My peripheral vision caught gunmen on both sides pivoting low around corners. Neither fired. They'd wait for me to stop so they could get a clean shot. Straight ahead was a single steel door. A lot depended on its strength.

"STAAAAWWWWWW!" screamed Sprinter, looking straight ahead at the rapidly approaching door. I didn't stop. Instead I ducked my shoulders behind both forearms and rammed the steel door at twenty miles an hour with seven hundred pounds of armored flesh-and-bone.

The collision was immense. My skull slammed into something hard and my neck jarred and everything flashed black and then I was stumbling forward and falling, the bodies attached to each forearm cushioning the blow. Without hesitation, my adrenaline in overdrive, I loosed my arm from Black Beard and rolled to my back, pulling Sprinter over top of me. Using my heels, I scuttled backward across a concrete floor into complete darkness. I was in. The bright orange light pouring through the smashed doorway obliterated any view of the warehouse's insides. Through that doorway, I heard fast-approaching footsteps.

Sprinter was lying directly on top of me, the top of his skull pressed up beneath my chin.

"Scream," I whispered.

"Fuyoo-" he began, but the words got stuck in his throat.

I'd palmed his skull and edged the tip of my forefinger into the corner of his eye socket. Sprinter bucked and shrieked as if, well, someone with serious grip strength was gauging his eye out. He tried lifting his head and smashing it into my ribcage while ripping at my finger with both hands. He had zero chance of dislodging me. Incrementally, I edged the tip of my finger deeper into his skull. The pitch of his shrieks increased exponentially. I dialled up the pressure until I felt his eyeball teetering on the edge of popping. The sound emanating from his throat reached a level of intensity reserved only for a man tortured to the edge of sanity. Then, without warning, I smashed my left fist into the point of his chin. His blood-curdling shrieks ceased instantly. A deafening silence fell in their wake. I held my breath, listening. From just outside the door, came whispers.

"What the fuck was that?" mouthed a voice.

I heard a ruffling of fabric, which I took to be a shake of a head. A beat of silence.

"You know who that was?" breathed the same voice.

"I . . . I think . . . " hushed a second voice. I could hear panic in it. "I think it was Sledge Laukkanen. You see how fucking big he was? He ran through a fucking steel door!"

Silence.

"Fuck that," said the first voice, stronger now. More certain. "I'm not fucking going in there."

Silence for another second.

"Me either," piped a third voice. "I'm not getting near that big fucker. They don't pay us enough for that."

Silence again. Longer this time. The first guy, the squadron leader, was making a decision.

"Fuck it," he said.

I braced for a hail of bullets. It never came. Then the quiet tap of receding footsteps echoed outside the door. I breathed a sigh of relief.

Then, from the darkness behind me, a sound. My heart lurched. Someone was in here with me. I jerked around, adrenaline spiking once again. Out of the darkness walked a man, suppressed Rattler aimed at my forehead.

"About fucking time," said Gow.

38

I rolled out from under Sprinter's unconscious body, extricating my left arm en route, and climbed achingly to my feet. My head was still ringing from the collision with the door. I headed over to where it lay flat on the warehouse floor.

"Fucking shite mate," said Gow, eyeing the door for the first time. "That door opens outward."

I looked down, checking the hinges. Sure enough, the door was still locked shut in it's frame. The collision had blasted both door and frame out of the concrete block wall. The weakpoint had been the concrete, not the door. No wonder my head hurt.

I hefted the door, levering the mass of steel back into its hole. Turning back to the now-darkened warehouse, I squeezed shut my eyes to engage my night vision.

When I opened them, I said, "Fuck."

"Figured you'd say that," said Gow. He was looking around behind his thermal scope. "What'd you expect?"

"Not that," I said.

At my feet, Sprinter stirred. Somehow, he'd survived. I nudged him with my boot. He groaned through his mangled jaw. His eyes opened. The one I'd nearly gouged out didn't look great. I doubted he could see from it. He blinked a couples times, groaned again, then levered himself up to an elbow. His one good eye found who was standing over him. He let out a high-pitched yelp and tried scrambling backward. Right into Gow's boots. Gow aimed the rifle at him.

"Don' shoo'!" Sprinter yelped, flinching behind outstretched hands. He put a hand to his bad eye. "I can' see!"

"Relax," I said. "We're not gonna hurt you."

Sprinter did not appear convinced.

"I can' see!" he yelped again.

"Yes you can," I said, pointing behind him. "Look, we're inside the warehouse."

Sprinter shot a furtive glance over his shoulder, not wanting to take his good eye off the rifle, but when he saw what I'd seen, he let out a small gasp. He looked back at me.

"Iss fuckin' emp'y?" he slurred with a scrunched brow.

"As the Virgin Mary's snatch," said Gow. "Nothing but a mile of concrete, and about a thousand fucking cameras."

"Glad you enjoyed your little tikki-tour, Fuckstick," I said. "Was this before or after I took on six guys with machine guns barehanded?"

"Not my fault you don't like guns," said Gow.

I considered punching him in the face.

"And Fuckstick?" he said. "Honestly?"

I shrugged.

"Best I could do on short notice."

I walked up to Sprinter and offered him a hand.

"Sorry about the eye," I said, throwing out my warmest smile, which, I'll admit, needs work. "And for using you as a human shield . . . and for ramming you into a steel door . . . and for breaking your jaw. Twice."

Sprinter didn't respond, just stared at me with a slightly open eye and a slightly crooked jaw. I dropped the grin. Visible relief washed over his face. Jeez. My smile really is bad. Sprinter looked around again. It was dawning on him that he was alone in an empty warehouse with Sledge Laukkanen and an obvious ex-soldier with a silenced rifle and very few scruples. He clasped my hand and let me pull him unsteadily to his feet.

"What's your name?" I said, supporting him with an arm as he found his legs.

"Jas'n," he said, without moving his jaw. "Guy' call me Jase."

"Jase," I said. "My name is Einarr Laukkanen."

"I 'ow who you are," he said. He looked like he was about to cry.

"Good," I said, letting him go. He stayed upright on shaky legs. "What you might not know, Jase, is why I'm here."

Jase shook his head.

"Turns out there's a pack of pricks who want me to fight to the death inside this warehouse next week."

Jase's eye opened wide.

"You shi'in' me?" he said.

"I am not," I said. "See those cameras?"

I pointed to a vertical I-beam supporting the lofty roof, from which leered the familiar grin of infrared LEDs.

"That's a Uefy Cam 6X," I said. "They're mounted throughout this entire fucking place, beaming footage up to the darkweb. Somebody's watching us right now. And listening."

"You fucki' seriou'?" said Jase, staring wide-eyed into the camera.

"As fondling the Queen," said Gow.

"They fucked up though," I said.

"How's that?" said Gow.

I walked up to the I-beam, crouched down, then leapt, grabbing hold of the baseball-sized camera in my fist and snapping it from its mount as I returned to earth.

"Underestimated my vert," I said.

"Not bad for forty," admitted Gow.

I held the camera up to my face and stared hard into the lens.

"I don't know who you are," I said, "but I'm going to find you. And when I do. I'm going to fucking kill you."

I slammed the camera into the concrete floor, smashing it into a thousand pieces.

"Pretty good," said Gow. "Little Liam Neeson to it. Gave me chills."

"Fuck you," I said.

I headed to the next camera and ripped it down.

"Wanna try?" I said, offering it to Jase.

He put up his hands and backed away fearfully.

"Suit yourself," I said.

I offered the camera to Gow.

"Why not."

He smashed it into bits.

"Now let us get the fuck out of here," he said. "This place gives me the creeps."

I shook my head.

"No," I said. "I got an idea."

"That's never good," said Gow.

"It's a spectator sport, right?" I said, leaping up to the next camera and yanking it down.

"Yeah, so?"

"So if they can't see it . . . " I said.

It took a moment, then Gow started nodding.

"No cameras . . . " he said. "No fight."

For the next fifteen minutes we escorted Jase from pillar to pillar, snatching and smashing camera after camera after camera. There were hundreds, all mounted exactly twelve feet off the ground. We were about half-done when Jase spotted it.

"Wha's tha'?" he said, tapping me on the shoulder.

I followed his finger to the floor, where lay a small white

rectangle. I looked at Gow.

"Fuck," he said.

I leaned down and picked up the envelope. A4 width. Unlicked. With a sinking feeling I opened the flap and pulled out the folded piece of paper.

Congratulations on your successful incursion of this secured location at Depth 6 of The Labyrinth. You have been awarded a bonus of +1000 Labyrinth souls. Good luck on your next Descent.

q8dsofkh387lkadhscxciyvi

39

"They knew you were coming," said Kiira, eyeing me over the top of the sheet of paper. We were back in her room in Maldonado's second guest house. Kiira hadn't been home in over a week and it was starting to show a little around the edges. She still looked good, but so does Queen Anne's lace.

"Tell me something I don't fucking know," I said with more edge to my voice than I intended.

Gow and I had driven back from Elk River through the night. I'd tried to get some sleep along the way, but vehicles and my legs have a long, sordid history. The sleep deprivation hadn't improved my mood. In the six hours since I'd found the letter, my irrational rage meter had been been slowly ticking toward redline.

"Did you see anyone else?" said Kiira.

"Other than the six guys with machine guns?" I said.

"No," said Gow. "We did a full check of the warehouse. There was no one else there."

"What about a vehicle?" she said. "Anyone drive in or out? Pass by on the road while you were on site?"

"No," I snapped. "You got a fucking point?"

"I do," she snapped back. "Someone had to physically drop this letter there. So if no one else was in the warehouse, and no one left while you were on your way in, then the letter was put there *before* your dumb ass hopped the fence."

I glanced at Gow. He squeezed the bridge of his nose. She was right.

"The fuckers knew we were coming," I said.

Kiira rolled her eyes.

"Once again, they were one step ahead," she said.

"Just one?" said Gow.

My rage meter ticked up another notch.

"They're fucking with me," I spat between gritted teeth. "And we don't have a fucking clue who they even are."

"Correct," said Kiira.

I pulled in a deep breath through my nose, trying to settle the monster growing inside me.

"Growling's not going to help, Einarr," said Kiira, unaware of the mindless beast simmering behind my eyes. "They're toying with you. I can feel them watching right now. Laughing at how stupid you are."

Welp. I let loose a guttural roar, spun, and punched a hole through the wall.

"Jesus Christ!" said Kiira. "What the hell is wrong with you?"

"Fuck you!" I roared. "Fuck you! Fuck them! Fuck *all you cunts*!"

I stomped to the nearest piece of wall-hung art. A smear of pastels a retarded third grader could have produced, most likely priceless, and hammered a fist through both it and wall. Glass and sheetrock exploded everywhere.

"What the fuck!" said Kiira. "Stop!"

I saw her glance at Gow, but he knew better than to try and stop me. I stalked to the next painting, some abstract piece of shit, eyed out where the stud would be. Both art and two-by-four were annihilated.

"Einarr please!" screamed Kiira.

But I'd completely lost my shit. The rage monster was loose. And it felt fucking *great*. I needed the release. I also needed the training session.

One of my big advantages in hand-to-hand combat is my adamantine bone density. The systematic strengthening of bones under tension, bending, torsion, fatigue, and sheer was a key element of my grandfather's unorthodox training regimen. Bones respond to stress the same way muscles do. Injure them slightly, and they heal back stronger. Continue that process systematically for twenty-five years, and what you get is a skeleton made of drastically different stuff than yours. Think of the difference between you and the winner of last year's World Strongest Man competition. Can you flip a 8,000 pound Dodge Ram onto its roof with your bare hands? Didn't think so. That's the same disparity between the density of your bones and mine. Put simply, I punch you, you break. *You* punch *me*, you break.

Cue the training montage.

I stalked the room's perimeter, dropping the first four studs with fists. Jab, right hook, straight right, left hook. The next two snapped with knees. Right, left. That was almost cheating. Elbows took the next four. Snap, cross, up, down. Then head butts. Two. Then shins. Low left round kick, low right, high left, high right. I made a full circuit of the three interior walls, completely obliterating them, then got to the door. I turned that into a grappling session, ripping the heavy chunk of solid oak from it hinges and snapping it over my knee as if it were someone's spine. Chest heaving, I dropped the pieces to the floor and wheeled on Kiira and Gow, who were standing slack jawed in the center of the demo'd room.

"Round kick's looking good," said Gow.

I breathed in and out for a while, the monster inside me slowly retreating into his cave.

I nodded.

"Think you're ready?" said Gow, glancing at the letter.

"Ready as I'll ever be," I said.

I wasn't.

40

<u>VICTIM PROFILE</u>

Code Name: Sledge
Height: 6′10″
Weight: 266 lbs
Labyrinth Depth: 6
Labyrinth Rank: 39 of 100
Labyrinth Souls: +11,750
Career earnings: $875,000 USD

<u>Power Grid</u>

Toughness: 6/8
Strength: 7/8
Speed: 1/8
Fighting Skill: 4/8
Intelligence: 2/8
Cunning: 5/8

<u>Depths Descended</u>

1 - Death Threat (rank 86-100, bounty $5000 USD, +250 souls)

2 - Beating (rank 71-85, bounty $20,000 USD, +500 souls)

3 - Kidnapping (rank 61-70, bounty $50,000 USD, +1000 souls)

4 - Rape (rank 51-60, bounty $100,000 USD, +2,000 souls)

5 - Grievous Bodily Harm (rank 41-50, bounty $200,000 USD, +3,000 souls)

6 - Deprivation of Hearing (rank 31-40, bounty $300,000 USD, +4,000 souls)

.

.

.

~~10 - Final Boss: джаггернаут (rank 1, bounty ?, +? souls)~~

Bonus Kills - 4 (bounty $50,000 USD x 4, +1000 souls x 4)

Penalties - 1 (-3000 souls x 1)

Congratulations on your successful Exploration of Depth 6 of The Labyrinth. Your Depth 6 Bounty of $300,000 USD has been transfered to your account, and can be accessed via your Victim Profile page. In addition, you earned your fourth Kill Bonus of $50,000 USD and +1000 souls for the unsolicited murder of Greg Shipp. Excellent work, your players will be delighted.

Your Death Match Summons is still live, and has been updated with the location.

DEATH MATCH SUMMONS

You have been Summoned to a Labyrinth Death Match. You will fight to the death at midnight Friday, March 16th. The location of your Death Match is 47.38076333, -91.342806. You are afforded NO WEAPONS upon entry. Failure to comply with this rule will result in a Depth 7 attack on a close friend or family member. Victory in your Death Match will descend you to Depth 7 of The Labyrinth and carries with it a Depth 7 bounty of $400,000 USD and +5000 souls. Defeat will result in your death. Failure to comply with this Death Match Summons will result in the immediate release of Indemnity to all major national and

international media outlets, along with a Depth 7 attack on someone dear to you.

Good luck on your next Descent.

41

"This is it," I said. "47 degrees, 38 minutes, 10.8 seconds North, 91 degrees, 20 minutes, 34.1 seconds West."

Gow pulled the SUV to a stop. The dashboard clock read 11:38 p.m. Ahead of us, in the wash of the SUV's headlights, the unnamed track we'd been following for the last ten minutes dead ended. We were deep in the North Woods. The only name within a thirty mile radius on Google Earth was Eighteen Lake Rustic Campground, twenty miles to the northeast through dense forrest. Outside that it was nothing but trees.

"Twenty-two minutes," I said, rubbing my hands together in front of the heater. "Better warm up."

"It's seven degrees out," said Gow.

"Balmy," I said.

Gow turned off the headlights, but kept SUV's the engine running. Grabbing a night vision range finder from the backseat, he scoped the trees. I climbed out of the car, pulling in a deep breath of cold air. I hadn't been lying about the temperature. It wasn't too bad. My grandfather had a saying: "Cold weather doesn't exist, merely inappropriate clothing." I was dressed for fifty below, with an insulated water skin across my back and a water-proof pocket full of chocolate chips, beef jerky, and peanuts. Cold weather pulls heat energy from your body. That's what kills you. As long as I stayed insulated and consumed as many calories as I burned, I could survive out here indefinitely. I doubted the same could be said for my opponent.

Pulling down my flecktarn balaclava, I got up on my toes, rolling my neck and throwing out a few warm-up punches. Gow rolled down the window.

"There's a fence," he said, nodding out the windshield. "Straight ahead. Stretches off east-west as far as I can see through the finder. Can't see anything else through the trees."

"How much time I got?" I said.

"Fifteen minutes."

I nodded.

"What you thinking?" said Gow.

"I'm thinking they fucked up letting me fight outside."

"Home court advantage," said Gow.

I nodded.

"My grandfather raised me out here."

"He had a rifle," said Gow.

"They said no weapons," I said. "Suits me."

"They said no weapons on entry. There might be weapons inside the fence."

"Same as the refinery," I said. "They had shit lying around. I expect it'll be the same."

"That's what I'm worried about," said Gow. "They seem to know what you expect."

I shrugged.

Gow shook his head, letting out a breath through his nose. I could see the stress on his face.

"Good luck," he said.

"Luck's got nothing to do with it."

"You sure about that?"

"No."

"How about don't die?" said Gow.

"Now there's a plan I can get behind."

Gow searched the woods with the range finder again.

"How long?" I said.

"Eight minutes."

"I'd better head out."

Gow let out another breath, nodded. We had that weird moment where we both realized this might be the last time we saw each other alive, but neither us acknowledged it. Instead we bumped knuckles through the car window, nodded to each other, then I set off into the woods.

I came upon the fence a hundred yards into the trees. I'd recently scaled a similar model in Elk River: 6-gauge chain link, ten feet high, concertinaed razor wire angling outward along the top edge. It looked recently installed. No rust anywhere. I looked left and right along its face, listening. I heard a quiet beeping. I followed the fence-line east toward the sound, crunching through calf-deep snow. The beeping grew gradually louder. A minute later I found a Uefy Cam 6X mounted to the fence, facing outward. Below it, a door-sized gate. I smiled into the camera lens. A moment later, an electromagnetic lock clicked. I cracked my neck from side to side, pulled in a breath, and ducked through the gate. It swung shut behind me and locked tight. The beeping stopped.

Go time.

42

I stood still, listening. I imagined my opponent on the far side of the fenced enclosure, near a similar gate, doing the exact same thing. But how far away was that? A hundred feet through the trees? Two hundred? Half a mile? Ten miles?

I listened.

The night was dark. No moon. No stars. Low hung cloud devoured the tops of the trees. What ghostly light there was came from below, diffused by the snow. I could see maybe thirty feet in front of me. What lay beyond in the darkness was anyone's guess. I listened. Heard nothing but the eerie creaks and cracks of the woods in winter.

I figured the weapons would be located in the interior of the fighting arena, most likely at the very center. But that was only a guess. They could be anywhere: randomly dispersed within the trees; hidden in caches beneath the snow. I didn't like the thought of wading through dense forrest, searching blindly. Too many opportunities for ambush. I didn't want to do a Skinpeeler all over again. I decided to stick to the fence. I needed the lay of the land. Figure out how large an area I was dealing with.

I set off, cracking and crunching through the snow, fence at my back, making a lot of noise. There was no way to avoid it. Luckily sound doesn't travel far over snowy ground. Refraction at its finest.

Every fifty feet or so a fence-mounted Uefy 6X grinned down at me. I glimpsed more leering from the darkness in the trees. They were watching. I paused, listening. Nothing. Even in the dark, with no moon or stars, my sense of direction told me I was travelling almost directly west. It didn't take long to realize this was a very large enclosure indeed. It took me forty-six minutes to reach the first corner. By rough estimate I'd covered nearly three miles. If the entry gate had been positioned in the center of the south fence, a reasonable assumption, that meant the enclosure was six miles on a side. Assuming it was square, that made a thirty-six square-mile fighting arena. Two guys could run around in here for weeks and never get near each other.

Fuck that.

Playing hide-and-seek in the woods wasn't my style. I wanted this fucker face-to-face. Now.

Cupping gloved hands to my mouth, I bellowed, "OVER HERE!"

My booming voice echoed through the silent night, then all was quiet. I counted silently to one hundred. Nothing. Maybe he was too far away. I marched north along the fence line, staying out in the open, not caring how much noise I made. Every few minutes, I loosed another roar.

"COME ON! I'M HERE!"

Nothing.

"I'M HERE! KILL ME! DO IIIT! DO IT NOW!"

Another mile. Two. Maybe there wasn't anyone in here with me at all. Maybe it was all a joke. Lock me in a cage and watch me freeze to death. I wondered what would happen if I hopped the fence and headed home. That's when I heard a noise, up ahead. A crunching footstep. Then the snap of a branch.

"Finally!" I yelled. "Let's do this."

More crunching through the snow in the trees ahead. Fifty feet away? Twenty? Like I said, sound does funny things in cold air. I couldn't gauge the distance. Nor could I see that far in the darkness.

"I'm here!" I yelled. "Come get m—"

A black shape emerged from cover. Thirty feet away. Just close enough to make out the form of a man in black tactical gear, face hidden behind a visor. At his shoulder . . . was that . . . ?

Another crunch of snow. *Behind* me. I spun ninety degrees, my back to the fence, keeping the guy in my peripheral vision. A second shape emerged from the cover of the trees thirty feet to my right. The quickest of glances in his direction was enough to confirm my fear:

There were *two* guys in here with me.

And they had fucking *rifles*.

43

Time to let you in on a little secret.

You know when you hear about a ninety pound mother lifting a two ton car off her kid? That's an actual phenomenon. It's called hysterical strength. It's a function of our evolutionary fight-or-flight response that has helped us survive as a species since back in the day when sabre-toothed tigers wanted a bite of our ass every time we left the cave.

It's an amazing process. When the human body is faced with a sudden dangerous situation, the hypothalamus sends a signal to your adrenal glands, activating your sympathetic nervous system, flooding your body with epinephrine and norepinephrine. Those hormones' chemical function is to drastically shunt blood from your stomach and skin to your muscle fibres. Which is why you get chills and butterflies when you're scared. Your muscles are flooded with oxygen, supercharging their conversion of your body's fuel source, glucose, into energy. Put simply, your muscles suddenly function at an elevated, seemingly superhuman level . . . for a very limited amount of time.

Hysterical strength and I go way back. To The Pit. For my debut fight I was faced up against a guy named Vasily Dimitriev. He'd spent his formative years as an enforcer-slash-hitman for the Russian mob. Nice guy, straight out of your worst nightmare, with a row of skull tattoos adorning his torso, one for each of his murders. It was a long row. This would be his eleventh descent into The Pit.

It's impossible to describe the soul-ripping terror of entering the blood-spattered arena. The walls of The Pit were darkened glass, behind which sat a live audience of assholes who'd paid massive sums of money to watch me die.

The fight did not begin well. I'd had years of training, but nothing can prepare you for the real thing. The moment The Pit gates lowered, I peered across the blood-stained concrete, directly into Dimitriev's eyes. Big mistake. What I found there . . . was nothing at all.

No fear. No empathy. No uncertainty. No humanity.

Only the inevitability of my own death.

The fear overwhelmed me. I froze. Stood there like a moose caught in headlights along the Gunflint Trail. Dimitriev stalked across the Pit and levelled me with a right hook. At least I think it was a right hook. Either that or a meteor. I was on my back, Dimitriev sprawled on top of me, his immense weight pinning me to the ground, crushing the breath from my chest. Mind still frozen, I did nothing but await death.

Then, slicing through the fog: laughter. Straddled on top of me, Dimitriev started chuckling. Mocking me. Playing to the hidden crowd. Drawing out the horrifying final moments of my life. What I didn't know then was that if he didn't get me to fight, they'd feed me to the dogs.

"*Beeeg* man, *leetle* balls," he chortled in his thick Russian accent. "*Noo* fight. Just die. Like *leetle girrl*."

He was still chuckling when he reached back and squeezed my balls.

As far as I know, that's what triggered it.

The instant his meaty fingers grasped the source of my manhood, something primordial inside me awoke. My sympathetic nervous system detonated like a billion megaton bomb. With a savage roar, I ripped my arms from their confinement and tossed Dimitriev's body six feet into the air.

By all accounts, it was an impossible feat of strength. Lying on my back, with no leverage to speak of, I'd hefted a three-hundred pound man and tossed him into the air as if he were a cardboard cut-out. Through the supposedly sound-proof glass encircling the Pit, I heard gasps. By the time Dimitriev fell back to earth I'd sprung to my feet. My legs were pistons. My arms hydraulics. My blood molten steel.

From the bloodied concrete where he landed, Dimitriev lifted his head, peering up at me. He tried to grin, but in the very same eyes in which I'd glimpsed the inevitability of my own death mere seconds before, I now saw fear.

I leapt on him. So quick was my movement it felt as though I'd disappeared from one place only to appear in another. My fingers, which were no longer fingers at all, but steel locking pliers, secured themselves to Dimitriev's neck. Then, laughing maniacally, I ripped his head off.

Yeah. *Off.*

So astounding was my colossal feat of strength that word quickly spread throughout the prison that I was some form of inhuman monster, capable of impossible carnage. They weren't far off. My grandfather had taught me that the mind controls the body. Not the other way around. Inside The Pit, I learned something vital: somewhere, lurking deep within my brain, was the key to unlocking my true physical potential. I call it *The Leviathan*.

Since then, I've systematically trained myself to consciously trigger my sympathetic nervous system. It's by no means easy, and it comes with a heavy price tag, but it really is that simple:

Flick the switch . . . and The Leviathan awakes.

44

Adrenaline has a weird effect on the brain. At first, time cranks itself down to zero. I've learned to use that to my advantage.

Over a near-eternal first millisecond, I assessed the situation. The two shooters stood roughly thirty feet from me on opposite sides, the three of us forming an obtuse triangle with me at the peak. The guy to my left was blocky, with bunched traps and bowling-ball shoulders crowding a muscled neck. His HK416 looked like a styrofoam toy in his meaty bare hands. The guy on the right was taller. Wiry. Like a four-hundred meter runner. From his angled stance and perfectly still upper-body he looked more proficient than Blocky at putting holes in me.

They wore identical outfits: black tactical gear with visored helmets like you'd see on a snowmobiler. Either they'd separately stumbled upon identical caches of gear that just happened to fit their drastically different body shapes, or I'd been set up.

Those helmets though . . . ? You couldn't get a cheek to a rifle wearing one of those. Not that it mattered much at this distance. And those visors were great for keeping your eyeballs from freezing solid atop a snowmobile, but you couldn't see shit to either side. If I could survive the next ten seconds, maybe, just maybe, I could use that to my advantage. A colossal if. Even with the helmets, the low light, the sub-zero temperatures, the chances of both of them missing a large, slow-moving target at thirty feet was damn near zero.

All this went through my head in the first thousandth of a second. Over the next thousandth, the adrenaline flooded my muscles, and The Leviathan awoke.

I'm big. I'm slow. I'm lumbering.

Until I'm not . . .

Time, which had been inching forward almost imperceptibly, blasted ahead in a gut-lurching blur. My pneumatic quadriceps launched me straight ahead. I was fifteen feet from the tree line, an impossible distance to cover without taking a bullet. Machine guns erupted on both sides. I dove, rolled once, and came up directly between the two shooters. In a blink of the eye I'd flattened our triangle to a straight line. They hadn't expected me to move so quickly, not in calf-deep snow, and now they were in each other's crossfire.

The gunfire ceased. I didn't. A savage impulse threw me straight ahead into the trees. I dodged left then right around birch trucks, my rocket-fuelled legs churning like pistons. I don't remember forming a plan. I didn't have one. It was all instinct. Savage memory from epochs past. Survive. I angled toward Blocky. I couldn't have voiced it, yet I knew his ungloved trigger finger would be slowed by the cold.

Through the trees I saw Blocky pivot toward me. His gun come up, spurting fire. But I'd zigged to the right behind an eight inch birch. Bullets sprayed the snow where I'd been. I'd be dead in a second unless I came up with something drastic. My eyes fell upon the birch. Its once paper-white bark was spotted with cubical rot. Was it possible? Probably not. Did I have a choice?

No, I didn't.

I lowered my shoulder and rammed the tree, hoping to fell it straight atop Blocky just like the steel warehouse door. Pain exploded in my hardened colar bone as the rot-brittled trunk buckled with a deafening crack. The tree shook, angled forward . . . and held.

My one shot at survival had air-balled.

With death imminent, I spun off the the tree to the right. Blocky stood ten feet from me now. Nothing between us but snow. All he had to do was put a bullet in me. But suddenly it was snowing. No. Not snowing. A thick blanket of white glommed down onto Blocky's helmet from the branches of the birch I'd just slammed, momentarily blocking his already limited vision. His left hand released his rifle to clear his visor of snow. He shook his helmeted head, right, then left, and found me barrelling down on him. His hand flew back to his rifle, but the falling snow had bought me the extra quarter second I needed. Fist and helmet collided as the HK416 erupted beneath me.

Was I hit? Who fucking knows. The Leviathan had taken over, and he didn't feel pain. My flying superman punch had knocked Blocky's helmet clean off his square head. We fell to the snow in a tangle of limbs. A savage wrestle ensued, life and death hanging in the balance. He was strong. Incredibly strong. Bucking and jerking beneath me, he hammered my head and neck with heavy blows, any one of which would have felled a normal man. But at the moment, I was no man. My forged steel fists reared back wide, then descended like twin wrecking balls onto the sides of Blocky's snarling face. Knuckles collided where once had been brainstem. Loosing a savage roar I ripped free my hands and surveyed the wreckage. Blocky was very, very dead.

Then, all at once, a colossal weight descended upon me, as if the air itself had turned to lead. Every superpower has its drawback. The last molecule of adrenaline inside my body had been used up. An overabundance of tryptophan flooded my cells and I collapsed backward into the snow. I lay there, barely able to lift an eyelid. A crunch of footsteps reached my ears. The second shooter edged slowly into view, rifle raised.

I searched desperately within me for The Leviathan, but as quickly as he'd arrived, he was gone.

45

Full-blown central nervous system fatigue is just as shitty as it sounds. As I said, every superpower has its drawback. Hysterical strength is great, but in just over a minute I'd burned through every last molecule of glycogen in my body, and now my cells were quite literally running on empty. I'd mega-bonked. I felt as though I'd been hit by a cement truck. My brain, which had been functioning at hyper-speed, was suddenly stuffed with cotton, and despite the machine gun aimed at my face, the best plan I could come up with on short notice was taking a nap.

I closed my eyes. It was very quiet. Peaceful. I almost drifted off but a crunch of snow jolted me back to consciousness. I kept my eyes closed, pulled in a lungful of air through my nose. Let it out. After a couple more I found the strength to force one eyelid open a crack. It felt like sprinting a mile.

The second gunman edged toward me through the snow, aiming his rifle as best he could in that ridiculous helmet. He tip-toed, carefully, as if on thin ice. Thirty feet away. Twenty-five. I closed my eye again and focused on my breathing, trying hard not to fall asleep. Somewhere far off the careful crunching continued, the only sound in the silent night. I breathed in and out. It was extremely hard work. I searched high and low for a couple molecules of ATP. Found enough to crack my eyelid again. The guy had stopped twenty feet away. I wondered why. It was almost a guaranteed killshot from that distance, even with that stupid helmet, but closer was better. I had no clue why he hadn't pulled the trigger yet.

I tried to speak, but all that came out was a weird moaning sound and a bit of drool. The effort awarded me a brief spat of unconsciousness. When I came to, the guy was still standing there.

I needed energy. It took me a good few minutes to process the next thought:

In your pocket you fucking moron.

Oh yeah. The chocolate chips.

Pulling my right hand back six inches felt like free-climbing El Capitan, but somehow I managed to get my right hand to my jacket pocket. The gunman didn't react. Again, I wondered why. The zipper was next. The coordination needed to pinch my fingers and pull the fucking thing felt like solving the Unified Field Theory. Part of me hoped the guy would just shoot me.

More time passed. Mysteriously, I stayed hole-free. I got a thumb to the zipper. Then an index finger. Somewhere I found the strength to paw it down a few inches. Chocolate chips cascaded in mini-avalanche into my open palm. Bingo. Now I just had to get hand to face.

Still no new holes. What was the guy doing? Probably laughing as he watched me spend my last few seconds on earth trying to eat a few fucking chocolate chips. I scraped my hand across the snow toward my mouth. One inch. Two. It made a hell of a racket in the silent night.

Just fucking shoot me you prick.

Half way there. I realized he was going to wait until I got my hand an inch from my mouth to pull the trigger. What a dick.

Finally, after a soul-sucking effort, I tasted chocolate. I didn't have the energy to chew. I let the chocolate melt on my tongue, welled the energy to swallow. It would take a while for the sugar to hit. Still, placebo cleared my brain the slightest bit.

I opened my eyes.

The guy was still standing there, twenty feet away, in that stupid fucking helmet, not shooting me.

"Take tha' fuckin' thing off," I croaked.

The effort to speak nearly killed me.

"I can't," he said.

His voice was high and clear.

"Fuck th' camera'," I breathed.

My brain was coughing in fits and starts.

"It's not the cameras," he said.

"Huh?" I mumbled.

He was quiet a moment, then he said, "I can't take it off."

"Why 'ot?"

"There's a bomb inside it."

46

My eyes opened a little wider. It was suddenly very quiet. We both experienced the terror and stillness that come in the presence of imminent death.

"Explain," I grunted.

Talking was still a Herculean effort, but I felt the sugar starting to circulate.

"Pressure trigger," he said. "I take if off. Kablam."

Oh. Now I knew why he'd been tip-toeing like such a jackass. He didn't want to blow his fucking head off.

"You agreed to put it on?" I croaked.

"'Course not," he said. He kept his head very still as he spoke. "Instructions said to put on the gear, then enter the gate. The helmet has a built in mic which would provide further information once I was inside. Helmet seemed normal. I got one at home just like it, built in headphones and everything. I figured I'd just take it off once the instructions were done."

"Bummer," I said.

He didn't nod.

"Why don't you have a gun?" he said.

"They told me no weapons," I said.

"And *you* listened?" he said.

"I'm not the one with a bomb strapped to my head."

He muttered something under his breath and started to shake his head then quickly stopped himself. We stared at each other for a while. I was getting very cold. Snow had leaked down the back of my neck, inside my jacket. I imagined he was the opposite, sheeting sweat inside that helmet. I swallowed more melted chocolate. Glucose, do your thing. I still felt as though I'd gone a hundred rounds with a cement truck. It'd be a while before I could do much more than grunt.

"How come his helmet didn't blow?" I said, shifting my eyes to the decapitated corpse lying beside me. The gooey remnants of Blocky's face had frosted over. His helmet lay face down in the snow near the base of a birch tree ten feet to my left.

"I've been wondering that for the last ten minutes," said the gunman. "Why do you think I haven't shot you yet?"

"No idea," I said.

He looked at me. Very still.

"When I came through the gate," he said, "a woman came on through the helmet. I'm not sure if she was pre-recorded or speaking to me live. She told me I'd just engaged a pressure trigger connected to five hundred grams of C4, which had been packed inside the helmet lining. If I take it off too soon, it'll vaporize everything in a twenty foot radius."

I thought about that.

"She say anything else?" I said.

I saw him begin to nod before he remembered the bomb strapped to his head. He went rigid. The helmet didn't go off. I heard him pull in a shaky breath.

"She said the detonator is wirelessly controlled via satellite," he said, pointing upward into the night sky."

"So maybe they turned the other one off remotely?" I said.

"Yeah," he said. "They must have."

"Or maybe they're just fucking with you," I said. "Maybe

there is no bomb. Sounds like something these Labyrinth assholes would do."

"I could test it out," he said. "Blow us both sky high."

I said nothing. We were quiet a while. I still had no idea why he hadn't shot me.

"You got any idea who they are?" he said.

"No," I said. "You?"

"Maybe," he said.

"What do you know?"

"Been doin' some searching online."

"And?"

"I found a video," he said. "It showed two guys locked in a room with a crow bar on the floor. I guess the deal was if one of them killed the other, they'd be initiated into the Russian mob. If they refused, they'd both be killed. Tortured first. So one guy picks up the crow bar and fucks the other guy up. Bashes his head in. The video was collateral. It gets leaked if the guy ever tries to leave the mob."

"Sounds familiar," I said.

"No shit," he said.

I looked at him.

"You know who I am?" I said.

"I do," he said, careful not to nod his head.

We were quiet a minute.

"What else?" I said.

"I heard on reddit they sell access to the live streams as entertainment. Like the ultimate NFT. Digital rights to watch us die. And they bet on the results. Huge money. All anonymous."

"Who's they?"

"I heard Medvyed's involved."

"Vladimir Medvyed?" I said. "The Russian President?"

"Yup," he said. "Supposedly the prick loves it. Maybe he started it, I don't know. He wants somebody offed, he just hires some anonymous asshole to do it for him. No way to trace it. If the money's real, people will do anything. And as you know, the money's real."

I said nothing.

"And I heard Medvyed let his buddies in on it," he continued. "Including our very own Ratfuck in Chief. Everyone knows they're butt buddies, right? They both use it to do their dirty work. And they bet huge money on their favorites. I'm talking billions. Entire economies rising and falling depending on who kills who."

"Fuck me," I said.

He looked at me carefully behind his helmet.

"So who you think's backin' you?" he said.

I said nothing. Neither of us moved. The sugar had hit my system, but I was still too wasted to do anything except lay there and die.

"Why haven't you shot me?" I said.

He studied me for a while before answering.

"I wanted to see what you knew," he said. "The mighty Sledge Laukkanen. The man, the myth, the legend, right here in the flesh. I didn't think it could be that easy. Thought you might have something up your sleeve."

I held up both my palms. My sleeves were very empty.

"Someone really wants you dead," he said.

"Tell me about it."

"For what's it's worth," he said. "I would've bet on you."

I said nothing.

After a moment, he raised the rifle.

"Sorry," he said.

I gave a thumbs up.

"Don't worry about it," I said.

The bullet struck home before I ever heard the shot.

47

"So what was the plan?" asked Kiira.

We were back at Maldonado's eating what was for Kiira and Gow an early dinner and for me a very late breakfast. After returning from the Death Match I'd skulled a gallon of chocolate milk, thawed out in the sauna for half an hour, then slept most of the day. I felt ok, all things considered.

"Stay near the fence," I said, forking steak and eggs into my mouth. "So Gow could put a bullet in anyone who looked likely to kill me."

"That's it?" Kiira said.

"We like to keep things simple," I said.

Kiira gave me a look that said she'd seen more intelligence in some rodents.

"How did you know there wasn't really a bomb in the helmet?" she asked.

"Lucky guess," I said.

Kiira looked aghast.

I finished chewing, then said, "Half a kilogram of C4 has a blast radius of over a hundred metres, not twenty feet."

"So it's *more* dangerous than he said?" said Kiira, screwing up her face.

I nodded.

"And *that* convinced you?" she said.

"It told me whoever was talking through the helmet was full of shit."

Kiira's look of incredulity intensified.

"And you were willing to risk your life on that?"

I shrugged again.

"He also said he had a similar helmet at home," I said. "If there really was half a kilo of C4 in there, it's likely he would have noticed the weight difference."

"Likely?" said Kiira. "How much is half a kilo?"

"One-point-one pounds."

"That's nothing!"

Shrug. Kiira let out a an exasperated breath.

"Then there was Blocky's helmet," I said.

Kiira raised a skeptical eyebrow.

I said, "There was no cell service out there, so the digital feeds of a thousand high-definition video cameras had to be uploaded straight to satellite. Then the satellite had to beam the feeds back down through some fancy encryption, probably ping around through a bunch of VPNs and what-not, before finally reaching the bad guys' screens. Then, if they inputted a command to, say, turn off the detonator, it had to beam all the way back through all the same shit in reverse. I figured there'd be a couple seconds lag in all that, minimum. So there was no way they could have turned off Blocky's helmet in time. It would have exploded the moment I punched it off his head."

Kiira stared at me. I watched the skepticism in her expression lessen in intensity, but only slightly.

"You got lucky," she said. "Again."

I looked at Gow. He shrugged.

"How did you know he wouldn't just shoot you?" said Kiira.

"I didn't," I said. "I had to trust that Gow was in position on the other side of the fence."

Kiira looked at Gow. He shrugged.

"You're insane," said Kiira. "Both of you."

"We've been told," I said.

"And you still have no idea who wants you dead," she said.

It wasn't a question.

"We know more than we did," I said. "If the guy was right, this thing goes all the way up to Medvyed and the President. That explains why they're so well-funded. And so arrogant. They think they're untouchable."

"Because they are!" said Kiira. "This is not good news Einarr. If the President of Russia wants you dead and our fuckhead in charge is working with him, then what chance do you have?"

I looked at Gow, who, you guessed it, shrugged.

48

Deckert called an hour later. Kiira and I were lying on the bed in her room, over the covers, so no, we hadn't. I had ice bags on both knees and a big bandage on my shoulder but overall I was feeling pretty good due to the prospect of what might happen once Deckert got off the line.

"Did you find the crowbar video?" Kiira asked him.

She was in black yoga pants and one of my old Pistons sweatshirts that was so big it could have fit six of her inside it and still have room for me. Her laptop lay between us on the bedspread.

"No," said Deckert.

Deckert's eyes flitted left on screen. To me. He wore the expectant smile of a labrador sitting next to a barbecue sizzling with ribeye.

"Put your tongue back in your mouth, Deckert," I said. "What'd you find?"

"Nothing." Big grin.

"Then why are you grinning like a fucking spastic?"

Bigger grin. I looked over at Kiira. She rolled her eyes. We waited.

"Okay," said Deckert. "Fine. Here's the deal. If this video was on the internet, which we're assuming it was at one time, then it's statistically impossible for me not to be able to find it."

"And yet you didn't?" said Kiira.

"Correct," said Deckert. *Biggerer* grin.

"Get to the fucking point, Deckert," I said.

He didn't, of course. He paused excruciatingly. I spent the time envisioning how his face would look if I punched it once for every second of wasted time.

Finally, he said, "If I couldn't find it, or even any mention of it, anywhere, the only conceivable explanation is that it was scraped."

Biggest grin.

"What's that mean in English?" said Kiira.

"It means it, or any mention of it, has been completely erased from the publicly accessible internet," said Deckert.

"That can happen?" said Kiira.

"Yes," said Deckert. "Remember when that nutcase shot up that mosque on Facebook live? The video went viral, right? Yet within a day the footage was entirely deleted from all major platforms across the internet."

"But it's still gotta be out there, right?" said Kiira. "I mean, nothing can be truly deleted from the internet, can it?"

"No," said Deckert, "which is why this is so odd. And by odd, I mean terrifying."

"What are you talking about?" I said.

Deckert balked.

"Haven't you been listening?"

I let out a low growl.

"Fine," he said. "I'll spell it out for you. To do something like that takes huge processing power, an entire fleet of people using the world's most powerful search engines, and the authority to de-platform and delete information in the public domain."

"So?" I said.

"So that basically proves that the guy was right. This goes all the way up to the tippy top. I mean, think about it. Who has the money, time, manpower, and authority to scour the entire internet for a single mention of something? Only the world's most powerful governments, or a secret group of world leaders acting above the government . . . The Labyrinth."

Kiira and I exchanged a glance.

"So you think Medvyed and the President are really behind this fucking thing?" I said, turning back to the monitor.

"I'm almost positive," said Deckert.

"Just because you couldn't find a video?" said Kiira.

"No," said Deckert, rolling his eyes. "Of course not."

And of course he didn't just tell us. He paused and did the expectant puppy dog thing again. In my mind, his face was slowly becoming a hole. Eventually, he continued.

"I spent the entire day combing the web for any mention of The Labyrinth, darkweb codes for hit work, underground cage fights, etcetera, etcetera, and once again I didn't find a god damn thing. I mean there were a few obviously bullshit conspiracy theories, but other than that, nada. Nothing. Not a mention. Not until . . ."

He held up an index finger and tapped his temple.

"We get it, Decker, you're a fucking dork," I said. "Go on."

"Thank you Sledge. I'm glad you appreciate the entire day I just spent figuring out who's trying to murder you."

"If only you'd fucking tell me," I said.

"I will," he said, "but first you need a little lesson on encryption."

I pinched the bridge of my nose and focused on my breathing. Eventually, Deckert started in.

"I've been wondering how all these fights you've been in, which are supposedly live streamed, can't be found anywhere on the internet. Not even snippets. That doesn't seem possible in this day and age. I mean, Sledge Laukkanen in a fight to the death? That's a viral video if ever there was one. So how come it's not out there?"

"That is odd now that you mention it," said Kiira.

"Obviously," said Deckert. "So I looked into it a bit. Most livestream videos are encrypted at the source, so it's reasonably hard to pirate the feed directly. And nowadays the more sophisticated streams are encrypted at the end monitor, so you can't even screen record them. Cool, right? But it still doesn't make sense that there's no sign of the videos anywhere, unless the same people that erased any mention of The Labyrinth are being put to work to scour the internet for the fight videos as well. And it makes sense that they would. They don't want anyone finding out about what they're doing. So chalk it up as even more evidence that someone mega powerful is behind this whole thing, covering it up.

"But then I thought, wait a minute, at the end of day, a video still has to come out of the screen as light into people's eyes, and nothing can stop someone holding up a camera and recording that light, and then putting *that* video on the internet. And that video wouldn't have the same digital footprint as the livestream video, so it would be much harder to trace!"

"And you found one of those videos!" said Kiira, unable to keep the excitement out of her voice.

"No," said Deckert. "Not even a snippet."

Kiira's grin vanished.

I said, "Deckert, if you don't get to the fucking point I'm going to drive down there and beat you to death with your own dick."

"That's oddly specific," he said.

"Just tell us what you fucking found," I said.

"First let me tell you how I found it."

I clenched my fist so hard Kiira's knuckles cracked.

"Make it quick," I growled through clenched teeth.

"So the video of a video idea got me thinking. Search

engines only look for what you enter. For example: The Labyrinth and TheLabyrinth, no space, will come up with different results. And clearly someone had scoured the internet for any mention of such a thing. But had they searched for The Labyrinth spelled incorrectly? Or spelled with symbols? Probably, but I figured even if they had it would be more likely that they let something like that slip. Or maybe, just maybe, The Labyrinth spelled in a specific coded way is how they talk about it over the internet. Kind of like a secret message that only the select few are let in on. And that's when I found it!"

Pause. *Biggestest* grin. Longer pause.

There was no point rushing him. He was at the moment of climax.

Finally, he said, "A reply to a forum post on the r/ deepweb subreddit by u/m@n@s&c0wt1pper."

He cleared his throat, then held up a piece of paper and read aloud:

"After that win I'm willing to put a $200M bounty that $13dg3 descends to the bottom of Th3L@byr1n+h by the end of the month. Any takers, you know where to find me."

49

"So it's for real?" said Gow. "Medvyed and the President?"

We were in Maldonado's sauna, which was, of course, exquisitely designed. I stretched along flowing curves of ergonomically-shaped raw Himalayan cedar, gazing out at the horizon through a wall of fog-proof glass while Gow tended to the stove.

"Deckert seems to think so," I said, pulling myself down into a deep hamstring stretch.

"Based on a single jumbled internet post?" said Gow.

"According to him, that's the proof," I said. "And it's not just one internet post. It's hundreds. Hidden in various forums. Th3L@byr1n+h, always spelled the same way. It's how they communicate online without being detected."

Gow ladled another scoop of water onto the rocks. Steam sizzled outward in a billowing cloud. It hit me like a physical thing, scary hot for a moment, then dissipating to a dry warmth that wrapped around me like a hug, seeping deep into my muscles, relaxing them at their core.

"So you believe it?" said Gow.

I shrugged.

"Don't know," I said.

"What's your gut tell you?"

I was silent awhile. Then I said, "My grandfather was the

Soviet Union's Osama Bin Laden, if Bin Laden had killed more people and never been caught. Think about that for a minute."

"The ultimate bad guy," said Gow. "How's it go? In Moscow, the boogeyman checks his closet for Vidal Laukkanen."

"Exactly," I said. "He destroyed the psyche of an entire generation of Russian people. Similar to what happened in Germany after World War I. My grandfather embarrassed Russia as a nation. And here I am, The Boogeyman's grandkid, who they tried to kill a while back and failed. *Again*. More embarrassment. More humiliation."

We were quiet a moment.

"They called it a haunting remember?" I said.

"When?" said Gow.

"In the original letter," I said. "The one Kiira brought to me. It said, 'Your haunting will begin in three days.' My grandfather haunted Russia. So that motherfucker's trying to haunt me back. Killing me for sport's probably been Medvyed's lifelong aspiration."

Gow thought about it.

"Fuck me," he said. "How's he expect to get away with it?"

"He's the fucking president of Russia," I said. "They got Tannen the presidency through the internet, remember? Cambridge Analytica. I imagine he plans on the doing the same thing with me. Have his fun, make some money, kill me, then leak specific videos to the internet along with a bunch of twitter chatter, and write the narrative. I'm an inhuman monster murdering mayors with my boot heel. I'll go down in history as a mass-murderer who could only be defeated by the might of glorious mother Russia. And with that video, not a single person will be able to argue."

Gow tipped another ladle onto the stove.

"Less than ideal," he conceded.

I said nothing. We were quiet awhile.

"Okay, assume it really is Medyed," said Gow. "How do we get to him?"

I rolled my neck around. I'd been thinking about that.

"You know anyone who can get me on the phone with the President?" I said.

Gow ran a hand down his face, clearing sweat.

"No," he said, looking over at me. "But Shawn does."

I tilted my head.

"Fuck," I said, slapping myself on the forehead. "Fucking *Audhild*."

I spat the name, for a bigger douchebag than Roman Audhild can be found precisely nowhere.

"Can't wait to listen to this one," said Gow.

Half and hour later we were towelled off and knocking on the double front doors of the mansion-cabin Maldonado'd put Shawn and Ariana up in. The left-hand cedar door opened and there stood Shawn in a bathrobe at least four sizes too small.

"The fuck you want?" he said.

"How's Ariana holding up?" I said.

"Fuck you think?" he said. "This a woman used to flyin' private wherever the fuck she wants, whenever the fuck she wants, and you got her locked in a chicken coop."

I glanced inside the the 4000 square-foot mansion.

"Not exactly a chicken coop," I said.

"Don't gimme that shit," he said. "Nobody gives a fuck about a million dollar hot tub when you can't leave the motherfucker."

I rolled my eyes.

"Motherfucker don't act like we privileged," said Shawn.

"I'm not," I said. "Hopefully you won't have to stay 'cooped up' in this hellhole much longer."

Shawn raised an eyebrow.

"You figure out who's behind this shit?" he said.

"Maybe," I said. "That's where you come in."

Shawn looked non-plussed.

"I'm listenin'," he said.

"I need to talk to your favorite right wing nutbag," I said. "You know, the one that lives in the White House."

Shawn screwed up his face.

"Roman?" he said. "The fuck you wanna talk to that prick for?"

I said, "I need to persuade him to spy on the President."

Shawn's eyes opened very wide.

"*Dayumn,*" he said. "You *proper* fucked."

50

Roman Audhild went to York with Shawn. Due to his rich prick father, Richard Audhild, owner of America's largest hedge fund and the Miami Heat, Roman was handed a walk-on spot on York's basketball team, where, according to Shawn, he slithered so far up Coach X's ass that every time Roman jerked off it gave Coach X a runny nose.

A triple major in political science, economics, and felatio, after college Roman suckled his way up the conservative food chain all the way into the White House, where today he can be found wiping the President's ass with hundred dollar bills soaked in the tears of illegal immigrants. I'd met the guy only once, when he'd sauntered into the Pistons locker room after a loss to the Knicks, doling out advice like Jackie Moon.

I gave Shawn his phone back, without the sim card, and let him turn it on long enough to get Roman's private number from the contacts, then dialled Roman on a burner. As it rang I pulled in a calming breath. Douchebaggery aside, Roman had the ear of the so-called 'most powerful man in the world.' I'd have to play this one carefully.

Roman answered on the third ring.

"Hullo?" he drawled.

"I've seen the video," I said, my voice an octave lower

than normal.

Silence on the other end.

"Who *is this*?" said Roman. *Is* and *this* had two syllables when Roman said them. "How'd you get this number?"

"You should have asked her for ID you stupid fuck," I said. "I know it can be hard to tell these days."

More silence.

"Who the *fuck* is this?" said Roman. *Fuck* and *is* came out like *fayuck* and *ayuz*. He didn't sound scared. Just stupid and overconfident.

"Video's got a nice angle to it," I said. "Good clear view of your face. And, just as importantly, hers."

"*Ahm* gonna *hayng* up now," Roman said.

"No," I said, "you're not. Not until you figure out who's about to go to the New York Times with pictures of you fucking a fifteen year-old in an extremely inappropriate place."

Silence. According to Shawn, Roman's weakness was women. Specifically young, *black* women. More specifically, he liked to denigrate young black woman. On video. Fuck 'em in the ass and feed them lines to say. Shawn had heard first hand from a couple strippers Roman had paid handsomely for the experience back in college. The bet was that he hadn't been able to kick the habit.

More silence on the other end.

Then:

"*Yer* full a *sheeit*," Roman said, but I noticed his voice had lost a little hauteur.

"I can send a screen shot," I said. "One to the wife as well."

"I ain't married," he said.

"By wife I meant New York Times," I said. "CNN too. All your favorite commie librags get a copy. The ones just *aching* to cancel your ass. I'm seeing a front page spread with you balls deep in a black teenage asshole."

Across the room, Gow and Shawn nearly burst out laughing. I wasn't sure who at. I bit my lip and tried to ignore them. On the other end of the line, I could almost hear Roman wracking his brain. Which one hadn't he paid enough to keep quiet?

I said, "How long do you think it'll take the President to feed you to the leftists? He can't survive another pussy grabber incident, not with a child. Black Lives Matter, bro. Me Too. They're about to shove their big black dick right up your lilly white ass."

Too much? I crossed my fingers and waited.

"What do you want?" said Roman. His voice was dead serious now.

I grinned.

"Meet me tomorrow night at Lake Vista private airport in Wayzata," I said. "Bring cash."

In the silence on the other end of the line I heard Roman searching for a way out. It sounded like hard work.

"How much?" he said. His voice had lost all its fight.

Across the room, Gow and Shawn put their fists in the air.

"Enough," I said, and hung up.

51

The Gulfstream III touched down in Wayzata just after eight the following evening. From the shadows inside the hangar I watched it taxi along the tarmac and pull up in front of the hangar doors. The engines whined down and after a minute or two the plane door dropped open and the stairs descended and out popped Roman Audhild. He looked slightly older than I remembered, but just as douchey in an expertly-tailored grey suit, perfectly quaffed golden hair, and a deep mid-February tan. He glanced around at the top of stairs, then boldly started down. Toughest guy in the world. Behind him, three men exited the plane. Secret service types. Black suits over white collars. They even had the little ear pieces. One of them carried a duffel bag. All three would be armed.

I watched the four men reach the bottom of the stairs and stand there on the empty tarmac looking around. I wanted to see what they would do. They didn't do much except stand there looking around. Eventually one of the secret service guys pointed toward the open hanger doors and the four of them started toward me. The guy who'd pointed took point, the other two flanked Roman three paces behind.

The guy on Roman's left had a shaved head and a square

jaw and an overly serious expression on his face. His eyes darted too and fro, seeking threat. The guy on Roman's right had slicked black hair and a neatly trimmed black beard and the same deep tan as Roman. He looked unconcerned. The guy out front was older, weathered, with a close-cropped flat top the color of granite. He looked alert, and weary. My guess is he'd seen the real thing before. Of the three, I figured Deep Tan for the weak link, Baldy the most trigger-happy. Sarge would be the hardest.

The hangar doors were tall and wide enough to fit a decent sized airplane, but I'd pulled them nearly all the way shut, leaving a gap the breadth of my wingspan. Just wide enough for four guys to walk through unencumbered. As they approached I retreated into the darkness. I'd locked the roof-top fire escape and chained the sliding escape ladder. There was only one way in.

I watched Sarge closely. He figured it out pretty quick, but not quick enough if I'd been up top with a rifle. He glanced up and saw the line of sight and his whole body jolted and he yanked his P229 from a hip holster and at the same time grabbed Roman by the shirt collar and yank-sprinted him sideways. Roman yelped and fell but Sarge got him around the waist and the two of them disappeared from view.

I retreated to a sidewall and ducked behind a vertical I-beam. I'd stolen that one from Skinpeeler. I counted to a hundred while Sarge deliberated with himself, then saw him edge his eye around the hangar door, low near the ground where a waiting rifle would have to adjust. He'd worked out the kinks. I knew he couldn't see far in the darkness, just far enough to spot the folded piece of A4 paper I'd placed on the floor ten feet inside the door.

Here, kitty kitty.

I counted another hundred as Sarge conferred with himself again. He did not have the proper firepower nor the proper team to infiltrate a darkened, open environment like this airplane hangar. It was suicide if the people inside were anywhere near competent. But I figured he hadn't dealt with much in the way of competence lately working for Tannen. And he was getting paid to do whatever the useless fuck next to him told him to do. I heard Roman whisper to him urgently, so loud I could make out their exact location behind the steel door. I could have shot the stupid fuck straight through the corrugated any time I felt like it. Roman wanted that video. Badly. And there was only one way for Sarge to get him to shut the fuck up.

Sure enough, ten seconds later Sarge came in low and fast while Baldy and Deep Tan spun in from either side covering the darkness with their P229s. Very fucking stupid. I could have taken them out with a sling shot. As it were, I just stood there and watched it unfold.

Sarge snatched the paper and was quick-stepping back toward the opening when there came a loud *zzzziiip*! Then Roman screamed and came flying in through the doors off his feet. Deep Tan and Baldy spun, but too late. The enormous corrugated iron hangar doors slammed shut. It went dark and I heard the big steel latch come down and Roman and someone else, Deep Tan I guessed, started screaming and banging at the doors in the darkness.

Well played Gow. He'd repelled down from the roof in a single leap and double-heel kicked the stupid fuck straight through the doors. Pretty damn slick.

Roman and Deep Tan freaked out for the first fifteen seconds while Baldy and Sarge flicked on their flashlights and searched the darkness behind the sights of their P229's. Their flashlights had strong narrow beams but the hangar was enormous and had a few decent spots for cover which I'd paced out earlier.

It took Roman and Deep Tan another minute to realize they were wasting energy on a hopeless exercise. They let go of the doors and turned to stand alongside Sarge and Baldy.

Deep Tan got his flashlight out, but Roman didn't have one, so he cowered behind Sarge, sneaking occasional looks over his shoulder at the silently beckoning darkness.

I watched to see what they'd decide, or rather, what Sarge would decide. If they split up, I'd have to keep track of multiple lines of visibility, which could be problematic for someone my size trying to hide behind shit in a wide open space. If they stuck together, it'd be easier to stay in the dark, but it'd be four on one, three guns to none, which didn't sound like a whole lotta fun either.

"*Thank* yer pretty fucking slick, huh?" said Roman. His voice was loud and brash in the darkness, but he couldn't hide the waver in it. "Fucking *Labyranth.*"

"Shut the fuck up, Roman," said Sarge.

I couldn't have agreed more. In the darkness behind his flashlight beam I saw Sarge signal to Baldy and Deep Tan. They split up, Deep Tan edging along the front wall, toward me, Baldy edging the other way, their backs to the hangar wall, guns and flashlights levelled at the darkness. Roman stayed behind Sarge and they broke for the nearest cover behind a refuelling truck parked near the entrance. Sarge knew the game. Protect the asset, send the other dumbasses out to die if it was going to be that way. Eventually, if it was Roman we wanted, we'd have to come to him.

I stayed behind the I-beam and let Deep Tan make his way slowly toward me. I lost Baldy on the far side of the hangar behind a tow car. I listened. Deep Tan was breathing loudly through his mouth, making it easy to pinpoint his location without have to stick my head out. I waited. When he got close enough I pulled a small picture-hanging nail from my pocket and tossed it into the darkness at his feet. It made a tiny metallic ping on the concrete floor. His breath caught and I heard him freeze, right in front of my pillar. I stepped out and swung the edge of my stiffened hand into his neck. If you hit the carotid artery with enough force it shuts the brain down instantly, which is exactly what happened.

Deep Tan's legs gave out and he fell and I slid behind him and caught him under the armpits and caught the flashlight. But I missed the gun. It slipped through my fingers and clattered deafeningly on the concrete floor. I held Deep Tan up and played him like a puppet, moving the flashlight around in the same pattern he'd been using.

"Don?" said Sarge. "You OK?"

"Fine," I said.

I looked backed toward the refuelling truck. Sarge had turned his flashlight off. I held my breath and bobbed Deep Tan's flashlight around and listened intently.

That's when all hell broke loose.

52

Sarge was good. He'd known something was off immediately and slipped into the darkness. Now he knew my location, and I didn't know his.

Three things happened in quick succession after that. First, I hefted Deep Tan under the armpits and tossed his unconscious body along with the flashlight through the air, back the way they'd come. Then I dove the other way, headfirst, low and fast across the floor. Third, Baldy started shooting.

The stupid trigger-happy fuck must have spotted me, but he was way over on the other side of the hangar. A three hundred foot shot at a moving target with a .357 takes great skill. Baldy didn't have it. But Sarge might, and he was right there.

His flashlight came back on and he spotted me lying on the floor not twenty feet from him and I was pretty much dead. Then Baldy's dumb ass fired again and the bullet pinged somewhere close-by and I saw Sarge flinch and I was up on my feet with legs full of high-octane adrenaline, sprinting at Sarge and imminent death.

Sarge must not have expected me to move so quickly because he fired from point blank range and missed. From the flash I saw the .357 pointed low at where I'd been and then I was on him.

He was one tough son of a bitch. I'll give him that. He brought the gun up and fired at my head but I got an elbow in the way and the bullet must have missed by an inch because the gunpowder blast seared across my scalp and I went both deaf and blind. The world was searing white and a high-pitched whine and a hard fist and another two gun shots very close by and then I got my forearm locked around his and wrenched and felt his elbow dislocate and through the high-pitched whine I heard him yelp in pain and the gun drop to the floor.

I couldn't see and could barely hear but I could feel and even with one arm Sarge was really putting me through it. I took a heavy fist to the temple and another to jaw, which wobbled me, and then a knee to the groin which folded me at the waist. He was right up next to me now which was right where I wanted him if only I wasn't doubled over in gut-wrenching pain. Somehow I got both meat hooks into his armpits as he pounded on my face with his fist and I wrenched him away and reared back my head and pulled him in and slammed my forehead into his face once then again and again screaming and roaring and raging until he went limp.

I dropped him there and spun, teeth barred, spittle flying, in full Leviathan-mode now, blinded by gun and blood and bone, beckoning death. It came in the form of Baldy, sprinting through the darkness, gun blazing. He was panicked and screaming and shooting for his life and missing but not for long. I still had my grip in Sarge's pits and as Baldy got near I spun a hammer-thrower's pirouette and tossed Sarge blindly into the oncoming gunfire. I didn't wait to find out what happened but dove again wide and low, hopefully under the firing line. I came up to the sound of colliding bodies. Baldy must have taken the hit and spun and kept firing because I heard gunshots spraying in a wide arc across the hangar. I blinked and blinked and my vision started coming back and I skirted fast and low across the concrete with nowhere to hide and came up behind Baldy with hammer unsheathed as he turned and fired. Hammer met skull and the firing ceased.

Everything went quiet.

I felt in the darkness for Baldy and grabbed a limp wrist then pulled the zip ties from my back pocket and secured him to Sarge. I found Deep Tan in the darkness further on, still unconscious, and secured him as well. Then I stood and listened.

Somewhere far off: whimpering. I followed the sound through the darkness and found Roman cowering in a back corner of the hangar. I smelled piss.

"*Pleeeeyuz*!" cried Roman as I approached. He couldn't see me in the darkness. "Don' kill me! *Ah'll* do anythayng! *Ah* have money! *Ah'll* pay! *Ah'm* rich! Whatever you want, it's yours! My dad owns the Miami Heat! *Ah* can pay! Trust me. Please don't kill me oh please God!"

"Shut the fuck up," I said.

In the darkness, Roman started sobbing.

"Take out your phone," I said.

Roman kept crying. I loomed up out of the darkness and kicked him. I'm not sure what I hit. He yelped and tried to stifle the crying but didn't do a very good job of it.

"Take out your phone," I said again.

I heard him fumbling in the darkness, then a phone screen blinked on, illuminating his face.

"Unlock it," I said.

Roman tapped in a 4-digit code and the phone unlocked.

"Open the internet," I said.

He tapped an icon.

"Type this in," I said, and slowly spelled out Th3L@byr1n+h. As he typed it out I watched his reaction in the ghostly illumination of the phone screen. It was hard to tell much behind his pathetic sobbing. He pressed search. The hits came up. He looked up at me. I couldn't read his face in the darkness.

"Tell the President I know," I said.

Then I left him there, sitting in own piss, sobbing quietly.

53

Three hours later Gow and I were driving north on 35 back toward Gunflint Cove. The roads were plowed and freshly salted and the driving was easy. I was behind the wheel, my body still vibrating with adrenaline, trying to keep the speedometer under eighty.

"You locked the fire exit," said Gow.

His voice came out cold and steady.

I shrugged.

"That was reckless," said Gow. "Reckless and fucking stupid, even by your standards."

I said nothing. I could feel his eyes on me, hard and unblinking. I kept mine on the road. We were north of The Cities now, cutting through pine forrest on the way to Duluth.

"Why?" said Gow.

I didn't reply. Probably because I didn't know the answer.

"Tell me," said Gow.

I let out a breath through my nose.

"Needed the reps," I said.

"Oh bollocks," said Gow.

I shrugged. Gow waited. I waited longer.

"Tell me," he said. "Tell me why, or I'm out."

I looked at him. I'd never seen him so angry. I felt I owed

him an answer, but damned if I knew what it was.

"So?" he said.

"It needs to be real," I said finally. "If I'm going to get anything out of it."

"*Real*?" said Gow. "What the fuck does that even mean?"

"It means if you're up in the rafters with a rifle . . ." I shrugged. "It's not for real. It's cheating. Like in the woods."

Gow snorted.

"Don't give me that shite," he said, shaking his head. "It's not cheating. It's operational awareness. This is your life we're talking about."

"I'm aware of that," I said. "That's why I need it to be real. Confidence comes from what you do consistently, not what you do occasionally. If I have pros coming for me, I need to be ready in real-time. Not just when you're there behind a scope. I can't gain proficiency if I know there's a safety net. And I need the preparation, because they're coming for me, whether I like it or not. That's my life. Always has been. I've come to terms with it."

Gow went quiet a while. I listened to the hum of the engine and rush of the road beneath the tires.

"You enjoy it," said Gow.

I said nothing.

"You enjoy the challenge," said Gow.

I shrugged.

"Three secret service clowns isn't exactly a challenge," I said, cracking a mirthless smile.

"From the sounds of things it wasn't a walk in the park," said Gow. "You nearly murdered two of them."

I raised an eyebrow.

"Sarge?" I said. "Grey hair? The guy I headbutted?"

"So that's what it was," said Gow. "He had a hard skull. Obviously not as hard as yours. But congratulations, you fractured two of his vertebrae."

I said nothing. Gow was silent a minute, watching me.

"You don't feel anything about it?" he said.

"Of course I do," I said.

"You want to know his name?" said Gow.

I let out a breath.

"Not really," I said.

Gow didn't reply for a moment. I felt him weighing up whether to tell me about Sarge.

"I'll say this," I said, before he could finish weighing. "He was good. It was hard. I was scared and I had to fight through it. He made me better. And I value that very highly. I respect him."

Gow looked at me.

"I'm sure he'll be overjoyed to hear that," he said. "If he ever walks again."

I said nothing.

A silence drew out.

"Richard Kickert," said Gow. "People call him Kick. Delta Force '91 to '05. Grunt to master sergeant, two years paid at Westpoint, then all the way up to Major. From all accounts, a good man. Wife. Three kids. Son's at Westpoint. He's been out fifteen years, protecting Presidents for all fifteen. He's one of us, Sledge. A warrior. And now he might be fucked. Proper fucked. All because you wanted practice."

I said nothing. There was no point. I couldn't take it back.

I felt Gow's eyes on me.

"You crave it," he said. "Don't you?"

I said nothing.

"You can't be away from it for too long, or you get antsy. Then you go looking for it."

I kept my eyes on the road.

"That's it," said Gow, nodding his head. "You're a junky. Except your drug isn't heroin. It's manslaughter."

I laughed at that one.

"Nothing?" said Gow.

I let out a breath.

"What do you want me to say?" I said. "This has always been my life. If I turn it off, I die. Tomorrow."

"That's exactly right," said Gow. "It's a drug. You need it, because the withdrawal will kill you."

I shook my head.

"Fine," I said. "Not your worst analogy. But it's also . . . home."

"*Home*?" said Gow, scrunching his face. "What the fuck does that even mean?"

"Oh fuck off," I said. "You, of all people, should know exactly what that means."

Gow went quiet a while. On the right the pines opened up and I saw a gibbous moon reflecting off the snowy surface of Cross Lake.

"Come on," said Gow. "Give me something."

I kept my eyes on the road. We passed Cross Lake and the pines came back, high and close along the highway.

"My grandfather explained it very simply," I said. "He said, 'The only way to survive being hunted, is to become a hunter yourself.' Otherwise, you're just prey. Always fleeing. Always afraid. The only way to conquer the fear, is to become something fearsome."

Gow looked at me.

"And that takes practice," he said. "Real-time reps."

I said nothing.

Gow let out a sigh, shook his head. His anger had dissipated somewhat.

"Fine," he said. "Now what?"

"Now we let Roman fly back to the White House and talk to the President."

"His phone's got Decker's spyware on it?"

I nodded. "Downloaded the moment his phone jumped on the wifi. Now we can turn on his life and watch it like reality TV."

"Not bad," said Gow. Then, after a pause, "Still shouldn't

have locked that fucking fire exit."

54

Gow, Kiira, and I listened to Roman's phone for the next three days, working in shifts. Our sudden access to the inner workings of the White House was startling. Roman spent the majority of his day within sniffing distance of the President's asshole, stroking the Commander in Chief's ego and whatever else he could get his tongue on. He took his phone with him everywhere. By day three, we had the President's schedule down pat.

"Fat Cunt off Twitter yet?" said Gow as he entered the living room of Kiira's guest house, which we'd set up as a temporary control center for snooping on the world's most powerful man.

"Nope," said Kiira. "Still 'Executive Time.'"

Gow shook his head.

"Lazy fuck hasn't been off the couch before eleven all week," he said.

"Then a thirty minute shower," said Kiira. "And he never misses second breakfast."

"What time's he ignoring the Chief of Staff today?" said Gow.

"Roman's reminded him six hundred times to be ready by eleven," I said.

"So twelve thirty," said Gow.

"If he rushes through lunch," said Kiira. "Which is unlikely."

Gow grabbed a Diet Coke from the mini-fridge and sat down next to us on the couch.

"It's shocking how little the 'most powerful man in the world' does in a day," he said.

"You're surprised?" I said.

"A bit," said Gow. "I mean, he does appear to be a lazy sack of shit on TV, but this is fucking ridiculous. Forget the fate of the world, he's literally only interested in his re-Tweets."

"Correct," I said.

"I take it Roman hasn't sacked up yet?"

We'd been waiting with baited breath for Roman to broach the subject of The Labyrinth with the President, but thus far no dice. The three secret service agents I'd maimed were still out of rotation. Roman had explained their absence with a bad case of food poisoning from a sushi restaurant they frequented. Thus far the President appeared to have bought it, but who knew how long that would last.

"Maybe today's the day," said Gow without much enthusiasm.

As it turned out, it was.

Four hours later I was in the gym doing some one-arm rope pull-ups while surveying Kiira's ass in cat pose, when Gow's voice came over the intercom.

"Get your arses in here," he said. "Roman just spilled the beans."

We got to the room in time to hear Roman say, "I . . . I can explain, sir."

Gow said, "He just told the President he was blackmailed and attacked."

Roman's phone must have been in his pocket because the TV screen showed nothing but black, but we could hear him loud and clear.

"You better start fuckin' explaining yourself," said the President.

He sounded exactly like he does on TV: i.e. a pompous, inbred moron with delusions of grandeur.

"I just thought they wanted money!" said Roman. "Like the last one."

"You paid them?" said the President. "How fuckin' much?"

"No!" said Roman quickly. "They didn't take it!"

Silence for a moment.

"Let me get this straight," said the President. "Someone blackmailed you for money. You brought it. Then they didn't take it?"

He sounded completely flabbergasted by the concept.

"No, sir," said Roman. "I mean yes, sir. I mean . . . yes, they didn't take the money."

It went quiet for a moment. I heard Roman breathing in and out.

"What do they have on you?" said the President.

Roman swallowed.

"Uh . . . a video, sir," Roman said.

"A video of *what*?"

When the President said what he pronounced the h.

"Of . . . uh . . . me, sir," said Roman.

"Of you doin' what?" said the President, his voice sharpening.

"Of . . . uh . . . you know."

"No, Roman, I don't fucking know," snapped the President. "What do they have a video of? More pictures of you in a frat house with nuts on your forehead?"

"No sir!" said Roman. "This one is . . . uh . . . with a gir- . . . a woman, sir."

Silence for a moment.

"And . . . ?" said the President.

I heard Roman pull in a shaky breath and let it out

through his mouth.

"I-I snuck a . . . a woman . . . into the White House . . . sir," said Roman.

He sounded like he wanted to crawl into a hole and die there.

The President went quiet a moment.

"*Snuck her in*?" said the President.

"Yes, sir."

"One of those niggers you like fuckin'?" said the President.

Kiira's mouth fell open.

"Yeah, I know about them, Roman," said the President. "I know everything. In case you fuckin' forgot. I'm the President of the God damn United Fuckin' States."

Roman said nothing.

"Answer the question, Roman," said the President.

"W-what question, sir?"

"Was it a nigger?" said the President.

My eyes opened wide. I'd figured the president for a racist cunt, but this was on another level. No wonder the country was country was coming apart at the seams.

"Uh . . . y-yes, sir," said Roman, his voice tiny now.

"How?" said the President.

"Sir?"

"How did you sneak a piece of nigger snatch into the White House?"

Kiira gasped. I couldn't blame her.

"Uh . . . Don helped me, sir," said Roman.

"Don?" said the President. "Who's conveniently off work with food poisoning at the moment?"

"Uh . . . y-yes, sir," said Roman.

Don was Deep Tan. He and Roman had probably hatched the plan while sharing a tanning bed.

"What else?" said the President.

Roman went quiet. I heard him figuring how to play it.

"They . . . uh . . . they said she was underage, sir," said Roman. "And . . ."

He paused. He pulled in another shaky breath. He sounded like he might cry.

"And *what* Roman?" said the President.

"And . . . " Roman let out a defeated breath. "I had relations with her in the oval office, sir."

"Holy fuck," said Kiira.

"O-on your desk, sir," said Roman. "They said if I didn't bring cash they'd send the video to *CNN*."

Dead silence. When the President next spoke, his voice was deathly serious.

"You're telling me they have video from inside the oval office of you fucking an underage nigger on top of my desk?"

"That's . . . uh . . . what they said, sir."

The President was quiet a moment. I could hear the gears turning.

"They used specifics?" he said.

"Sir?"

"They told you specifically that they had video of you fucking an underage nigger on top of my desk in the oval office?"

"Uh . . . I can't remember exactly, sir," said Roman.

"What the fuck do you mean you can't remember?" said the President. "Did they or did they not say 'We have a video of you fucking an underage nigger on top of the president's desk in the oval office'?"

"They didn't use those exact words," said Roman.

"What the fuck did they say then?" said the President. *"Exactly."*

"They said . . . uh . . . that the video had a good view of my face . . . and . . . uh . . . hers . . . and that . . . uh . . . that she was underage . . . and uh . . . I can't remember exactly, sir, but . . . uh . . . they said something about me fucking her in an inappropriate place . . . so . . . uh . . . so I figured . . . ."

The President let out an exasperated moan.

"For fuck's sake Roman, did it ever occur to you that they could have been fucking with you? How the fuck would they get a camera inside the oval office anyway? That's gotta be the most secure location on the goddamn planet outside the room we're sittin' in right now!"

"I . . . I . . . I don't know, sir," stammered Roman.

"Yer one dumb sum'bitch, you know that Roman?" said the President. "You took daddy's airplane with a sackful of money to pay off some dumb fuck who probably doesn't even have shit on you."

"I . . . I don't think they really wanted the money, sir," said Roman.

"No shit, Sherlock," said the President. "What was yer first fuckin' clue? What *did* they want, anyway?"

"I-I think they wanted to send you a message . . . sir," said Roman.

The President went quiet then.

"What message?" he said. Serious now.

"He said, 'Tell the President I know.'"

"Know *what*?"

"I don't know," said Roman. "He made me search something on my phone. A bunch of letters and symbols and stuff. It was weird."

The President went very quiet.

"Do you know what it was?" said the President.

Gow and I exchanged a look.

"No," said Roman quickly. "No idea, sir. But one guy took out all four of us out with his bare hands. Including Kickert, sir."

"*What*?" said the President. "Kick was with you?"

"Yes, sir," said Roman.

Silence for a moment.

"Fuck me," said the President. "Who was this guy?"

"Sir," said Roman. I heard him swallow. "I . . . I think it was Sledge Laukkanen."

Silence.

"Jesus H. Christ," whispered the President.

55

An hour later Gow and I were debriefing at the Manitou. Shane brought us gallon-sized urns of his moose reaper chilli with fresh-baked crusty bread rolls and fists of garlic butter, then casually edged to the far end of the bar to wash glasses and pretend not to eavesdrop.

Gow tried the chilli.

"Fuck me!" he yelped, eyes bulging.

"Reaper peppers," I said, smirking.

Gow's tongue wagged. His eyes started watering.

"Drink the beer," I said. "It helps."

Gow guzzled a third of his Camp Misery Imperial Stout and let out a satisfied sigh. I skulled two pints back to back and washed them down with some Lagavulin.

"I still don't get how you can drink like that," said Gow. Then the heat came back and he had to guzzle more beer.

I shrugged.

"Liquor doesn't do much to me," I said. "Never has. I just like the taste."

Gow shook his head, then took another gulp of stout.

"So the President knows?" he said.

"You heard how quickly the Fat Cunt jumped off the couch when Roman said my name," I said. "Pretty clear who he called."

"Medvyed," said Gow.

I nodded.

"Still pretty thin," said Gow. "We didn't hear the call."

I shrugged.

"President hears my name, runs to make a call," I said. "Scared the shit out of him. He knew what it meant. One of the pawns in his fucked up little game is on to him."

"Too bad Roman didn't listen at the door," said Gow.

"That would take actual testicles," I said.

"We need to tap the President directly," said Gow. "He doesn't trust Roman now. Not after the hangar fuck up. We won't get anything else."

"We'll keep listening," I said. "But you're right. We're probably at a dead end unless Roman grows a pair and eavesdrops on the President without his knowledge."

"Which we know won't happen," said Gow. "The only reason Fat Cunt won't fire him directly is to keep him close to make sure he doesn't blab. I wouldn't be surprised if he uses The Labyrinth to have Roman offed."

I raised my eyebrow at that. Gow guzzled the last third of his stout and set down the empty glass. I reached behind the bar and poured him another. Shane, I'd noticed, was re-washing an already perfectly clean glass while making a point of not looking at us.

"So," I said, "we work on the premise that Fat Cunt and Medvyed, maybe a few select others, are the money and influence behind this thing. They make up a cute name so it sounds like some mysterious shadow organisation in order to scare people, and they use it make people disappear without getting their hands dirty."

Gow nodded, slurped another tentative spoonful of chilli, then franticly gulped more beer.

"Jobs are put out anonymously on the darkweb," I said. "The money's real, so anyone willing to risk jail time or death for the cash will go for it. You start small, but once you find out how easy the money is, you keep going. Eventually they set you up, because they're a bunch of cunts who like to play god, which keeps you locked within The Labyrinth, doing their dirty work. At any time, if you get too nosy, or try to get out, they put out a contract on you and take you out of the game."

Gow finished his second beer and poured a third himself.

"And that's where the betting starts," he said. "The gladiator aspect."

"Exactly," I said. "That's where the real money always changes hands. Fat Cunt versus Medvyed versus whoever else in the ultimate dick swinging contest. The whole thing must cost millions to run. It's like buying a sports team, except you get to play with people's lives. Specifically, my fucking life."

"My bet is you're Fat Cunt's prize race horse," said Gow. "The All-American ass-kicker. That would piss Medvyed right off. I wouldn't be surprised if Tannen's bet the farm on you. Which explains why he's so shit scared that you're on to him."

I cleaned my chilli urn with my sixth bread roll and washed it down with the end of my fourth stout.

"So how do we get you out?" said Gow. "And take the whole fucking thing down?"

I sipped my beer and thought about it.

"I got no idea," I said.

Shane, who was still re-washing the same glass, finally set it down and made his way over, reaching into his back pocket as he approached.

"I might be able to help," he said, and pulled out a letter.

56

Shane handed me the letter. White envelope, unlicked. I opened it and pulled out the piece of paper. It held a darkweb code printed in the middle of the page. Nothing else. My eyes went from the letter to Shane.

"How'd you get this?" I said.

"I found it," he said. "This morning."

"Where?" I said.

"In the toilet," he said, nodding down the far end of the bar toward the restrooms.

"Which one?"

"Men's."

I looked at Gow. He was studying Shane's face. I turned back to Shane.

"Show me," I said.

Shane walked down the end of the bar and led us into the men's toilet. It was freshly cleaned. The tile floor shined. The urinals sparkled. The mirror gleamed, streak-free.

"How often do you clean in here?" said Gow.

"Every morning," said Shane. "Shocking how much piss gets on the floor per day, even in a high-class establishment such as this."

"Drunk dudes can't aim," I said.

"Sober ones aren't much better," said Shane.

"Where'd you find the letter?" I said.

Shane pointed to the garbage can to the left of the door, below the paper towel dispenser.

"In with the used paper towels?" I said.

Shane shook his head.

"No, at the bottom, between the garbage bag and the can. Changed the bag this morning. Saw the letter at the bottom when I went to put in the new one."

I looked at Gow.

"Why here?" he said.

"Easy," said Shane, pointing up.

"No cameras," I said.

Shane nodded.

"How often do you change the bag?" I said.

"Every couple days," said Shane. "On average. Fills with paper towels pretty quick, but not every day."

"When was the last time you emptied it before this morning?" I said.

Shane tilted his head.

"Day before yesterday," he said. "I think."

"Don't fucking think," I said. "Remember."

Shane scratched the back of his neck, eyes on the ceiling.

"Yeah, it was the day before yesterday," he said, nodding. "Yesterday I remember checking the can and it wasn't quite half full, and nothing nasty in it, so I left it. So it would have been the day before."

"And the letter wasn't there then?" I said.

"No," he said. "I would have seen it when I put the new bag in."

"So whoever left it, did so in the last forty-eight hours," I said.

Shane nodded.

"Must've," he said.

"Show me the security footage," I said.

We followed Shane back out into the bar. He ducked into

the kitchen and came out with a pad of paper and a pen. Then he pulled out his phone and led us to one of the alcove booths near the fire. I made Shane go in first and I slid in next to him on the same side. Gow sat across from us.

"Camera feed goes to my phone," said Shane.

He set the phone down flat on the table so we could all see the screen. He opened an app.

"Eufy Security," I said.

Gow's eyes flicked to mine across the booth.

"Best security camera on the market," said Shane. "Year-long battery life. 4k video streamed directly to the cloud in real-time. Fully encrypted."

"So I've heard," I said.

Shane tapped the events tab at the bottom of the screen. A new screen popped up. At the top was the current date. Shane tapped the most recent event. A video started, showing Gow and I arriving at the unmarked alley door and knocking.

"You got any cameras inside the bar?" I said.

Shane shook his head.

"Not in the Manitou. Over in the Tavern I got them in the corners. Figure part of the allure of this place is the privacy. I only let in who I want, so no need to spy on anyone."

I stared at Shane until he met my eyes.

"You lying to me?" I said.

Shane's eyes widened.

"No Sledge, I swear to God," he said, putting his palms up. "No cameras in here. Have a look around."

I held his gaze another long second.

"Okay," I said. I glanced down at the phone. "Go back three days. Start on the morning you last cleared the garbage bag. Write down the name of every person who enters."

Shane did as he was told. It took ten minutes to compile the list.

"Eighty-one people," said Gow. "That's a lot of door

knocking."

"Three of them work for you," I said.

Rupert, Clancy, and Ajax were regulars. They'd come in the last three nights at shift's end, like clockwork.

"They're here every night," said Shane.

"We'll grill them first," said Gow. "Maybe they saw something. Then start at the top of the list."

"What about Walkely?" I asked Shane. "He come here often?"

Shane shook his head.

"No, haven't seen him in a while. We had a good catch up last night, though."

"What'd you talk about?"

"You know Errol," said Shane. "Mad scientist. Don't you cook chemicals with him up at the high school?"

I didn't reply. I'd never shared that information with anyone other than Gow and Errol.

"Anyone else on the list isn't a regular?" I said.

Shane went down the list of names and put a tick next to everyone he hadn't seen in a while. Of the eighty-one names, sixteen were here less than once every few weeks.

"We'll start with them," said Gow.

"No," I said. "We won't."

Gow raised an eyebrow.

I said, "Who would drop this letter here?"

Gow thought about it.

"Someone they paid," he said.

I nodded.

"Five grand," I said.

Gow nodded.

"Depth 1," he said.

"Exactly," I said. "Doesn't matter if we find out who dropped the letter. They won't know anything more than we did at the start of this thing."

"Dead end?"

"Not entirely," I said.

Gow raised an eyebrow.

"We know at least two people still alive at lower Depths," I said.

"Marx," said Gow. "And Kowalski, a.k.a The Wraith."

I nodded.

Shane looked from Gow to me, his brow furrowed.

"Great," he said, "but don't you have a more pressing problem?"

He pointed at the letter.

57

<u>VICTIM PROFILE</u>

Code Name: Sledge
Height: 6′10″
Weight: 266 lbs
Labyrinth Depth: 8
Labyrinth Rank: 11 of 100
Labyrinth Souls: +21,750
Career earnings: $1,875,000 USD

<u>Power Grid</u>

Toughness: 6/8
Strength: 7/8
Speed: 1/8
Fighting Skill: 5/8
Intelligence: 2/8
Cunning: 5/8

<u>Depths Descended</u>

1 - Death Threat (rank 86-100, bounty $5,000 USD, +250 souls)

2 - Beating (rank 71-85, bounty $20,000 USD, +500 souls)

3 - Kidnapping (rank 61-70, bounty $50,000 USD, +1000 souls)

4 - Rape (rank 51-60, bounty $100,000 USD, +2,000 souls)

5 - Grievous Bodily Harm (rank 41-50, bounty $200,000 USD, +3,000 souls)

6 - Deprivation of Hearing (rank 31-40, bounty $300,000 USD, +4,000 souls)

7 - Deprivation of Vision (rank 21-30, bounty $400,000 USD, +5,000 souls)

8 - Paralyzation (rank 11-20, bounty $500,000 USD, +6,000 souls)

.

~~10 - Final Boss: джаггернаут (rank 1, bounty ?, +? souls)~~

Bonus Kills - 6 (bounty $50,000 USD x 6, +1000 souls x 6)

Penalties - 2 (-3000 souls x 2)

Congratulations on your successful Exploration of Depths 7 and 8 of The Labyrinth. Your Depth 7 Exploration—deprivation of vision of target Stephen Hansson—was successful. Nice head crush! Your Depth 7 Bounty of $400,000 USD has been deposited in your account and you have been awarded +5,000 souls. You also earned your fifth Kill Bonus of $50,000 USD and +1000 souls. Excellent work, your players will be delighted.

Further congratulations are in order for your successful Exploration of Depth 8 of The Labyrinth. Your Depth 8 Exploration—paralyzation of target Richard Kickert—was successful. Your Depth 8 Bounty of $500,000 USD, along with +6,000 souls, has been transferred to your account.

Unfortunately, we are disappointed to confirm that assistance from outside The Labyrinth was required in your Labyrinth Death Match for the murder of target Matthew Bowie. A penalty of -3000 souls has been deducted from your account. A further penalty has also been included in your Depth 9 Labyrinth Descent (please follow the link below).

Your Depth 9 Labyrinth Descent awaits you. Good luck.

Descent (Depth 9)

Welcome to your Descent into Depth 9 of The Labyrinth. During this Descent you will be visited upon by four fellow Victims at varying Depths of The Labyrinth. A Depth 4, a Depth 7, a Depth 8, and a Depth 9. The Depth 4 has been added as a penalty for your transgression during your Labyrinth Death Match. The four Victims have been tasked with your rape, blinding, paralyzation, and severe torture to death, respectively. To descend to Depth 9 of The Labyrinth you must survive all four encounters. Should you succeed, please await Summons for your Final Descent.

Good luck.

58

Marx and Wraith agreed to meet at my cabin at six the following evening. I got there early, got the fire going, and set up. They bobbed out of the trees right on time beneath a light but steady snowfall.

I'd told them the deal over the phone: four assholes were en route, so come prepared. Marx came in carrying a duffel bag with something heavy in it. Wraith had a black canvas backpack slung over one shoulder filled with god knows what. They set their stuff down near the fire and we sat and drank coffee and waited for shit to hit the fan.

"They're shending *four* at onshe?" said Marx. His jaw was still wired shut. He looked nervous.

I sipped my coffee, nodded.

"What's the set up?" said Wraith.

"I got my guy outside," I said. "Behind a scope."

"Where?" said Wraith.

I looked sideways at him.

"Where he needs to be," I said.

"What if dey get him?" said Marx.

"They won't," I said.

"You sound sure," said Wraith.

"I am."

"So by your thinking," said Wraith, "by the time they get

to us it'll be four on three. Maybe four on two if your guy's as good as you say he is."

I nodded.

We were quiet awhile, drinking coffee and listening to the crackling of the fire.

"You got any idea who's behind it yet?" said Wraith.

I took a sip of coffee.

"Yeah," I said.

Wraith raised an eyebrow.

"Who?" said Marx.

"Tannen," I said.

Marx's eyes bulged.

"Preshident Tannen?" he said.

I nodded. "And Medvyed."

Wraith studied my face in the flickering fire light.

"How'd you find out?" he said.

"Bugged Tannen's aide," I said.

I told them about the secret service guys, the phone bug, and my latest Labyrinth code.

"So they knew what happened in the hangar?" said Wraith.

I nodded.

"And the only way that works is if the President has something to do with it," said Wraith.

I nodded.

"And they can't have you knowing," said Wraith.

"No," I said. "They can't."

"So they're sending four at once, to erase you."

I nodded. We were silent for a moment.

"That fuckin' shucks," said Marx.

I shrugged.

"So who do you think they'll send?" said Wraith, eyeing me.

I met his gaze.

"A Depth 4, a Depth 7, and Depth 8, and a Depth 9," I

said.

Wraith blinked a couple times.

"Fuckin' 'ell," said Marx.

"You're at Depth 9?" said Wraith.

"Eight," I said. "If I handle all four, I'll be at nine."

"Only one guy above you then," said Wraith.

"You mean below," I said.

He smiled.

"What Depth are you at Marx?" I said, turning to him.

Marx coffee cup paused half-way to his mouth. A little coffee sloshed over the side and dripped down onto the floor.

"Uh . . . four," he said. "I think."

"You think?" I said.

I got up and went to the fire and grabbed the coffee pot off the hearth where it had been warming. When I turned back Marx's duffel bag was unzipped and he had a crow bar in his hand. I looked from him to Wraith. Wraith had his silenced MK-23 in his right hand, pointed at me.

"And you're Depth 7," I said to him.

He nodded.

"Sorry," he said.

I looked at Marx.

"You gotta rape me?" I said.

He swallowed, nodded quickly. He looked very nervous, but a glance at the silenced handgun in Wraith's hands seemed to give him a little confidence.

"I figure jamming thish up your ash'll count," he said, brandishing the crow bar.

"You plan on doin' that before I'm dead?" I said.

He swallowed.

"If I'm already dead," I said, "it ain't rape."

Marx's eyes widened slightly.

"What do they got on you?" I said.

His eyes went to the ground.

"They know about the family businesh," he said, hanging his head. "And they got me for murder. And the cover up."

I nodded.

"Worth more than me," I said.

He glanced up at me, shrugged. I couldn't really blame him.

I turned my attention to Wraith.

"It's unfortunate," he said. "It's you or my mother. Not really a choice, in the end."

Couldn't argue with that one, either.

"What's the plan after I'm gone?" I said. "How are you going to get out?"

Marx glanced at Wraith for support. Wraith wasn't much help.

"Who the fuck knows," said Wraith. "How do you get to the President?"

I shrugged.

"Still trying to figure that one out myself," I said.

We were silent a while. It was an odd moment.

"How you supposed to blind me with that thing?" I said, nodding to the pistol.

"Figure I'd hobble you first," he said. "Then shoot your eyes out."

Keeping the gun trained on my gut, he smiled at me without warmth.

"What'd you use?" he asked.

"My fists," I said.

He let out a low whistle.

"You're something else, Sledge," he said, shaking his head. "Bummer we couldn't figure this thing out together."

"We still could," I said.

Wraith let out a breath.

"No," he said. "We can't."

A moment passed, then he pulled the trigger.

59

I'd been concentration on Wraith's eyes with the hyper-alertness that rides alongside life and death. Wraith owed me. I'd spared his life. Twice. Yet he'd still decided to betray me. My guess was the final decision to pull the trigger wouldn't come easy. And I bet my life I'd be able to see it in his eyes.

As I've said, I'm not fast, but anticipation beats speed every day of the week.

Wraith's pupils dilated and his gaze went far away, to something unseen, then I saw the muscles in his jaw shift beneath the skin. His eyes came back hard and found me and I slung the coffee pot at him underhand. The boiling liquid arched and he pulled the trigger and I dove right, across his body, toward Marx. The gunshot rang out loud inside the cabin even with the suppressor and I hit the floor and rolled and the boiling coffee must have got Wraith because he screamed and leapt back tipping over his chair. I came up, as yet un-shot, and there was Marx, all six foot eight three-hundred-fifty pounds of him, clutching the crowbar overhead in two meaty hands and swinging down with all his might. I took a colossal blow across forearm and skull and the world went bright black and I staggered and almost fell and cast a glance at Wraith who was swinging the gun back around. I threw a backhand fist into Marx's broken jaw and he squealed and I ducked behind him as Wraith fired. The bullet went wide. I snaked a hand around Marx's mandible and squeezed, using the bone-shredding pain to steer him in front of me and keep him there, a three-hundred pound human shield.

"Bullet won't go all the way through," I said to Wraith, pivoting Marx as Wraith circled with the MK-23.

"I know," said Wraith. "Sorry Marx. You're worth an extra fifty k anyway."

"Huh?" Marx had time to grunt, then the back of his head exploded.

So much for my human shield. With no brain to control him, Marx's muscles turned off and he dropped like a very large stone. I got a fistful of the ass of his pants and clamped a hand across his decapitated throat and managed to hold his immense headless bulk upright. Fuck was he heavy, even without a head. Wraith used Newton's First Law to his advantage and sidestepped quickly to the right to flank me. The MK-23 spurted fire but I got Marx around just in time to eat the bullet in the gut.

"How long can you hold him up like that?" said Wraith, dodging back-and-forth like a shifty point guard, trying to deke me out.

"Long as I fuckin' need to, you prick," I said. "Why'd you do it?"

"Told you," said Wraith, skirting back toward the fire place before stopping on a dime and leaping back to the right. "It's you or my mother."

"Bullshit," I said, pivoting behind Marx's heavy corpse, which was getting heavier by the second. "I saved your ass, twice. You think you can take them down on your own? No fucking way. You need me."

Wraith snorted.

"You really that stupid, Sledge?" he said, shaking his

head. "Can't you see? You *are* the way out."

I said nothing. It took all my focus to keep a grip on Marx's headless corpse.

"Whoever's running this fucking thing wants you dead," said Wraith, dancing left. "Not just any *dead,* either. They want to piss on your corpse and shit on your name. They want you raped and blinded and fucking crucified. On camera. You think they're just gonna let us go before they get what they want? They want *you,* buddy. *Bad.* And if that's the case, it might as well be me who reaps the reward."

I said nothing, mainly because I couldn't really argue with his logic. This whole thing *was* about me. My haunting. Wraith was just one of the assholes hired for the job.

We danced our little dance a while longer. Marx wasn't getting any lighter. My deltoids seared. My grip on his bloody throat was slipping. Wraith could sense it. He redoubled his herky-jerky circling, jab-stepping one way, leaping back the other. I didn't want to kill him, but what other option did I have?

"You sure about this, Wraith?" I said.

In answer, he leapt back right, toward the fireplace. Exactly as I anticipated. I'd stopped pivoting and suddenly he found himself mid-hop, flying toward me. Too close. I let go of Marx's neck and lunged, shooting out my left palm. Wraith's eyes went wide and the heel of my hand smashed him in the solar plexus and he let out a loud *oof* and fell ass-first into the fireplace. He screamed and forgot the gun and put his hands to the floor, desperate to climb out of the coals but I stomped his chest and kept him burning. He remembered the gun then and went to raise it but I'd already stomped my other boot to his wrist. I heard the bones crack even above his screams and I stood there letting him burn.

"Done trying to kill me yet?" I said.

He thrashed and screamed and I leaned down and hammered a right into his face and with that hand grabbed the MK-23 and tossed it across the room. Wraith screamed and thrashed and I held him there and counted a slow ten until the terrifyingly appetizing smell of burning human flesh reached my nostrils. I meant to let him up then, but turns out Under Armor clothing is extremely flammable. No sooner had I pulled my boot from his chest than his acrylic base layer ignited and he burst into flames. He loosed a blood-curdling shriek as his head combusted and he burned alive.

I reached down to yank him from the fire and the cabin door opened. I turned and saw Gow. There was arm around his neck and gun to his temple. His hands were secured behind his back and he looked like he'd been roughed-up pretty good. The guy with the gun pushed Gow roughly into the cabin. I wondered why Gow wasn't fucking him up. Then the second guy came in. His gun snapped from Gow's head to mine with no wasted movement. I looked at Gow.

He shrugged.

"They're good," he said.

He nodded toward the second guy and a shot rang out and something stabbed me in the throat. I slapped a hand to the spot and pulled something out. Tranq dart. Son of a bitch.

Then the world faded away.

60

I woke up some time later with a throat full of razor blades and a brain dipped in battery acid. Opening my eyes only made it worse.

I was seated in my maple Adirondak chair in the exact center of my cabin floor. The rest of my furniture had been removed. It was dark. A flickering fire cast wavering shadows across the floor. They danced like demons, nipping at my feet. Speaking of feet, something was very wrong with my legs. I looked down. Ratcheted steel cables sliced across my knee caps, securing my lower legs to the chair. An identical set cut mercilessly into my shin bones. A third ground against ankle. Now that I saw them, the pain hit hard. I tried extending my legs at the knee. Not a hope in hell. I tried wiggling my toes. Just. The pain was immense and growing by the second.

Things got appreciably worse when my eyes found my arms. Ten sets of steel cables, five to each arm, secured my elbows, forearms, wrists, hands, and fingers to the thick maple arm planks. My fingers were splayed wide. My left hand had been secured palm down. The right, palm up. I didn't want to think about what that might mean.

I tried rotating my hands at the wrist. Couldn't. I tried curling my splayed fingers. Couldn't.

Depth 8, I thought. Paralyzation.

Which left only . . .

I looked up. Marx's body still lay on the floor near the fire place. An eight foot lake of blood radiated from his exploded head, coagulating on the floorboards. Gow and Wraith were nowhere to be seen. Two men were in the room with me. They'd taken off their ski-masks. They didn't care that I saw their faces.

Initial impression of the situation: not good.

The nearer guy, the one who'd tranq'd me, met my eyes. He was dressed in winter-camo tactical pants and a white dry-fit t-shirt with a one-blade buzz-cut and a parkour build. His dark eyes were very still. An icy spider scuttled down my spine. I recognized a trained killer when I saw one. The other guy stood in the shadows in a far corner of the room. I couldn't see his face, but his silhouette resembled a stack of boulders stuffed into tight clothing. The Thing.

"File said you were strong," said One-Blade, nodding at the cables. "The exact wordage the government geek used was '*otherwordly* physical strength.' Otherwordly. I liked that."

He smiled without warmth. His voice was flat, business-like.

"File mentioned you ripped a man's head off with your bare hands," he said. "I didn't think that was possible. We figured it best not to take any chances. Our tech guy special-ordered the ratchet systems. Max pull force of six-thousand pounds. You may be strong, but you're not that strong. If I want to I can cinch those fuckers straight through bone."

I tried to tell him to go fuck himself, but my throat was too dry to make a sound.

"Oh," he said.

He walked over to where he'd set his fatigue jacket and came back with a bottle of water. He walked up, unscrewed the blue cap, and held the bottle over my head. I tilted my head back and opened my mouth. He pulled the bottle away, smiling that dead smile.

I glared up at him.

"My bad," he said. "Here."

He reached out again and waited for me to open my mouth then pulled the bottle away again. Fucking prick. I lunged at him, teeth first. He danced back, water slopping from the mouth of the bottle onto my neck. The chair tipped and after a teetering pause I crashed hard to the floor. An arm plank hammered me in the ribs edge-wise. Steel cables ripped down to bone. It fucking hurt.

"Come on now," said One-Blade. "If your file's anything to go by, you know how this goes."

I did.

Depth 9. Severe torture to death.

One-Blade walked round, knelt behind me, and jerked my chair upright in one violent motion, slamming me back onto four legs. My freshly-ripped lacerations ground against steel. One-Blade stalked back in front of me and looked at me with empty eyes. He'd just showed me everything I needed to know about his proficiency in combat. He was quick, strong, and ruthless. It'd be one thing to get out of the chair, another to get past him. Then there was the big guy in the corner. He'd handled Gow without a scratch. Even I couldn't do that.

Hmm. Maybe I could charm them.

This time One-Blade gave me the water. I guzzled and choked and sputtered and guzzled some more. He poured out the entire bottle. I swallowed as much as I could and let the rest splash over my head and neck. Then One-Blade stepped back and threw the empty bottle into the fireplace. The acrid stench of burning plastic wafted through the room. I sat there dripping and hurting and waiting to see what came next.

"Ready?" said One-Blade.

"Fuck you," I said.

I wondered what he'd use. Coals? Blades? Acid?

He held up a finger. A hand went to his pocket and came out with a thin black case. He unzipped it and opened it like a paperback. Inside were three syringes. He pulled out the first, held it up in front of me.

"Sodium amobarbital," he said. "And a micro-dose of LSD."

I knew about that little cocktail. The amobarbital slowed the speed at which the spinal cord sent messages to your brain. The LSD skewed the messages altogether. The result was a total loss of inhibition. Truth serum.

One-Blade placed the needle on the webbing between my pinky and ring finger on my left hand. The palm down one. He looked at me, then sunk the needle deep into the meat of my hand and plunged in the liquid. It didn't feel great. He extracted the needle and placed the empty syringe back in the case.

"Doesn't matter," I said. "I don't know a fucking thing."

He smiled.

"You spied on the President," he said. "That's a big no-no. It's my job to find out why."

"He fuckin' knows why," I said. "I found out he's behind the fucking Labyrinth."

One-Blade squinted at me.

"We'll get to that bit," he said.

He pulled out the second syringe. It was much larger than the first.

"Human Growth-Hormone," One-Blade said.

He stabbed the huge needle into the webbing between my ring and middle finger. I felt it slide three inches into the center of my hand. Something cold pumped into me. I had no idea why he'd given me a performance enhancer.

"Keeps you alive," said One-Blade, answering the look on my face. "Can't have you dying too quickly from all the acute trauma."

Oh, I thought. Fuck.

The third needle went in between my middle and index finger.

"Haloperidol," said One-Blade.

I looked at him.

"What's that one do?" I said. My words came a little slurry. The amobarbital was already hitting.

"Let's keep it a surprise," he said, smiling.

He walked over to a small black duffel bag on the floor near the door, unzipped it, and pulled out two things.

A hammer. And a bag of nails.

61

"Want to hear something fucked up?" said One-Blade.

I didn't, but figured he was going to tell me anyway. He stalked toward me. I had to forcibly remove my eyes from the hammer and nails to meet his gaze. What I saw there wasn't encouraging.

"They got a guy does studies on this shit," he said, nodding to the bag of nails. "Stuck a heart rate monitor, ecg, blood pressure cuffs on guys while they were being tortured. Recorded stats. Which nail size causes the most pain? Which length induces the most fear on sight? What material works best, galvanized, stainless, or plain old raw iron? In the end, he crunched the numbers and came up with these."

He hefted the large bag. The veins of his bicep writhed under the weight.

"60D's," he said. "Raw iron."

He dropped the bag to the floor. It landed with a heavy jangling thud.

"Six-inchers," he said. "The big ones. They were deemed the most painful *and* the most terrifying on sight. As you'd probably expect. But that's not the fucked up part." He shook his head. "It's the material. Raw iron. Any idea why?"

I had to blink a few times to get my eyes to focus. When they did, I found his unblinking stare looking right back at me. He was trying to scare me. It was working.

"Rust," I said. The word fell out as if of its own volition.

One-Blade smiled.

"Very good," he said. "The research geek had us spray them with hydrogen peroxide, vinegar, and salt water, then leave them outside for a week. The result . . ."

He bent down and pulled out a single nail, then held it up in front of me. Nice and close. The nail was fucking enormous, it's once-smooth surface completely covered in jagged flakes of blood-colored rust.

"Nasty right?" said One-Blade.

"Yup," I said.

"It's the rust, isn't it?" he said. "The fear of that shit getting into your blood stream. As if tetanus is your biggest concern right now."

I nodded in agreement. The drugs were definitely getting to me.

One-Blade studied me for a moment, the thinnest of smiles on his face. The fucker was enjoying himself.

"Who's the last person you murdered?" he said. "Before the guy in the fireplace."

It took me a second to find my tongue, then the words spilled out effortlessly.

"Some guy named Hansson," I slurred.

"How'd you do it?"

"Punched his skull in from both sides. Never done that before. Works pretty good. Makes a mess though."

One-Blade's smile widened.

"Tongue's loosened up I see," he said. "Good. But before we get to the questions, we need to see how you handle a little trauma."

"No thanks," I said.

He kept smiling.

"Tell you what," he said. "I'll let you choose which hand."

He tapped the tip of the nail on the back of my left hand,

then the palm of my right.

"There *is* a correct answer," he said.

I looked down at my hands. Palm up. Palm down. Which would I rather have a giant rusted nail pounded through?

"Don't s'pose none's an option?" I slurred.

One-Blade snickered.

"Sorry," he said, shaking his head. "What's your pick?"

"Palm down," I said. The words just came out.

One-Blade's eyes opened, surprised.

"Wow," he said. "No one ever picks the back of the hand. But that's the right choice. Let me show you why."

He pinched the tip of the nail and placed it onto the back of my left hand, in line with my middle finger.

"The goal is to fracture the metacarpal," he said, pressing down. "Obviously that causes the most pain, and maximizes trauma. When you go through the palm, the meat of the muscle sort of locks the nail in place, keeping it right in line with the bone. I can crack it damn near every time. But on the back of the hand . . . see how even though the bone is right there beneath the skin, the nail keeps slipping to the side? You just can't get it to stay on track. I've only split the bone once. Maybe you'll be lucky number two."

He brought the hammer down fast and precise. Despite the brain fog, the pain was all-consuming. I screamed and jerked and roared and accomplished nothing but more pain. Maybe it was all in my head, but I swear I felt the jagged flakes of rust scraping off inside my hand, ripping their way down my veins, coursing into my blood stream. The nail jerked all the way through and jammed firmly into the maple arm plank.

"Damn," said One-Blade, pulling back the hammer and shaking his head. "See. Slid right past the bone."

While I screamed and yanked ineffectually against the cables he hammered the nail four more times in quick succession until the fat nail head lay flush with the back of my hand. Rivulets of blood leaked from beneath it. I screamed and jerked and roared some more but there was absolutely nothing I could do to stop the terror and the pain.

One-Blade stepped back to admire his handywork.

"Nice chair," he said. "Where'd you get it?"

I screamed some more. I couldn't talk, but through my screams my tongue still tried to tell him I'd built the chair myself because stock Adirondaks didn't fit. The headrest stopped half-way up my back.

One-Blade let me scream and grunt and live in the pain for a while. Then he grabbed another nail and pounded it into my right hand. It sunk into the meat of my palm and hit bone. He held it in place and hammered hard one, two, three, four times, then something gave and nail burst through. I jerked and grunted and screamed and clenched my jaw so tight my teeth nearly shattered.

One-Blade pulled back the hammer, looking confused.

"What the fuck?" he said, tilting his head to the side. He knelt down and looked beneath the arm plank.

"The nail bent," he said. "*How*?"

"Hard bones," my throat grunted through clenched teeth.

One-Blade's head emerged from beneath the chair arm. He eyes had opened a little wider.

"File did mention that," he said, tilting his head. "But it's another thing to actually see it."

He studied me with renewed interest.

"How'd you do it?" he said.

"Whacked hard stuff," my lips spat.

One-Blade's brow furrowed, then he laughed to himself and leaned in over the slightly angled nail head sticking out of the back of my right hand.

"It'll be interesting to see what happens when we get to your knee caps," he said.

"You won't be alive then," I said.

"Oh yeah?" said One-Blade, a smile creasing his face.

"Why not?"

"File say anything about my carpentry skills?"

Ever since he'd mentioned it, my swirling brain had been reliving the construction of the Adirondak chair. I'd run out of decking screws about three-quarters of the way through, but instead of heading in to Ace's to buy more, I'd finished it off with a pack of brad nails I'd found in the garage. To secure the arm planks, I'd nailed the brads upward through the base so no nail heads showed. Gave it a nice clean look. As far as I could recall, the nail points only sunk in about half an inch.

"No," said One-Blade, tilting his head up to meet my eyes. "Why?"

"They're shit," I said.

I yanked my left arm upward. The steel cables' incredible tensile strength held, of course. The brad nails' thin points didn't. With a high-pitched screech the arm plank ripped free. One-Blade's eyes went wide. He jerked backward, but not before four-inches of raw iron stabbed into his right ear.

He died with a look of complete shock on his face.

With One-Blade's head still fixed to the nail, I ripped the right arm plank off the chair in similar fashion and rose to my feet. My lower legs were still firmly attached to base of the chair. On each forearm I now had two hardwood shields with four-inch iron spikes sticking out the front. One-Blade's head slid off the nail and his body thumped to the ground.

I turned toward The Thing. He emerged from the shadows . . . and smiled.

Then the Haloperidol hit.

62

Haloperidol's a hell of a drug.

The Soviets were the first to administer it for pharmaceutical torture back in the eighties. It's an antipsychotic used for treatment of acute psychosis, delirium, and alcohol withdrawal, amongst other things. But the real fun begins when you overdose someone who isn't insane. It takes about twenty minutes to kick in, then your muscles begin to spasm violently. You look and feel like you have Parkinson's. But that's not the worst part. Not even close. After the shakes hit, your mind is slowly enveloped by an inescapable foreboding. Put simply, you quite literally *quake with dread*.

Standing in a lake of blood, I began to scream.

Not in pain. In *fear*.

Somewhere far off, The Thing started laughing.

"Halo's got you," he said, his voice distorted into a demon's snarl. "The Nightmare Juice."

I tried to run, forgetting that my legs were manacled to the chair, tripped, and fell face-first into the blood lake. It did nothing to improve my mood. Face down in sanguine hell, I screamed and thrashed and tried to flee the nightmare, but it was everywhere and all at once.

"Breathe," boomed The Thing.

As if that were an option.

"Focus on my voice," The Thing said. "I'm going to ask you some questions now. Answer truthfully, and I'll make the nightmare go away. Lie . . . and it will get worse."

Did he say worse?

"Why were you spying on President Tannen?" growled the demonic voice, deep and terrifying.

Even deep within the nightmare, the amobarbital still had control of my tongue.

"He's behind The Labyrinth," I said.

"And what is The Labyrinth?" said The Thing.

"Fucked up death game," I said. "Murder for hire. On the darkweb. Killing for sport."

"The Labyrinth hired you to murder the President?" said The Thing.

"No," I said. "President's torturing me for sport. Him or Medvyed. Not sure who one wants me deader."

"Vladimir Medvyed," said The Thing.

"Yes."

"How do you know that?"

"He hates me," I said. "For what I did to Taktarov. And for my grandfather."

"So President Tannen and Vladimir Medvyed are colluding together to terrorize you, personally, and they're using The Labyrinth to do it?"

"Yes," I said.

"How do you know all this?"

"Because you're here right now," I said. "Doing it."

The Thing smiled.

"You're Depth 8," I said. "Paralyzation. Fucker with the nail in his head was gonna torture me to death."

"That's more or less true," said The Thing. "You're not getting out of here. I'm the guy they send when they need someone disappeared."

"Figured," I said.

It was about then that a funny thing happened. Slowly, gradually, I was becoming aware of myself again. The sticky blood on the floor beneath me, soaking into my beard. The wooden planks gripping excruciatingly to each forearm. The tight pain in my lower legs where the base of the chair was still connected.

The nightmare was fading. No. Not fading. I was becoming aware of it. Like that moment of clarity in the bathroom mirror when you're particularly high.

"Wha' is this shit?" I said, my voice frayed. Full of panic.

The Thing laughed. "They use it for booze dependancy," he said. "And crazy fuckers. At about a tenth the dose."

"How long," I whimpered, "will it last?"

The Thing chuckled.

"For the rest of your life," he said.

"Make it stop!" I screamed.

The Thing laughed some more.

"Sorry pal," he said. "That's not how this works. You fucked with the President. Inside his home. There's no coming back from that."

I started screaming in earnest, as if caught in the deepest, darkest recesses of the nightmare. I thrashed my legs, flexing at the knees, smashing my manacled shins against the cabin floor over and over again. It hurt horrifically. The mass of maple chair base rattled and shook against my restraints. I heard a crack. Felt something give. Kept thrashing.

"You're going to die now," said The Thing, leaning in close to snarl in my ear.

"I got a better idea," I screamed.

"Oh yeah?" said The Thing, chuckling his demon's chuckle. "What's that?"

"This."

I shot to my feet. The severely damaged chair was still attached to my lower legs. I raised a foot, heard another crack, then stomped at The Thing's upturned, gaping face.

He was down on all fours, leaning over his hands to whisper sweet nothings in my ear. He tried leaping back but his hands slipped in the coagulating blood. My heel bashed his cheekbone, knocking his chin into the floorboards. The chair base cracked in two. Mangled bits were still attached to each leg, but I had the use of both feet again. The steel cables cut unmercifully into the bone, but I went for The Thing again, a second brutal stomp. He rolled away, scrambling to his feet in the lake of blood. For someone so large, he moved incredibly fast.

He backed away across the lake in a fighter's crouch, eyes locked on mine. I stepped backward until my feet found dry footing.

"That was enough halo to kill an elephant," he said, confused. "You should be dying."

I shrugged.

"Not your day," I said.

The Thing settled his eyes on me. I tried not to think about how he'd handled Gow without a scratch.

"Sure it is," he said, grinning.

And it began.

63

On an average day I'd wager my life in mortal combat versus any man on earth. That's not being cocky. That's simply a fact.

But today was not an average day . . .

And The Thing was no ordinary man.

We faced each other across the crimson lake, our eyes unblinking. The fire had burned low. Darkness encroached on all sides. The air was stifling. The stench of blood a physical thing. In one precise motion, The Thing extracted an 8-inch Ka-bar from a sheath on his left hip and an M48 Tactical Tomahawk from his back.

"No bazooka?" I said.

Thing said nothing. I guess we were past jokes. He spun the blades once in each hand, practiced fingers dancing like spider's legs.

"Where's the camera?" I said. "They wouldn't miss this."

The Thing shrugged, his traps bunching like lake rock. By silent agreement, we began circling. I watched his hands. No telling how fast he could throw those blades. Slowly, we inscribed an orbit of the bloody lake. On our second pass my eyes darted to the two islands at it's core. One-Blade. And Marx.

"Son of a bitch," I murmured. "Body cams. Like in the

SUV."

The Thing said nothing.

"How long you been in?" I said.

I was trying to get him talking. Distract him. The Thing didn't smile. When he spoke, his voice was deep, flat, lifeless. The voice of death.

"Ten years," he said.

I guessed his age at thirty-five. Late physical prime. With a decade of hit work under his belt. Wraith had been right. The Labyrinth was a proving ground. The guys at the lowest Depths were the best of the best. Seasoned killers. Government-funded assassins. The guys Presidents sent to take out their highest-value targets.

"How many?" I said. I didn't have explain what I meant.

The Thing took his time answering.

"Who's counting?" he said.

"You are," I said, watching his eyes. "We all count."

He laughed through his nose without moving his face. His focus was unrelenting. We orbited the lake, keeping our distance, gauging the terrain. The blood was a death zone. No footing. The fight would go there only as a last resort. Which left the winding track of dry flooring along the shadowy edges of the room. A twisting wooden viper, upon which one of us would die.

"Sixty-eight," The Thing said.

That was a large number. He was trying to distract me with it. I watched him. Closely. He was relentlessly present. Right here. Right now. He knew exactly what this was. What it took. He'd been here many times before. Sixty-eight, to be exact.

We circled.

Soon the nasty bit would come. We were both curious how it would go. Keenly aware of what we were up against. That neither of us had ever lost. And that today, one of us would.

"Do you crave it?" I said, trying my own hand at distraction.

The Thing said nothing.

"Someone asked me that the other day," I said. "I didn't know what to say."

"Guy behind the scope?" said The Thing, without blinking.

I watched him study my movement patterns. I was older. Slower. My brain fogged with nightmare and truth. Four limbs manacled. Hands crucified. He wasn't offering to help.

"How'd you spot him?" I said.

"Drone," he said.

"Thermal?" I said, frowning slightly.

He shook his head. We stopped, started circling the other way.

"He was good," he said. "Not a blip on heat. Not even his breath. I thought we'd lost him."

"Lost him?" I said. "How'd you get him in the first place?"

The edges of The Thing's mouth curled.

"Drone's been up there all week," he said, tipping his head toward the sky without unlocking his gaze.

He let it sink in.

They'd been watching us the whole time. We'd walked right into it.

"Don't feel bad," he said. "You couldn't have spotted it even if you were looking. Not the one we got."

"Why not?" I said.

"LEDs," he said. "Project down what the cameras see on top. Damn near invisible at ten feet, and up so high you'd need a telescope."

"Where is he?" I said. "What'd you do with him?"

The Thing said nothing, but something moved behind his eyes.

I knew in that moment that Gow was dead. I hadn't

pulled the trigger. But I'd killed him. Simple as that.

The Thing let the the weight of it hit me. I pivoted around a peninsula of blood in the far corner, opposite the fire. The darkest spot in the room. My concentration slipped for a fraction of a second, my mind going to Gow and how they must have worked it. The Thing would have snuck up behind him, making a little too much noise. Gow would've had to make a choice: give away his position, or take a knife in the back. The moment he raised his head, One-Blade would have been there with a tranq. Too easy. What they did with him after that, I didn't want to think about.

The Ka-bar came in low and fast. I had one foot in the air, mid-pivot, all my weight on my left leg. The Thing closed the distance between frames. Impossible to track in the dim light. I stuck out my left shield to deflect the flashing blade. The Thing watched me commit, then the Ka-bar changed direction, darting around the edge of the plank like a scorpion's sting. A four inch gash appeared on my forearm. I was still waiting for the pain to hit when the tomahawk swooped down. I took it on the right shield. A savage blow. And there was the knife again, darting in from an impossible angle. A second slash materialized across my side.

Fuck me. I'd never seen someone so skilled with a blade.

The tomahawk had lodged itself in my right shield, the apex of its blade penetrating my forearm to the bone. I pivoted, wrenched down, hoping to twist the axe from The Thing's grip. He yanked back savagely. The tomahawk dislodged from wood and bone. The sudden shift in momentum made him stagger. I lunged, slapping at his throat with the crooked nail protruding from my right hand. He dodged, looking bored, and the tomahawk came up in a vertical arc into my exposed groin. I chopped down with my left shield. The axe cleaved three inches into the edge of the maple plank, biting into my forearm. Then the Ka-bar flashed over the top. At my heart.

I was dead.

I let go of my legs and dropped knee-first to the lake of blood. The knife plunged between my ribs. A kill shot. But I was falling, my hardened ribs chopping down on the face of the blade as it slid inside me, pulling it down with me. The Thing leaned in over his front leg, desperate to sink the killing blow. And four-inches of rising iron nail met his exposed crotch.

"NO!" he grunted.

"Yes," I growled.

The knife retracted. Blood gouted. I might already be dead. I met The Thing's eyes. Saw no fear. Only rage. My right-hand nail was still sunk deep in his groin. The Ka-bar spun in his palm, fingers locking it into place, blade down. I closed my right fist and yanked myself forward using the crotch-sunk nail, knees sliding atop the slick coagulating blood, left arm slipping between The Thing's legs, nail-side up. Then The Thing roared and stabbed down. I looked up. Saw the blade descend. Watched, as four inches of hardened steel penetrated my forehead.

64

"How the fuck are you not dead?" said Gow.

We were lying on neighbouring ICU beds in Maldonado's medical facility. We'd been there a day-and-a-half while Code and his crew fussed and fawned over us, keeping us alive. I felt like I'd been recently tortured to death. Gow, who'd only woken up an hour ago, looked worse. On the bright side, the President still wanted to kill me.

"I should be asking you the same thing," I said.

"It appears they spared me," said Gow.

"Makes no sense. You're worth an extra fifty k."

Gow shrugged. "Maybe they were saving me for later. When they were done with you."

I started to shake my head, then remembered the hole in it. Beside us, our vital monitors beeped gently.

"How'd we get here?" said Gow.

"I found you unconscious on the porch next to Wraith's corpse. Chucked you over my shoulder and headed straight here."

Gow frowned. "With a knife sticking out of your head?"

"Yup."

One of the nurses, a spicy ginger I'd been eyeing since she came on shift, came in to check our wounds and record our vitals on a chart. I had major lacerations on every limb, a few bone chips where the tomahawk had bit me, and a large hole in my skull. Gow'd had surgery on a dislocated shoulder and was still showing severe symptoms of benzodiazepine overdose. After she was done the nurse smiled and walked out. We both watched her exit.

"That smile was for me," said Gow.

"*Riiight.*"

We were quiet for awhile, then Gow looked over at me, his face serious.

"How'd you get him?"

The Thing, who's name we'd yet to learn, was in an induced coma in the next room.

"Slapped him on the back," I said.

Gow raised an eyebrow.

"Helped that I had a six-inch nail pounded through my hand," I said, holding up my bandaged palm. "From the way he convulsed, I'm pretty sure I nicked his spinal cord."

"Ouch."

"Can't say I feel too bad about it."

Gow didn't reply. He was still looking at me funny.

"What?" I said.

"You still haven't told me how you're not dead."

The edges of my mouth curled.

"He stabbed me exactly in-line with my scar," I said, holding an index finger up between my eyes.

"I know," said Gow. "I'm looking down the hole."

"Great shot," I said. "Takes incredible strength. But he didn't know his cerebrum anatomy."

Gow cocked his head.

"What on earth are you talking about?"

"I looked down the blade," I said.

Gow blinked a few times.

"Come again?"

"Story Code told me," I said. "Guy came into the ER in Pretoria with a machete hacked through the top of his skull.

Blade was sunk in four inches. Damn near cleaved his skull in half. Code figured the guy was already dead, just didn't know it yet. But when they removed the blade . . . ." I shrugged. "Guy was fine."

"What?" said Gow.

"The great longitudinal fissure."

Gow blinked a couple more times, said nothing.

"There's a groove between the hemispheres of your brain," I said. "A big cleft right down in the middle, maybe half an inch wide, about three inches deep. Just wide and deep enough for a blade to slide through without doing any serious damage."

Gow's stared at me for a while with his mouth open.

"Are you saying you let him stab you on purpose?" he said.

If I could have shaken my head, I would have.

"He was going to stab me anyway," I said. "He was too damn good with that blade. But I knew from my old x-rays that my scar was right in line with the fissure. Figured it'd make a good target. All I had to do was tilt my face and help him line it up. It gave me the opening I needed."

Gow stared at me.

"How'd you get the blade out?" he said.

"Yanked it," I said. "Code nearly feinted. Then rushed me to surgery and tied off the blood vessels. Pretty gnarly. I was awake the hole time."

Gow's mouth was hanging open.

"I should be fine," I said.

"Should?" said Gow. "With a fucking hole in your head?"

"Code's been ominously vague about long term side effects."

Gow shook his head, letting out a little laugh.

"What about the drugs?" he said. "Why didn't they work?"

"They did," I said.

Gow scrunched his brow.

"Too low a dose?" he said.

I did another invisible head shake.

"Code's got a theory," I said. "Something to do with my inhibitor pathways. Same reason I can drink ten whiskeys and still kick your ass. Stuff hits me, it just wears off quick."

"What the actual fuck," said Gow, marvelling. "You're lucky they didn't have that in your file."

"They do now," I said.

Just then the door opened and Code walked in.

"How's the brainless wonder?" he said.

I showed him my middle finger.

"Good to hear," he said.

He checked my chart.

"When can we get out of here?" I said.

"Take a shit yet?" said Code.

"Two," I said.

"Then you can go whenever you want," he said. "But you have a strong propensity of dropping dead at any moment. It's up to you where you want to be when that happens. If you're here, I may be able to save you."

I looked at Gow.

"Beer?" I said.

"Huzzah!"

We made to get up. Code shook his head despondently.

"What's that?" I said, pointing to the pocket of Code's lab coat.

He looked down.

"Oh yeah," he said. "Cindy found this at the front desk. Has your name on it."

He handed me a white envelope.

65

<u>FINAL DEATH MATCH</u>

Code Name: Sledge
Height: 6′10″
Weight: 266 lbs
Labyrinth Depth: 9
Labyrinth Rank: 2 of 100
Labyrinth Souls: +31,750
Career earnings: $3,025,000 USD

<u>Power Grid</u>
Toughness: 8/8
Strength: 7/8
Speed: 1/8
Fighting Skill: 6/8
Intelligence: 2/8
Cunning: 6/8

VS.

Code Name: джаггернаут
Height: ?
Weight: ?

Labyrinth Depth: 10
Labyrinth Rank: 1 of 100
Labyrinth Souls: +10,691,733
Career earnings: $1,069,442,077 USD

<u>Power Grid</u>
Toughness: 8/8
Strength: 8/8
Speed: 8/8
Fighting Skill: 8/8
Intelligence: 8/8
Cunning: 8/8

<u>Depths Descended</u>
1 - Death Threat (rank 86-100, bounty $5000 USD, +250 souls)
2 - Beating (rank 71-85, bounty $20,000 USD, +500 souls)
3 - Kidnapping (rank 61-70, bounty $50,000 USD, +1000 souls)
4 - Rape (rank 51-60, bounty $100,000 USD, +2,000 souls)
5 - Grievous Bodily Harm (rank 41-50, bounty $200,000 USD, +3,000 souls)
6 - Deprivation of Hearing (rank 31-40, bounty $300,000 USD, +4,000 souls)
7 - Deprivation of Vision (rank 21-30, bounty $400,000 USD, +5,000 souls)
8 - Paralyzation (rank 11-20, bounty $500,000 USD, +6,000 souls)
9 - Severe torture to death (rank 2-10, bounty $1,000,000 USD, +7,000 souls)
~~10 - Final Boss: джаггернаут (rank 1, bounty $10,000,000, +25,000 souls)~~

Bonus Kills - 9 (bounty $50,000 USD x 9, +1000 souls x 9)
Penalties - 2 (-3000 souls x 2)

* * *

SOUL MERCHANT

Flashlight: +1,000 souls
Night Vision: +5,000 souls
Small Bladed Weapon (blade < 10"): +7,500 souls
Shield: +10,000 souls
Blunt Trauma Weapon: +20,000 souls
Body Armor: +30,000 souls
Large Bladed Weapon (blade > 10"): +40,000 souls
Firearm (handgun, single fire): +50,000 souls
Firearm (shotgun): +75,000 souls
Firearm (semi-automatic): +100,000 souls
Firearm (automatic): +250,000 souls

FINAL DEATH MATCH SUMMONS

You have been Summoned to a Final Death Match versus Final Boss джаггернаут. You will fight to the death at midnight, Friday, March 30th. The location of your Death Match is 47.16856654996787, -87.21196980233155.

Upon entry, you are afforded as many SOUL MERCHANT items as you can afford. The total amount spent must not exceed the amount of souls in your inventory. Overspending will result in Depth 9 attacks on multiple targets dear to you.

Victory in the Final Death Match will descend you to Depth 10 of The Labyrinth and result in attainment of Final Boss status, which carries with it a Depth 10 bounty of $10,000,000 USD and +25,000 souls, along with other yet-to-be-specified rewards. Defeat will result in your death.

Failure to comply with this Final Death Match Summons will result in the immediate release of Indemnity to all major national and international media outlets, along with multiple Depth 9 attacks on those dear to you.

Good luck on your Final Descent.

66

Gow and I were in Kiira's living room, Kiira and I hovering over the encrypted laptop, Gow on the couch with his eyes closed. He was still deep in the teeth of tranq withdrawal and his surgically repaired shoulder appeared to be killing him.

"Okay," I said, eyeing the laptop screen. "Let's see where these fuckers want me."

Kiira copy and pasted the GPS coordinates from the Final Death Match summons into Google Earth and pressed return. A satellite map of the earth tilted and rotated and zoomed in. Over the middle of Lake Superior. I stared at the lonely red marker in the middle of a sea of blue nothingness. I waited for it to keep moving. It didn't.

"You sure you did it right?" I said.

"It's right," said Kiira.

"It's in the middle of the fucking lake," I said.

"Appears that way."

"An ore ship?" I said.

Kiira shook her head.

"Ore ships don't cross this time of year. Too dangerous."

"Then what?"

Kiira leaned in over the laptop screen and clicked "more info." A new window popped open. It had a name of the location on it.

"What the fuck is that?" I said.

Kiira typed the name into Google and clicked on images.

"Oh. My. God," she said. She looked up at me with wide eyes. "Did you know that was out there?"

"No," I said.

She clicked the "all" tab, scrolled down to the first link, clicked it. An article opened, titled, "A rare glimpse into the 'grimmest place on earth.'"

"'Thirty-nine miles from land'," read Kiira. "'A desolate beacon guarding against an underwater mountain in the middle of the deadliest lake in the world. A place so unremittingly grim it robbed sea-hardened men of their sanity.'"

"Bit much," I said.

Kiira looked at me.

"What?" I said.

"You're so fucked," she said.

I couldn't argue. I left Gow on the coach and went to look for Maldonado. I found him in his library smoking a cigar in front of the fire, contemplating world domination.

"You know that thing you promised me?" I said, standing over him. "I need it. Yesterday."

Maldonado's teeth glinted in the firelight. Of all men on earth, he was the least frightened of me.

"Perfect timing," he said.

"It's ready?" I said.

"It's modular," he said.

I glared at him, jaw clenched. He took a pull of cuban, blew out a cloud of smoke and smiled at me through it. Prick.

"You're needed," he said. "In the lab."

"For what?"

"Final adjustments."

"Then it's mine?" I said.

Maldonado showed me his teeth again.

"About fucking time," I said.

I told him where I was going. He smiled once more and made a call.

I went to see Code next. It was late. He took me to his living room where he had a fire and two inches of Laphroaig going. He poured me one without asking.

I told him where I was headed and who would be there waiting for me. He laughed. After his time in the special forces, Code worked emergency trauma in Pretoria for six years. He once spent twelve hours piecing together a guy's machete-hacked body, only to get the same guy back three days later, burned alive and whipped. All over the guy's sneakers. Witnessing that kind of heartless depravity day after day robs you of your faith in humanity. Code gave very few fucks about very few things, and I wasn't entirely sure my life was one of them. But he knew his shit, and he'd hit me with it straight.

"I met a guy was stationed out there," he said. "Coast guard engineer."

"Call him."

"Can't," he said.

"Why not?"

"He's dead."

"Oh."

"You can't go out there, mate," said Code.

"I don't have a choice."

"No," said Code, chuckling. "I mean you literally *can't*. The lake is impenetrable this time of year. And even if, by some miracle, you make it there, you won't be able to get in."

"Why not?"

"You'll see."

I glared at him. He giggled.

"Maldonado's got a crew," I said. "He said they can do it."

Code laughed through his nose, sipping his scotch.

"You know better than to fuck with Lake Superior," he said. "Especially in March, with a big nor'easter coming though."

I shrugged.

"I have to go," I said.

"It's your funeral, mate."

I ran a hand over my beard.

"Say I make it," I said.

I told him about the souls thing. What I planned on bringing. Code cackled.

"Will it work?" I said.

"Against what?" said Code.

"Against this fucking guy waiting for me out there."

Code pursed his lips.

"Not really," he said.

"Why not?" I said.

"Work the physics."

I tried.

"It's got extremely high flexural strength," I said. "So it'll absorb a ton of kinetic energy and spread the force over the entire surface area, which should hugely decrease pressure at point of impact."

"Yeah," said Code, grinning, "but conservation of momentum still applies. If you get cracked in the head with something heavy, you'll get whiplashed, which will jostle your brain inside your skull, which, in case you've forgotten, has a large fucking hole in it."

"So . . . duck?" I said.

Code shook his head, giggling. Then he went quiet for a time and his face turned serious.

"You're not really thinking of going out there?" he said.

"I have to," I said. "This is government funded assassination. All the world's richest assholes working together in glorious harmony to watch me die. If I don't go, I ruin their little circle jerk. This is their Super Bowl. What do you think happens if I don't show up?"

Code eyed me over his scotch.

"You have a hole in your head, mate," he said flatly. "Which is fitting, because you're heading to a fucking tomb. You won't survive the trip, let alone a fight against the government's top killer."

"Did I mention he might have a machine gun?" I said.

Code snorted into his scotch.

"You can't win this one, mate," he said. "Not with a hole in your head. There's simply no way."

I didn't reply.

Code looked at me for a while.

"You're going to die in that lake," he said.

"That's encouraging."

Code drank his scotch.

"What would you have me do?" I said.

Code shrugged.

"Not go."

I pointed over our heads.

"There's a billion-dollar drone over us right now. Watching my every move. If I don't go, they'll send an army. Here. Multiple Depth 9 attacks. That could mean you, your family, severely tortured to death."

In the fire light, Code's eyes widened ever-so-slightly. Maybe he was afraid of something after all.

"Still want me to crash on your couch for the next couple days?" I said.

Code laughed maniacally.

"Well, when you put it that way," he said. "Where's the fucking boat?"

67

There was, of course, no boat.

Code was right, traversing Lake Superior at this time of year, in this weather, was suicide. Want nightmares? Look up the fate of the Edmund Fitzgerald.

I walked out of Maldonado's dressed for eighty below. Three layers under a gore-tex shell, gloves, balaclava, full-face visor, and Kahtoola K-10 crampons. I needed every inch of it. According to Kiira's weather app the current wind chill was negative sixty. And plummeting. Eighty mile-an-hour winds ripped out of the northwest across three-hundred-and-fifty miles of open water. Every few seconds a deafening concussion shook the ground as a thousand tons of ice water slammed into the granite cliff face beneath Maldonado's manor. I trudged up a snowy path through the trees along the back edge of the property toward the precipice of the cliff. The trees parted onto a large open space, the center of which had been cleared of snow, uncovering a large yellow octagon surrounding the letter H. Another colossal wave shook the ground. To my left, lake spray cascaded over the top of the cliff, a hundred feet above the lake, freezing instantly into shards of ice which clinked and clattered to the earth, forming piles of broken glass.

And I had to go out in this shit.

I'd gone to the lab that morning and made the final adjustments on the thing Code had told me wasn't going to work. I'd brought it along. That, and a flashlight.

"You sure about this?" said Gow, squinting at me through the brutal wind. He'd made it out of the house to see me off, but still looked like three shades of shit.

"Nope," I said.

"That makes two of us."

I cocked my head. Over the howl of the wind and crash of waves came the distant whoop whoop of helicopter blades. Gow and I huddled with our backs to the gale as the sound grew louder, then a Sikorsky S-92 SAR whooshed in low overhead and began its uneasy descent.

"Fucking hell," said Gow. "You seriously going up in that thing? It's getting tossed around like a fucking beach ball."

I said nothing. I hate flying at the best of times. Watching the bird swoop and sway in the hurricane-force wind already had my stomach churning.

"Isn't that the same helicopter Kobe died in?" said Gow.

My fists clenched over clammy palms. I shot him a look. Now wasn't the fucking time. He smiled mirthlessly.

"Have fun," he said.

The helicopter wheels touched down. The bird rocked and swayed in the brutal wind as the rotars slowed. A minute later the right-side sliding door pulled open and the pilot climbed out. He walked over to us, leaning into the wind, and pulled off his helmet. It was Maldonado.

"Is there anything you can't do?" said Gow.

"Very little," said Maldonado, deadpanned.

He looked at me.

"Do you have everything you need?" he said.

"Yup," I said, holding up my flashlight.

He showed me his teeth.

"Then let's go."

I turned to Gow. The weight of the moment hit us, as it

always did at times likes this.

"See you back here in a few hours," he said, slapping me on the shoulder.

I didn't feel it. I met his eyes, nodded once, then turned and left him standing there in the storm.

The guts of the copter were sparse. Utilitarian. Foldable seats lined the side-walls, providing space for stretchers to be secured along the middle walk-way. Elastic cargo nets secured various pieces of rescue equipment to the upper walls and ceiling. Hydraulic hoists stood sentinel above the sliding door and descendable rear ramp.

I pulled off my balaclava and strapped myself to a seat nearest the cockpit as Maldonado went through the pre-flight checks. Weather radar, a digital map, and thermal imaging screens blinked on, then the engines roared to life. Maldonado motioned over his shoulder to the headset strapped beneath my seat. I put it on. The roar of the wind and rotars died away.

"Ready to die?" said Maldonado's voice, high and clear inside the headphones.

I said nothing. I wasn't in a laughing mood.

Maldonado snickered, then yanked the throttle. With a tremendous lurch the helicopter tipped sideways off the edge of the cliff. We were going to die. Maldonado laughed and jerked the stick hard against gravity. We righted, but not for long. The hundred-and-fifty mile journey across the world's deadliest lake was my worst nightmare made real. The relentless wind plucked us up and tossed us down at the towering waves. We were dead a hundred times. Then a hundred more. Maldonado laughed the entire way. Then, up ahead in the distance, lit up by the frenetically jerking beam of the helicopter's search light, stood Stannard Rock Lighthouse.

"There she is," said Maldonado.

And now I saw what Code had known all along. It was a

tomb. Sixty foot waves hammered the desolate tower, the spray cascading over the lantern room 150 feet above the lake. As each colossal wave receded, they uncovered a base platform completely entombed in ice.

"There's no way in," I said.

Maldonado turned his head and grinned.

"Not from below," he said.

My eyes opened wide.

"Clip in," he said, motioning to the rescue joist above the sliding door.

I unfastened my seatbelt and stumbled drunkenly to the side-door as the helicopter swooped and swayed and lurched and dropped. With shaking hands I hooked myself to the winch.

"I'll lower you down as slowly as I can," said Maldonado. "But no promises. Be prepared for a heavy collision."

I said nothing, just pulled open the sliding door and leapt out into the storm. The wind's icy claws swung me on my steel lifeline like a madman's yo-yo as Maldonado struggled to hover the helicopter above the iron roof of the lighthouse lantern room. The cable descended, slowly. I was almost there when a brutal gust tossed me the wrong way. I swung out, high and wide, then lurched down and swooped in fast. The lantern room reached up out of the stormy sea like a leviathan's hungry maw, ready to swallow me whole. I slammed into wrought iron and hardened glass. Felt my brain slosh inside my shattered skull. Waited for death even as my fingers frantically fumbled at the hook securing me to the steel cable. If I couldn't get it undone, I'd be pulled back into the storm. Into the night. Into the deathly sea. The cable tensed, yanked at my guts, ripped at my fingers as they gripped desperately to the wrought iron rail encircling the lantern room. Then the hook disengaged and the cable yanked free, shooting away into the night.

I was free.

But not for long.

The lake still wanted me.

I turned my head and saw a massive wall of water, sixty feet high, rise out of the darkness and ram the lighthouse tower. White wash rocketed up the sheer ice-covered sides. The icy spray, half-water, half broken glass, tossed me up and over the railing, into the crows nest. I reached through the shocking cold, searching for purchase as the deluge washed me toward the far-side precipice. Toward death. My fingers found the edge of a smashed lantern room window. With every last inch of my might I held on against the massive force of ice and water. Held on and raged at Death itself.

And then it was gone.

With no time to waste before the next assault I pulled myself slithering through the broken lantern room window.

I fell down, down, into darkness.

Where Death awaited.

68

I fell quite a ways.

On instinct, I wrapped my forearms around my broken head in a make-shift helmet and braced for impact. Then something very hard moving very fast annihilated me. I blinked out for a while, but not long enough to avoid the pain. For a time it was all there was and I figured I was going to die then. But I didn't.

Eventually, the pain eased to something manageable and the world solidified again. I did a quick mental check. I appeared unbroken, outside of the hole in my skull. My bones are hard. And I can take a hell of a hit.

Outside the lighthouse, the storm raged. Every few heartbeats another concussion slammed the walls, followed a beat later by a clattering shower of ice shards as spray washed in the broken window above my head. I was too fucked to move out of the way.

I cracked open my eyes. It was almost pitch black. I was lying on something cold and hard. Stone. I tried pushing myself up but the moment I lifted my head the floor rolled as if I were still inside the helicopter. I went fetal, vomited once, then lay there holding onto my existence with everything I had.

Over time, I regained some of myself again. I uncoiled

and lifted my head the tiniest fraction. The ground stayed solid this time. I slipped a finger through the eye hole of my balaclava and ran it across the skin beneath my head wound.

A little blood might be ok. A lot would be very, very bad.

I pulled my finger out and rubbed it on my thumb in the darkness. What little wetness there was froze instantly. That was good. The cold might keep me alive. Frozen blood was clotted blood.

I stayed curled on the floor and let my night vision settle in. A faint glow, charcoal on black, floated in the open, southeast-facing window ten feet above my head. Ice clattered down around me. If the waves didn't ease soon, I'd be trapped in here. Entombed in ice.

Remind me again how I got myself into this?

I eased myself up to a sitting position, didn't vomit, and clawed my tactical flashlight from its belt holster, praying it hadn't snapped in the fall. I clicked the power button. The 2250 lumen beam lacerated the darkness. I flinched, snapping my eyes shut, which did nothing for my head. I puked again. With my eyes squeezed shut I clicked the flashlight down to quarter beam. When I opened my eyes, I could see.

I was seated on the dressed stone floor of the lantern room. The majority of the room was dominated by a massive central column of rusted iron. A skeletal steel staircase coiled around it, leading up to the lantern platform. I'd read on the internet that the Tideland Signal ML-300 incandescent lamp was still online. Battery-powered and solar-refreshed.

So why wasn't it blinding me?

I climbed to my feet in stages. It took a while. When I finally got there the stone floor wobbled and I had to snatch the stair railing to stay upright. Moving my head, even a little bit, sucked. Fortunately, I had to fight to the death in a minute or two.

When I could, I took a few tentative steps. The ground

stayed where it was supposed to be. Progress. I shuffled my feet, rotating until I faced the center of the room. I was just tall enough to see over the lantern platform. I pointed the flashlight at the Tideland lamp. It was smaller than I anticipated. I traced the beam down to its base and found the power cable. It was severed. I searched around and found a large south-facing solar array. I traced its power cord and found it stripped and connected via twist caps to a thick black wire leading to some electrical equipment. On top of that was a large black satellite dish, pointing straight out the open lantern room window ten feet overhead.

The Labyrinth had beefed up the internet.

We were live.

I eased myself backward across the narrow stone walkway that circuited the room until my back kissed the outer stone wall. I was moving a little bit easier. Maybe my bleeding brain had finally frozen over. I pointed the flashlight up to the ceiling and found the first Eufy 6X perched at the room's apex, its red eyes peering straight down like a vampire bat's.

They knew I was here.

And they knew I was fucked.

I imagined President Tannen in the White House bedroom swearing with unholy fury at his thousand-inch TV screen. He'd backed a dud.

I eased myself away from the wall and stepped gingerly along the stone pathway, careful to keep my head as still as possible. At the far side of the iron column the ground fell away and a curving stone stairwell descended down and around into darkness.

I didn't want to give the audience the satisfaction of seeing me afraid, so after a quick pause to let my brain solidify a little further, I started my descent. The stone slabs that made up the staircase spiralled down in a wide arc around the lighthouse's outer circumference. The curving inner wall was made of the same riveted sheets of rusted iron that made up the lantern platform. Every six feet or so the grinning face of a Eufy 6X leered down from the ceiling. I counted thirteen steps before I came to the first door. It led inward to the guts of the lighthouse, slightly ajar. Beyond the door the stairs continued their dark, winding descent.

Now I saw the game.

According to the floor plan Deckert had found online, the lighthouse had ten levels including the lantern room and basement. Ten Depths. Cute.

I put my back to the inner wall and slipped my fingers into the door gap and pushed it open. It swung inward on shrieking iron hinges. I stood still in the silence that followed, trying to listen between the colossal crashing of waves against the lighthouse walls. I couldn't hear a fucking thing. I reached the flashlight around the edge of the door and eased myself down, peeking a careful eye around the frame, then flicked on the light.

Nothing jumped out.

No one shot me.

I carefully ducked my head inside the room and did a quick search. It was empty. Nothing but dust and bits of broken wood. Maybe old furniture. The lone window opposite the door was completely iced over. I headed back to the stairwell and slowly descended down to the next floor. Did it all again.

No one on eight.

No one on seven.

Floors six through three no longer had doors, and were all just as empty. The second floor appeared to have once been a library. Rotted wooden shelves crumbled from the flaky, rusted walls. No one was in there.

On the ground floor I found the galley. An ancient pot-belly stove abutted the far wall. Rusted pots and broken cutlery and the rotted planks of a long-collapsed table littered the floor. No one murdered me.

Which left only the basement.

The lowest Depth.

Of course.

But where was it? The stone stairwell had ended in this room. I didn't see another way down.

"What the fuck?" I breathed.

Maybe Code had been right. Maybe this was all just a ploy to get my dumbass out here. By the time they chipped me out I'd be a popsicle.

But where was the entertainment value in that?

I searched the room, found a Eufy hanging dead center from the ceiling, just like in the lantern room.

"You pricks gonna jerk off watching me shiver to death?" I said, eyeing it.

No one answered.

Wait a minute . . . why was it pointed over there? I followed the Uefy's gaze to the base of the wall opposite the stove. Didn't see anything other than junk. I stepped through the wreckage. When I got near the wall, the sound of my footsteps changed. I looked down.

Of course.

I knelt down and found a small gap near the wall in which I could slide my fingers. I hefted up a heavy iron floor panel. Hinges shrieked. I got it vertical then dropped it backward with a resounding clang.

A rectangular hole in the floor led down into complete darkness.

Motherfuckers.

I leaned over the edge, shining the flashlight down. A steel ladder descended way down, maybe thirty feet, to a raw stone floor. A rusted iron cylinder encircled the top rungs of the ladder, blocking most of the subterranean room from view.

I leaned my ear over and listened. Heard nothing but the

muted crash of waves above my head. It didn't matter. I could feel him down there. In the darkness.

Waiting for me . . .

I looked up at the Eufy. I could feel the voyeuristic fucks on the other side leaning forward in their chairs.

This was it. Show time.

I clipped my flashlight to my belt with the beam on high power, pointing down. I sat down on the edge of the opening, feet dangling into darkness, then climbed onto the ladder and looked down. The flashlight holster had a small hole in the bottom for exactly this purpose. The beam cut a jittery swath across the stone floor far below. If he had a rifle he could've blown out both my knees right about now. But somehow I knew he wouldn't.

The Labyrinth wouldn't allow it. It wasn't part of their game. They wanted to know who was better. Me or him. And had millions riding on it.

The fight must go on.

I began my descent. It took me a long time. Every third or fourth rung the world lurched sideways, forcing me to cling on for dear life. I must've looked like a fucking twat. When my feet finally hit stone I held on to the cold steel rungs until the ground solidified, then stood up straight and pretended to be fine. Pretty sure I wasn't nailing it.

When I was ready, I un-clipped the flashlight and looked around. I was in the bowels of the underwater mountain atop which the lighthouse had been built. Walls of raw, reddish-black stone rose sheer and impenetrable on all sides. Evenly spaced along the walls grinned a satanic circle of Eufy 6X's. I wondered how they got their signal out of the solid stone, then realized there was a line-of-sight relay, winding from camera to camera all the way up and around to the top of the lighthouse and on out into space. Clever. I should've thought to break a couple of the fuckers on the way down and spoil the show. Damn.

I let out a long breath. I was here now. No going back. I lowered the flashlight beam to ground level and inscribed a slow circle.

And that's when I saw him.

The Dzhaggernaut.

It took only a momentary glimpse for one thing to become blood-chillingly clear:

I was about to die.

69

At first, I thought it must be some sort of optical trick. A forced perspective with the floor and the cavern walls. The Dzhaggernaut appeared to be standing level with me, maybe fifteen paces away, yet somehow I was looking *up* at him. *Way* up. No one could be that big.

Then, without warning, he leapt forward, halving the distance between us in a single bound. My heart lurched into my throat. There was just no fucking way. Nothing that freakishly large should be able to move like that. It was like watching a Tyrannosaur leap to your side of a river you'd thought uncrossable. He could be on me in an instant. From there. And now there was no doubting it. Dzhaggernaut was nearly *eight feet* tall.

An overwhelming urge to run nearly consumed me, but there was nowhere to go. I dawned on me then that this must be how I made others feel.

It sucked.

I stood there, frozen in shock and awe, gaping at him. He was now fully illuminated in the flashlight beam. Which only amplified the nightmare.

He was . . . *impossible*. He *towered* over me. His enormous body fully encased in gunmetal grey combat armor. A head-to-toe hard-plate system with over-locking joints and a four-inch thick steel neck plate. No weak points. And *heavy*. Which only made his astounding leap that much more terrifying. He was powerful. Explosive. Impenetrable. And, did I mention, *eight fucking feet tall*.

A god damned Juggernaut.

For the first time in my life, I felt . . . *puny*.

His armored helmet was counter-sunk into the neck plate so only the top half of his head showed, face hidden behind a tinted eye shield. I figured he could survive a nuclear strike to the eyeball in that thing. If that wasn't enough, attached to his massive suit of armor was enough weaponry to invade Russia. I counted a KA-BAR 2217 Big Brother combat dagger hanging from his left hip; a Desert Eagle 50 AE, the world's largest caliber handgun, holstered to his right; an M48 tactical warhammer, the meatier buddy of the tomahawk The Thing had hacked me up with, built in to a kevlar sheath on his left thigh; a 4-gauge TOZ KS-23M pump-action shotgun, a Russian monster large enough to level ten elephants with a single shot, in a similar built-in holster on his right; and, I kid you not, a fucking Hanwei Odachi samurai sword dangling from a low-slung sheath on his left hip. There was also something enormous attached to his back, but I couldn't quite make it out behind the towering steel neck plate.

I stared at him with my jaw hanging open.

"What *are* you?" I said.

He made his first utterance. It sounded like breaking stone. It took me a moment to register it as laughter. I shined my flashlight directly into his eye screen. He didn't flinch. My bet was he had self-adjusting infrared night vision in there. He'd be fighting in broad daylight. I was in the dark with a fucking flashlight and a hole in my head.

"You really need all that shit?" I said.

He laughed again. It sounded like boulders in a tumble drier.

"What's the fucking point?"

Silence for a moment, then he spoke his first word:

"Victory."

His voice was three octaves lower than any sound I'd ever heard. I didn't hear it. I *felt* it. In my bones.

His first attack came so fast I didn't even see it. The flashlight beam was high-powered, but narrow. I blinked and he unleashed a second incredible leap, this time sideways, and vanished into the darkness. I jerked the flashlight, desperate to find him, and caught a nine-and-three-quarter-inch serrated blade in the stomach. The force of the blow pitched me backward. I stumbled and slammed into the steel ladder, glanced off, spinning, and fell to the stone floor. The flashlight flew from my fingertips and clattered across the ground, throwing out a dizzying swirl of blinding light before slamming into something hard and blinking out.

I was on the ground, in complete darkness. With *him*.

At that moment, my adrenaline detonated like Tsar Bomba.

In a blink I was up, grasping blindly through the darkness, fingers searching desperately for the steel ladder, finding it, clutching it before me like a shield. The floor had solidified beneath my feet. I couldn't see, but my other four senses snapped into starling focus. The metallic taste of blood. The smooth coldness of fingered steel. The icy waft of stale air. Quite suddenly, I realized that seeing didn't matter. The Dzhaggernaut was too quick to keep in the flashlight beam anyway, and holding onto the damn thing eliminated the use of one of my hands.

Besides, something had just occurred to me.

Dzhaggernaut was bigger, faster, and harder than me.

But was he any better at being quiet?

I closed my eyes and *listened*. I had two hands on the ladder directly in front of me, knees slightly bent, weight on the balls of my feet. Dzhaggernaut was fighting in broad daylight. And he knew I couldn't see him. I played the scared blind guy and waited for him to pick his shot. In the end, he stabbed straight at my heart. I never saw it coming.

But I didn't have to.

I *heard* it from a mile away. His elbow joint flexed and his wrist torqued and the blade shot forward. I had aeons to yank myself to the side. I heard the clang and clatter of his elbow joint locking straight as he stabbed the air where I'd just been.

And I realized The Dzhaggernaut had just fucked up.

In his overzealousness to land the killing blow, he'd stabbed *through* the rungs of the ladder to get at my heart. Before he could retract his arm I let go of the steel bars and grabbed the thick steel plate of what must have been his forearm and yanked sideways. Metal clanged into metal and I spun and locked his extended elbow joint across the hardened steel ladder. Full arm bar. He roared and flexed his massive bicep and pulled against me. He was incredibly strong, his suit of armor even stronger, but I had my feet planted on stone and my hip braced against steel and an enormous mechanical advantage. I yanked for all I was worth. And I was worth a lot. Something gave with the sound of an axle breaking. The Dzhaggernaut bellowed and I heard the giant knife clatter to the stone floor.

One weapon down.

I kept hold of his buckled arm and waited to see what he would do next. He went for the warhammer. I heard the movement clearly. The unsnapping of the sheath, the articulation of his shoulder, elbow and wrist as he raised the hammer high and whooshed it down. I waited until the last moment then torqued his broken elbow and absorbed the hit on his own steel-plated forearm. He screamed and staggered and I felt through the darkness and got a hand on the head of the hammer and twisted it from his fingers and threw it aside.

Two weapons down.

Then, out of the darkness, the menacing *sllllliiing* of the fifty-inch Odachi blade exiting its scabbard. A samurai sword is the deadliest martial arts weapon ever created. Light, fast, strong, and deathly sharp. A good one can cut through damn near anything. Even hardened steel.

I ducked just in time. The blade *thwanged* over my head and I heard the grinding squeal of severing iron and then a beat of silence and I realized the blade had hacked into the thick steel ladder above my head and gotten stuck.

I stood and reached through the darkness and found Dzhaggernaut's left hand still trying to pry the blade loose. I gripped his thumb and torqued his wrist and his hand came away from the blade and I pivoted, turning my back to him, and yanked his left arm over my shoulder until his armored chest slammed against my back. I levered my shoulder beneath his armpit and flipped his enormous mass over top of me. He bellowed with rage as he slammed to the stone floor with the sound of a cement truck hitting a wall at a hundred miles an hour. I let go of his arm and dropped on top of him and fumbled through the darkness, searching for a weapon. I found the Desert Eagle on his right hip, but should have gone for the shotgun on his thigh. Both weapons unsheathed in the same moment and I heard him articulate his elbow and raise the 4-gauge barrel and I let go of the hand gun and dropped to his chest not a moment too soon.

The gigantic shotgun went off with the sound of a billion megatons of TNT, amplified and reverberated by the towering stone walls. He'd missed. And I wasn't sure he could rack another shell with his broken arm. In the darkness I found the shotgun and wrenched it backward and he yelped and it was mine. I leapt to my feet and racked a shell and leaned in. A 4-gauge shotgun blast is enough to decapitate a rhinoceros. I squeezed the trigger and blasted The Dzhaggernaut in center mass from point blank range.

"Eat that motherfucker!" I roared, as the enormous gun bucked in my hand.

I stood there, triumphant, ears ringing from the second still-reverberating concussion.

Which is why I never heard it coming.

70

The kick.

At least I think it was a kick. Either that or a fucking freight train. Something large and heavy moving very fast slammed into my chest and then I was flying backward into complete darkness. The 4-gauge shotgun blast from point blank range hadn't done shit. That was some serious fucking armor. I hit the ground on my butt and tumbled over my shoulder and came up on my feet but the world swam and I staggered and fell back down. I lay there in the darkness breathing hard, ears still ringing, trying to listen for him but hearing nothing.

Then, from the darkness, I felt deep, rumbling laughter.

"You really think you can beat me?" said Dzhaggernaut.

I heard him climb to his feet. I pried myself up onto an elbow, then slowly crawled up to standing. He let me. The adrenaline was wearing off fast. And there was nothing I could do about it.

"No," I said. "Not really."

"Yet you're still here," he said.

I couldn't see him. But I gauged his distance at twenty feet. Too far for me to do a damn thing. Close enough for him to kill me at any moment.

"Fuckin' a," I said.

A beat of silence.

"That's why we the play the game," he said. "You never know what's gonna happen."

Something twinged in my brain. I tilted my head to the side. Eyed the darkness. Said nothing.

"Aren't you afraid?" he boomed. "Now, at the moment of your death."

I shrugged my tired shoulders.

"Probably not as much as I should be," I said.

Dzhaggernaut chuckled again. My skull rattled.

"Let me see if I can fix that," he said.

Then he turned on his headlamp and showed me what he had strapped to his back.

"You've got to be fucking kidding me," I breathed.

He chuckled some more.

"What's the ROF on that thing?" I said. "A million?"

"What the fuck is ROF?" boomed Dzhaggernaut.

My blood went cold.

Just like that, I knew who it was.

But . . . it couldn't be.

Something must have crossed my face, because he laughed again.

"About fucking time," he said.

I stared at him through the harsh headlamp beam. It wasn't possible.

"Surprise," he said.

I just stood there, dumbstruck.

"But . . . *how*?" I said. "*Why*?"

He had an answer ready for me.

"It's time you finally saw what I truly am," he said.

I stared at him. I couldn't fucking believe it. This whole time . . .

I shook my head. Nearly barfed. My adrenaline was gone.

"Who *are* you?" I said.

He chuckled one more time. It made the hair on the back

of my neck stand up.

"The motherfucker who finally beat you," he said.

Then he pulled the trigger.

Ever seen Predator? Remember the scene where Jesse the Body mows down an entire forrest? Well, I was the forrest. The General Dynamics GAU-19/B six-barrel gatling gun fires .50 calibre NATO rounds at a rate of 1500 per minute. That's twenty-five bullets, each the length of your hand, every second.

I remember the first couple.

The swarm of death hit me high in the chest, spinning me around and lifting me off my feet. Then I was flying through the air, propelled by gun fire, floating on bullets like a kite in a hurricane. I hit the ground hard and there came a moment of respite and then the storm hit again, tumbling me violently across the stone floor like a twig in a leaf blower. I remember ramming something hard, most likely the far wall, and tumbling and turning and slamming against it for a while. Then the onslaught ceased.

Somehow I was still conscious.

I couldn't see. I couldn't tell which way was up. Something wet was in my eyes. Blood. Cascading from beneath my balaclava. Filling my eyes, coursing down the bridge of my nose, onto my cheeks. I could feel it freezing in its tracks on my neck.

Booming footsteps approached through darkness. Then The Dzhaggernaut's enormous boots shook the ground next to my head. His headlamp blazed down on me. The world went red through my blood-drowned eyes.

"You're still not dead?" he boomed.

It took me a time to find my mouth.

"Fuck," I said. "You."

He chuckled.

"Always the conversationalist."

I heard the sound of the Desert Eagle .50 cocking.

"Would you look at that," he said, shaking his metal head. "I finally got you."

Then he shot me in the forehead.

71

I woke up, days later, in a blinding light.

My first thought was this must be the pearly gates. Then I remembered who I was and all I'd done and that pleasant little dream shot itself right to shit. No, this was something else. Somehow, I was still alive.

I opened my eyes. High above me, a bank of stadium lights blazed down in a concentrated beam. I flinched, jerking my head to the side. The room backflipped. I puked.

Oh yeah, the hole in my skull.

It all came back then. The Labyrinth. The lighthouse. The Dzhaggernaut. The gattling gun. The bullet to the brain.

How the fuck was I still alive?

"He's awake!" yelled a voice, somewhere off to my right. It echoed slightly, giving me the impression of a large open space.

"That's nasty!" yelled a second voice, from the opposite direction.

Ever-so-slowly I lifted my head and looked down the length of my body. It wasn't great. I was lying on my back on a stainless steel surgical table. Naked. My arms, legs, and torso strapped to the table with the same cable-ratchet system they'd used on me in my cabin. This time they'd done a proper job of it. Steel on steel. I let out a long breath through my nose, then closed my eyes and gingerly set my head back on the table. From all accounts, I appeared genuinely fucked.

I pulled in a deep breath and titled my head to the side. Some distance away, in the darkness outside the spotlight, I could just make out a perimeter of heads and shoulders in silhouette. People. Seated in chairs.

A fucking audience.

A wooden floor stretched between us, disappearing into the darkness. I was reminded of Madison Square Garden, where they keep the crowd lights off, giving you the impression of being up on stage.

This was a show.

And I was the main attraction.

Then came another voice:

"That *is* nasty."

This one, I recognized. You would have too. I rotated my head toward it, dipping my cheek into a pool of cooling puke. She burst out of the darkness and into the spotlight. The crowd erupted in whoops and catcalls. As usual, she looked like ten million bucks. As usual, it came as a shock to see her in the flesh. The crowed hooted and hollered as she strutted across the stage in a booty-hugging, cleavage-revealing, venom green dress. The adulation of the crowd seemed to amplify her. As if she needed it for sustenance.

"Ariana," I croaked.

"Ain't that a bitch," she said, strutting up and standing over me with a hand on her outthrust hip. "I had a hundred k on you bein' braindead."

The crowd burst out laughing as if this were a stand-up comedy show. Which would make me the punchline. I looked up at her. Body heat radiated from her flawless caramel skin. She had on her super-megawatt smile. The one you see on billboards and Pepsi commercials. But when I looked in her eyes something inside me recoiled. In there, leering out, was the purest distillation of hate I'd ever seen.

The megawatt smile evaporated.

"Welcome home motherfucker," she snarled.

That's when I figured out where I was. Not a stadium. A home. Albeit a very extravagant one. I was lying in the center of the enormous foyer of Hooper's Heaven.

"Why aren't I dead?" I said.

Ariana glanced down at me and shook her head. Her dangly, diamond-studded earrings wish-washed back-and-forth across her slender neck and cheeks.

"*Sheeit,* I should be asking you the same fucking thang." She spoke loudly, projecting her voice into the crowd. Performing. "We left you in that cavern overnight. Thought about leaving you down there forever, but decided you deserved worse. Wasn't 'till we winched your cracka' ass out the next day we saw you was still breathin'. So you tell me motherfucker, how the fuck this shit work?"

She reached under the table and came back holding my balaclava. It held its shape, as if my head were still inside.

I let out an astonished breath.

"Son of a bitch," I breathed. "It worked."

"*What* worked motherfucker?" snapped Ariana. "What this shit made outta?"

"Diamene," I said.

Ariana recoiled. I was reminded of a viper readying to strike.

"The fuck you talkin' 'bout?" she hissed, barring her fangs.

The crowd laughed uneasily.

"A two-dimensional covalent network of double-bonded carbon atoms that transitions to a three-dimensional diamond structure on impact," I said. "On a molecular level, the strongest substance on earth. It's just never been made in a large quantity before, and no one thought to overlap the layers asymmetrically atop an energy-absorbing non-

Newtonian polymer gel, then attach it to ultra-high molecular weight polythylene fabric."

Ariana's face darkened.

"Except me," I added.

Ariana reached over the table and pincered my testicles in her inch-long magenta fingernails. The pain was exquisite. I screamed and bucked and writhed against my restraints but couldn't move an inch. The crowd whooped and hollered and cheered. Ariana kept pinching.

"In English motherfucker," she snarled, releasing my nuts.

It took a while before I could speak again.

"The world's first Level V ballistic armor," I gasped. "A thousand times stronger than steel, at a hundredth the weight. I had a full body suit fitted beneath my clothes."

Ariana slitted her serpentine eyes.

"You telling me this shit blocked all them bullets?" she said, staring at the stiff, lightweight balaclava in her hands.

"Looks that way," I said.

Ariana let out an exasperated breath, then shook her head. Her earrings did the wish-wash thing again. She took one more look at the ski-mask then tossed it over her shoulder and settled the full power of her gaze on me. My aching balls tried to crawl inside my stomach.

"I suppose you got some questions motherfucker," she said, eyeing me with her hands resting on the world's most famous hips.

"A couple," I said.

"Well," she said, "go on then."

"Where's Shawn?"

She looked off into the darkness expectantly.

"I'm here," said a deep, booming voice.

From the shadows an enormous shape emerged into the spotlight. Shawn was clad in a black tank top, athletic shorts and a pair of size 18 cobalt blue Schilling XI's. Even with his right arm in a sling, he looked magnificent.

"Were you serious with the fucking samurai sword?" I said as he walked up to my table and towered over me.

He shook his bald head.

"Don't even start, motherfucker," he said. "I beat your ass fair and square."

"We're calling that fair?" I said.

"You the one taught me fighting fair's for suckers," said Shawn. "Only way you could ever beat me was by cheating. Payback's a bitch, ain't it?"

"So that's what this is all about?" I said. "Settling old basketball scores?"

Ariana let out a guttural shriek. The full force of her incredible voice made my sphincter clench to the density of a neutron star. The crowd gasped.

"You done fucked with this man for the last fucking time!" she snarled. "Twenty-first best player in NBA history my black ass! You fucking kidding me? You ain't qualified to hold this man's jockstrap! Never have been. Never will be. Fucking rebounds. Like anyone give a shit about that. Yet all these fatass motherfuckers in their notebooks talking about Shawn wouldn'a been nothin' without you. Like you the reason he won three MVPs. You the reason he scored all them fucking points!"

She spat in my face. I blinked just in time, but could do nothing to wipe away the phlegm. I cracked open my eyes and squinted up through it.

"Wait a minute," I said. "Are you telling me all this is over a fucking ESPN list?"

Ariana leered down at me, fangs barred.

"You dumb motherfucker," she snarled, shaking her head. "You still got no idea what's going on, do you?"

I said nothing. She had me there.

Ariana began to saunter back and forth across the stage, swinging her hips, playing to the crowd.

"When I was young," she bellowed, "there was a bully on

my block just like this big motherfucker."

The crowd whistled and cheered, egging her on.

"*Biiig* bitch name' Dominique," she said, giving her ass a little shake. "Used to chase my scrawny ass home and steal my shit."

More cheering from the crowd.

"You tell him mamma!" someone yelled.

I thought I recognized the voice. Dayshawn, you lazy sack of shit.

"Bitch scared the fuck outta me," said Ariana. "Every *god damn* day. Made me feel *small*. Made me wanna quit school. Move out the neighbourhood. Give up."

"What'd you do about it mamma?" Dayshawn yelled.

"I'm'a tell you," she said, waggling her hips. "One day, I ran home, scared outta my *god damn* mind, crying to my mamma. Tol' her exactly what was happenin'. Said, 'Mama, this big bitch scaring me. She too *strong*. She too *mean*. If she catch me, she gone whoop my ass.'"

The crowd whistled and whooped.

"And you know what my mamma told me?" said Ariana.

The crowd catcalled.

"What she say mamma!" yelled Dayshawn.

"She said to me, 'Baby, you gotsta go out there and *fight* that big bitch. That the only way she gon' learn.'"

The crowd erupted in wild cheers. Ariana stopped sauntering and made her way back to my table, peering down hungrily at me.

"You took everything from Shawn," she said. "His career. His legacy. His one true love. I watched it happen right before my eyes. Watched this magnificent man become . . . *small* inside. You got any idea what that's like? To come home day after day and see the man you love, the most astounding man on the face of the earth, reduced to a shell of his self?"

She paused. Placed her taloned fingers over my testicles.

"Of course you don't," she said. "You can't see nothin' past that crooked fucking nose."

She let out a breath through her nostrils, shaking her head in disappointment.

"But what to do about it?" she said, fingering my balls. "What payback could be commensurate to the destruction of a man's soul?"

The tips of her talons nipped my nuts. I tried not to wince. Failed.

"Whatchu gon' do mamma?" said Dayshawn.

I really wished that motherfucker would shut up.

"In the end," said Ariana. "I decided I had to do to you exactly what I did to that big bitch Dominique back in the day. I plotted. I planned. I waited for just the right time. Then, when you least expected it, I grabbed me a heavy ass frying pan and hunted yo ass down like a fuckin' *dog*."

The crowd erupted in raucous cheers. I glanced over at Shawn. He refused to meet my eyes. Ariana leered down at me, triumphant.

"How?" I grunted. "How'd you do it?"

After considering me another moment with those venomous eyes, she told me.

72

"Dayshawn's the one came up with The Labyrinth," said Ariana, smirking. "And let me tell you something, *boy*. You underestimated that motherfucker *big time*."

She laughed. The megawatt smile was back. My testicles were trying to flee from it like mice from a viper, but finding nowhere to hide.

"Dayshawn a certified genius," said Ariana, all sass. "He the one created my whole social media empire. *And* Shawn's. Over a hundred million followers. A *billion* dollars in revenue. Enough to fund the whole operation a hundred times over. Think on that one a minute motherfucker."

I said nothing. Ariana looked at me, shaking her head back and forth. Disappointed.

"And," she said, "he just happens to play video games every single night with your boy Deckert."

"*What*?" I said.

"*Soulsborne* series," yelled Dayshawn from his spot in the crowd. "Gave me the idea for the Soul Merchant and the Labyrinth Depths!"

"Don't forget the Power Grid!" said a second voice.

"Deckert," I said. "You son of a bitch."

Ariana cackled. I couldn't see what was so funny.

"As you can see, the two geeks teamed up," she said.

"Deckert had his spy software. Dayshawn can code his ass off. He created the darkweb sites. Together, they make quite the team. Problem was, your barbarian-ass the only motherfucker in the world without a cell phone. So we needed a way to get to you."

"Kiira," I said, almost to myself.

Ariana laughed again. My nutsack recoiled.

"Dumb bitch came running straight for you," she said. "Just like I knew she would. Stupid ho actually think you got some redeemin' qualities."

"I don't?" I said.

Ariana snorted.

"Always a joking motherfucker," she said, shaking her head. "Even with your dick trying to shrivel itself out of existence."

"Damn," I said. "I hoped he was holding his own down there."

Ariana snorted again. I felt it in my scrotum.

"After that, it was easy," she said. "We were in the room with you the whole time. Either through that blond bitch's phone, or the laptop Deckert gave her. Or when you invited us, you dumb motherfucker."

I was speechless for a moment. Ariana leered at me, letting it sink in.

"You made it all up?" I said.

"Of course, baby," said Ariana. "And your dumb ass had no fucking clue. Why you think your Intelligence score stayed so low?"

I blinked a couple times.

"What about the video of the guy getting his guts ripped out his ass?" I said. "You did that?"

Ariana shook her head.

"No, that video was real," she said.

"That's where I got the name," yelled Dayshawn. "The Labyrinth. Sounds scary as fuck, don't it? And I figured eventually someone would show you that video, make you think it was real."

Ariana laughed. My testicles tried burrowing into my stomach.

I said, "So . . . you got all those people killed just to fuck with me?"

Ariana's smile transformed to a scowl.

"To *haunt* you," she snarled. "And who you callin' innocent? I'll admit, you made it further than I planned, so a couple extra people had to get fucked up, but no one inside The Labyrinth was innocent, baby. Not by a fuckin' long shot."

I said nothing. I didn't need to. She'd started rolling, her face alight, eager to show me just how deeply she'd fucked me.

"First we got that redneck asshole, Marx," she said. "My niece works a club down near the U. Told me he liked to get physical with the girls. Always got away with it too 'cause he was some big shot football player. So we stole footage of him punching a guy to death off his phone. Seems he liked to watch it while he jerked off. We used it to blackmail him. Thought he'd whoop your ass too. But he was a bigger bitch than we anticipated. So we had to go up a level."

"You mean down a Depth," called Dayshawn.

Ariana rolled her eyes.

"The Wendigo," I said. "Mikwam."

"He was a scary motherfucker," said Ariana, nodding. "We hacked his phone, found the name of the guy he killed to get into that fucked up voodoo gang. Used it to scare him into stalking your girl. But you threw his ass out the window. So once again, we had to go *lower*."

Ariana gave me the megawatt smile.

"Deckert told us about a guy named Duffy," she said. "Ran shit out of Duluth. We blackmailed a couple of his guys to kidnap Kiira. You tied them motherfuckers to a tree and let the wolves eat 'em. *That's* fucked up. Then we found your boy Wraith. Now he was a real piece of shit. Been killing people for money ever since he got kicked out the marine corps. But he was easy to blackmail because of his mamma. I was sure he was gonna get your ass. But again, I was wrong."

I blinked some more. It was coming so thick and fast I was having a hard time keeping track of it all.

"What about the mayor?" I said. "He was a jackass, but he didn't deserve to be murdered."

"*Sheeeit,*" said Ariana, tossing a taloned hand at me. "We got your ass good with that one, didn't we? Dayshawn didn't like the look of him. Too woke. Never trust a white man act like he love black people that much. Sho' 'nuff, we hacked his phone, found all sorts of shit. Seems he had a predilection for trafficking underage girls off the reservations. Sold 'em to Duffy after he had his fun with 'em. How the hell you think he paid for that big-ass mansion up on the lake?"

I opened my mouth to say something, but nothing came out.

"After you stomped the mayor we had your ass locked in," she said. "So we decided to have some fun with you. No point killing you if we couldn't watch."

Ariana laughed again. My nuts cowered underneath my dick.

"You came down here wondering where all Shawn's people was," she said. "Thought *I'd* scared 'em off. Dumb sumbitch. They been out dropping off letters, writing shit on yo' truck, and settin' up locations. You even saw a couple of 'em at the bar chattin' with your boy Shane."

My mouth was still hanging open. Ariana winked at me.

"Over the last couple months we bought us some warehouses, a gaming reserve, even a god damn lighthouse," she said. "Coast Guard sold that motherfucker to us cheap. Funny what money can do. We put cameras all up through everything and we was ready to go. We let you take us up north so we could stay close, move the operations right under your nose. To be honest, I thought that little Hmong motherfucker, Skinpeeler, was gonna carve yo' ass up first time out. He crazy. Lost me a shitload of money on that one. After that, I gotta admit, I started betting on you. Made a killing when I threw you out in the woods with those two rednecks without a gun. No one else knew about the fake bombs in their helmets. Everyone was wondering why they was walking so damn slow. Shit had me dyin'."

"I'm still mad about that shit!" yelled Dayshawn.

"*Fuuuck* you," said Ariana, snickering. She turned back to me, smiling her viper's smile. "How you feeling honey?"

I wasn't great. I blinked a couple times.

"Wait a minute," I said. "What about Tannen? Medvyed? Who took out Gow with the million dollar drone? They said the President sent them."

"He did," said Ariana. "They had nothing to do with us. We fooled you into thinking The Labyrinth had something to do with yo' grandaddy. Deckert came up with the Juggernaut thing for the Final Boss, wrote the shit in Russian. That was clever. Put you on the wrong track. What we didn't know was your dumb ass was gon' spy on the fucking President, *inside* his house. *That* shit was crazy. You pissed off the wrong white boy. He sent his best to kill you. What you expect? We just acted like they was part of it once Deckert found out they was on the way. You should'a kept listening to that phone feed."

I shook my head. It was too much. I glanced over at Shawn. He was still having a hard time looking at me.

"How long you been training for this?" I said.

"Nine months," he said, glancing at me for the briefest second. "Suit of armor heavy as hell."

I almost laughed. It felt weird with my nuts exposed.

"That one-legged leap was impressive," I said. "I should have known it was you right then. Only a couple people in the world could've made that leap. I just never would've expected to find you out in that lighthouse. You can barely swim."

"You talkin' to the greatest athlete of all-time!" snarled Ariana. Her taloned fingers pounced on my balls again. I screamed in agony.

Ariana leaned in close to my ear.

"That the man who bested you," she hissed. "So you gonna show him some *god damn* respec'!"

Her fanged fingers bit into my nuts a little deeper, then released. I groaned for a while.

When I could talk again, I said, "Are we done here?"

"Hell no we ain't done," said Ariana. "We just getting started motherfucker. Now comes the good part."

"What's that?" I wheezed.

"Shawn gone cut off your dick," said Ariana. "*And* your nutsack. Then feed them to you one by one. We all got money on how much he can get you to swallow before you bleed to death. I got five hundred thousand on the whole shebang, and I ain't try'na lose."

"Sounds like a blast," I said. "But something's been bothering me."

Ariana chuckled.

"What's that baby?" she said.

"You haven't mentioned Maldonado a single time," I said.

Ariana's face contorted.

"That foreign motherfucker own all them houses?" she said. "What the fuck he got to do with anything?"

I let out a long breath through my nose, and smiled.

The first bullet took her high in the right shoulder blade. It tossed her forward onto the table, her upper half flopping over my exposed groin. She had time to turn her head and look at me, an expression of utter shock on her face, then the second bullet got her somewhere low and she screamed and disappeared from view. Shawn froze like a moose in headlights. His eyes found mine. I winked. The third bullet got him in the hamstring. He gasped and spun and looked down as if he'd been stung by a wasp. Then he saw the blood and the hole and sucked in a frightened breath and put his hands in the air.

After that, the screaming began in earnest.

73

I was still attached to the surgical table with my dick out.

Noodin had shot three wannabe gangsters through the left eye as they went for their 9mm's. Yeah, the left eye. After that little demonstration of proficiency everything proceded rather smoothly. Mawka had the rest of the crowd lying face-down along the edge of the room while he paced back and forth, daring someone, anyone, to try him. Funnily enough, no one did.

"How long have you known?" I said.

"Long enough," said Maldonado, "to be quite entertained."

"I'm going to kill you," I said. "You know that, right?"

Maldonado showed his teeth.

"I think not," he said.

Ariana and Shawn were in the adjacent living room being tended to by Code. I could hear Ariana yelling something about getting blood on the suede. Gow had Deckert and Dayshawn in the recording studio, accompanied by Rupert, Ajax, and a large kitchen knife. Occasionally, a muffled scream could be heard through the soundproof door.

"I was keeping a close eye on the competition," said Maldonado. "You always seemed a good bet."

"You were betting on me?" I said between clenched teeth.

"Of course," he said. "I know a winning horse when I see one."

"You're going to die," I said. "Slowly and painfully."

Maldonado laughed.

"Untie me," I said. "See if you still find this funny then."

"Not just yet," said a voice.

Kiira strode out of the darkness, dressed to kill in black jeans and a tight t-shirt beneath a kevlar vest.

"You fucking *knew*?" I said.

Kiira saw the look in my eye and stopped.

"No," she said, putting up her palms. "It wasn't like that."

"Give yourself some credit," said Maldonado. "You felt it right away."

Kiira pulled in a careful breath.

"Something . . . wasn't right about her," she said. "She was sharp, but . . . slippery."

"You suspected her and you didn't fucking tell me?" I said between my teeth.

Kiira shook her head, eyes wide.

"No," said Maldonado. "She told *me*."

I rounded on him.

"She has a nose for these things," he said, shrugging. "Call it a writer's intuition. I queried her about our guests. She voiced a vague suspicion, but had absolutely no grounds upon which to base it. I told her to ignore the feeling. But after that I . . . stayed abreast of the situation."

I said nothing. I was trying to decide if Kiira needed to die too.

"I promise you, Einarr," she said, placing her hand on my chest. "I didn't know."

She had tears in her eyes now. I held her gaze until she looked away.

"Did Gow know?" I said to Maldonado.

He grinned.

"Not until after I dropped you at the lighthouse," he said.

My fists clenched.

"I needed hard evidence," said Maldonado. "Deckert really is quite clever. I couldn't pin anything on him. I had to catch them in the act. I figured once you reached the bottom Depth they'd mobilize. Which, of course, they did."

"You dropped me at that lighthouse to die," I said.

Maldonado shrugged.

"I was curious," he said. "To see who'd win."

My knuckles audibly cracked.

"Gow's rather displeased," said Maldonado, unperturbed by the murder in my eyes. "He's very protective of you. But Code assured him that the enormous dose of human growth hormone in your system, along with the impenetrable armor, would most likely keep you alive."

"Most likely?" I said.

Maldonado shrugged again.

"How much money'd you win off me?"

Maldonado's grin vanished.

"Not a single dime," he said.

I raised an eyebrow.

"You lost the final fight," he said. "Quite badly, I might add."

I glared at him.

"You saying I owe you?" I said.

Maldonado's teeth reemerged.

"Indeed I am," he said.

I shook my head, letting out a low growl. The balls on this motherfucker.

"And what about you?" I said, turning to Kiira. "Was Ariana right? You still think I have some redeeming qualities?"

A hesitant smile creased her face and she ran her fingers down me.

"At the moment," she said. "I suppose I can think of one."

I considered her for a moment, then grinned.

"One's enough," I said.

Kiira rolled her eyes, smiled, then began releasing my restraints. It felt glorious.

Gow came in a little while later.

"Got a full confession from the two nerds," he said. "Add that to the video of Ariana and Shawn confessing to the whole thing and we got all four of them by the bollocks for the foreseeable future."

"Indemnity," I said.

We bumped fists.

"How about these fucking assholes?" I said, motioning my head to Kiira and Maldonado. "We got anything on them?"

"Plenty," said Gow. "But it'll have to wait."

"Can't have everything," I said. "At least there's this."

I grabbed Kiira's ass. She rolled her eyes again, but the smile stayed.

"We done here?" she said. "I don't know about you guys, but I want to go home."

I eased myself down off the steel table and made sure everything still worked. Somehow, after a knife to the head and a drop through a lighthouse and a barrage of .50 caliber machine gun fire and everything else, I was still kicking.

"Who's the fucking Juggernaut now?" I said.

There came a beat of silence.

"About that," said Maldonado.

The three of us looked at him.

"There is one last thing," he said. His face had gone serious.

"What?" I said.

"The video of the man and woman getting their insides ripped out," he said. "The one that gave Deckert the name for The Labyrinth."

"What about it?" I said.

"I found the location where it was filmed."

I swallowed.

"And?" I said.

Maldonado levelled his gaze at me. I wasn't sure he could feel fear, but what I saw in his eyes made the hairs on my neck stand up.

"An abandoned prison in northern Siberia," he said. "One you know rather well."

Beside me, I heard Kiira gasp.

"What are you saying exactly?" I said.

He let it come to me. Tannen wasn't part of it. But we'd never got to Medvyed . . .

"Oh," I said. "Fuck."

Maldonado nodded, his eyes wide open.

"What?" said Kiira, glancing between us.

I looked her dead in the eye, and said:

"The Labyrinth is real."

Nick Horvath is the author of the *Sledge vs.* action-mystery series. A native of northern Minnesota, Nick double-majored in Physics and English at Duke University before embarking on a 12-year professional basketball career. Over that time he transformed himself from a timid finesse player into a rugged rebounding monster, much like his savage anti-hero, Sledge Laukkanen. Though he has yet to bludgeon anyone to death with his bare hands, anyone wishing to date his daughter should consider themselves forewarned.

He draws inspiration from 80's action and horror movies, Robert. E Howard's *Conan*, Frank Miller's *Sin City*, fighting games, the *Dark Souls* universe, and hard-boiled mystery novels in wintery settings.

He currently resides in New Zealand with his family.